Born in 1893, **Anthony Berkeley** was a journalist as well as a novelist. A founding member of the Detection Club, he was one of crime fiction's greatest innovators, being one of the first to predict the development of the 'psychological' crime novel. He sometimes wrote under the pseudonym of Francis Iles. He wrote twenty-four novels, ten of which feature his amateur detective, Roger Sheringham. His best-known Roger Sheringham mystery is *The Poisoned Chocolates Case*. Anthony Berkeley died in 1971.

BY THE SAME AUTHOR
ALL PUBLISHED BY HOUSE OF STRATUS

Death in the House
Jumping Jenny
The Layton Court Mystery
Murder in the Basement
Not to Be Taken
Panic Party
The Piccadilly Murder
The Second Shot
The Silk Stocking Murders
Top Storey Murder
Trial and Error

THE POISONED CHOCOLATES CASE

ANTHONY BERKELEY

This edition published in 2001 by House of Stratus, an imprint of House of Stratus Ltd, Thirsk Industrial Park, York Road, Thirsk, North Yorkshire, YO7 3BX, UK.
Also at: House of Stratus Inc., 2 Neptune Road, Poughkeepsie, NY 12601, USA.

www.houseofstratus.com

Typeset, printed and bound by House of Stratus.

A catalogue record for this book is available from the British Library and the Library of Congress.

ISBN 0-7551-0206-1

To

S H J Cox

Because for once he did not guess it

chapter one

Roger Sheringham took a sip of the old brandy in front of him and leaned back in his chair at the head of the table. Through the haze of cigarette smoke eager voices reached his ears from all directions, prattling joyfully upon this and that connected with murder, poisons and sudden death. For this was his own, his very own Crimes Circle, founded, organised, collected, and now run by himself alone; and when at the first meeting five months ago he had been unanimously elected its president, he had been as full of proud delight as on that never-to-be-forgotten day in the dim past when a cherub disguised as a publisher had accepted his first novel.

He turned to Chief Inspector Moresby of Scotland Yard who, as the guest of the evening, was sitting on his right, engaged, a little uneasily, with a positively enormous cigar.

'Honestly, Moresby, without any disrespect to your own institution, I do believe that there's more solid criminological genius in this room (intuitive genius, I mean; not capacity for taking pains) than anywhere in the world outside the *Sûreté* in Paris.'

'Do you, Mr Sheringham?' said Chief Inspector Moresby tolerantly. Moresby was always kind to the strange opinions of others. 'Well, well.' And he applied himself again to the lighted end of his cigar, which was so very far from the other that Moresby could never tell by mere suction at the latter whether the former were still alight or not.

Roger had some grounds for his assertion beyond mere parental pride. Entry into the charmed Crimes Circle's dinners was not to be gained by all and hungry. It was not enough for a would-be member to profess an adoration for murder and let it go at that; he or she had got to prove that they were capable of worthily wearing their criminological spurs.

Not only must the interest be intense in all branches of the science, in the detection side, for instance, just as much as the side of criminal psychology, with the history of all cases of the least importance at the applicant's fingertips, but there must be constructive ability too; the candidate must have a brain and be able to use it. To this end, a paper had to be written, from a choice of subjects suggested by members, and submitted to the president, who passed on such as he considered worthy to the members in conclave, who thereupon voted for or against the suppliant's election; and a single adverse vote meant rejection.

It was the intention of the club to acquire eventually thirteen members, but so far only six had succeeded in passing their tests, and these were all present on the evening when the chronicle opens. There was a famous lawyer, a scarcely less famous woman dramatist, a brilliant novelist who ought to have been more famous than she was, the most intelligent (if not the most amiable) of living detective-story writers, Roger Sheringham himself and Mr Ambrose Chitterwick, who was not famous at all, a mild little man of no particular appearance who had been even more surprised at being admitted to this company of personages than they had been at finding him amongst them.

With the exception of Mr Chitterwick, then, it was an assembly of which any organiser might have been proud. Roger this evening was not only proud but excited too, because he was going to startle them; and it is always exciting to startle personages. He rose to do so.

'Ladies and gentlemen,' he proclaimed, after the welcome of glasses and cigarette-cases drummed on the table had died away. 'Ladies and gentlemen, in virtue of the powers conferred by you the president of our Circle is permitted to alter at his discretion the arrangements made for any meeting. You all know what arrangements were made for this evening. Chief Inspector Moresby, whom we are so glad to welcome as the first representative of Scotland Yard to visit us' – more drumming on the table – 'Chief Inspector Moresby was to be lulled by rich food and sound wine into being so indiscreet as to tell us about such of his experiences as could hardly be given to a body of pressmen.' More and longer drumming.

Roger refreshed himself with a sip of brandy and continued. 'Now I think I know Chief Inspector Moresby pretty well, ladies and gentlemen, and the occasions are not a few on which I too have tried, and tried very hard, to lure him similarly into the paths of indiscretion; but never once have I succeeded. I have therefore little hope that this Circle, lure it never so cooingly, will succeed in getting from the Chief Inspector any more interesting stories than he would mind being published in *The Daily Courier* tomorrow. Chief Inspector Moresby, I am afraid, ladies and gentlemen, is unlurable.

'I have therefore taken upon myself the responsibility of altering our entertainment for this evening; and the idea that has occurred to me in this connection will, I both hope and believe, appeal to you very considerably. I venture to think that it is both novel and enthralling.' Roger paused and beamed on the interested faces around him. Chief Inspector Moresby, a little puce below the ears, was still at grips with his cigar.

'My idea,' Roger said, 'is connected with Mr Graham Bendix.' There was a little stir of interest. 'Or rather,' he amended, more slowly, 'with Mrs Graham Bendix.' The stir subsided into a still more interested hush.

Roger paused, as if choosing his words with more care. 'Mr Bendix himself is personally known to one or two of us here. Indeed, his name has actually been mentioned as that of a man who might possibly be interested, if approached, to become a member of this Circle. By Sir Charles Wildman, if I remember rightly.'

The barrister inclined his rather massive head with dignity. 'Yes, I suggested him once, I think.'

'The suggestion was never followed up,' Roger continued. 'I don't quite remember why not; I think somebody else was rather sure that he would never be able to pass all our tests. But in any case the fact that his name was ever mentioned at all shows that Mr Bendix is to some extent at least a criminologist, which means that our sympathy with him in the terrible tragedy that has befallen him is tinged with something of a personal interest, even in the case of those who, like myself, are not actually acquainted with him.

'Hear, hear,' said a tall, good-looking woman on the right of the table, in the clear tones of one very well accustomed to saying 'hear, hear' weightily at appropriate moments during speeches, in case no one else did. This was Alicia Dammers, the novelist, who ran Women's Institutes for a hobby, listened to other people's speeches with genuine and altruistic enjoyment, and, in practice the most staunch of

Conservatives, supported with enthusiasm the theories of the Socialist party.

'My suggestion is,' Roger said simply, 'that we turn that sympathy to practical uses.'

There was no doubt that the eager attention of his audience was caught. Sir Charles Wildman lifted his bushy grey brows, from under which he was wont to frown with menacing disgust at the prosecution's witnesses who had the bad taste to believe in the guilt of his own client, and swung his gold-rimmed eye-glasses on their broad black ribbon. On the other side of the table Mrs Fielder-Flemming, a short round, homely looking woman who wrote surprisingly improper and most successful plays and looked exactly like a rather superior cook on her Sunday out, nudged the elbow of Miss Dammers and whispered something behind her hand. Mr Ambrose Chitterwick blinked his mild blue eyes and assumed the appearance of an intelligent nanny-goat. The writer of detective stories alone sat apparently unmoved and impassive; but in times of crisis he was wont to model his behaviour on that of his own favourite detective, who was invariably impassive at the most exciting moments.

'I took the idea to Scotland Yard this morning,' Roger went on, 'and though they never encourage that sort of idea there, they were really unable to discover any positive harm in it; with the result that I came away with a reluctant, but nevertheless official permission to try it out. And I may as well say at once that it was the same cue that prompted this permission as originally put the whole thing into my head' – Roger paused impressively and glanced round – 'the fact that the police have practically given up all hope of tracing Mrs Bendix's murderer.'

Ejaculations sounded on all sides, some of dismay, some of disgust, and some of astonishment. All eyes turned upon Moresby. That gentleman, apparently unconscious of the collective gaze fastened upon him, raised his cigar to his ear and listened to it intently, as if hoping to receive some intimate message from its depths.

Roger came to his rescue. 'That information is quite confidential, by the way, and I know none of you will let it escape beyond this room. But it is a fact. Active inquiries, having resulted in exactly nothing are to be stopped. There is always hope of course that some fresh fact may turn up, but without it the authorities have come to the conclusion that they can get no farther. My proposal is, therefore, that this Club should take up the case where the authorities have left it.' And he looked expectantly round the circle of upturned faces.

Every face asked a question at once.

Roger forgot his periods in his enthusiasm and became colloquial.

'Why, you see, we're all keen, we're not fools, and we're not (with apologies to my friend Moresby) tied to any hard-and-fast method of investigation. Is it too much to hope that, with all six of us on our mettle and working quite independently of each other, one of us might achieve some result where the police have, to put it bluntly, failed? I don't think it's outside the possibilities. What do you say, Sir Charles?'

The famous counsel uttered a deep laugh. ''Pon my word, Sheringham, it's an interesting idea. But I must reserve judgment till you've outlined your proposal in a little more detail.'

'I think it's a wonderful idea, Mr Sheringham,' cried Mrs Fielder-Flemming, who was not troubled with a legal mind.

'I'd like to begin this very evening.' Her plump cheeks positively quivered with excitement. 'Wouldn't you, Alicia?'

'It has possibilities,' smiled that lady.

'As a matter-of-fact,' said the writer of detective stories, with an air of detachment. 'I'd formed a theory of my own about this case already.' His name was Percy Robinson, but he wrote under the pseudonym of Morton Harrogate Bradley, which had so impressed the more simple citizens of the United States of America that they had bought three editions of his first book on the strength of that alone. For some obscure psychological reason Americans are always impressed by the use of surnames for Christian, and particularly when one of them happens to be the name of an English watering-place.

Mr Ambrose Chitterwick beamed in a mild way, but said nothing.

'Well,' Roger took up his tale, 'the details are open to discussion, of course, but I thought that, if we all decide to make the trial, it would be more amusing if we worked independently. Moresby here can give us the plain facts as they're known to the police. He hasn't been in charge of the case himself, but he's had one or two jobs in connection with it and is pretty well up in the facts; moreover he has very kindly spent most of the afternoon examining the dossier at Scotland Yard so as to be sure of omitting nothing this evening.

'When we've heard him some of us may be able to form a theory at once; possible lines of investigation may occur to others which they will wish to follow up before they commit themselves. In any case, I suggest that we allow ourselves a week in which to form our theories, verify our hypotheses, and set our individual interpretations on the facts that Scotland Yard has collected, during which time no member shall discuss the case with any other member. We may achieve nothing (most probably we shall not), but in any case it will be a most interesting criminological exercise; for some of us practical, for others academical, just as we prefer. And what I think should be most interesting will be to see if we all arrive at the same result or not. Ladies and gentlemen, the meeting is open for discussion, or whatever is the right way of putting it. In other words: what about it?' And Roger dropped back, not reluctantly, into his seat.

Almost before his trousers had touched it the first question reached him.

'Do you mean that we're to go out and act as our own detectives, Mr Sheringham, or just write a thesis on the facts that the Chief Inspector is going to give us?' asked Alicia Dammers.

'Whichever each one of us preferred, I thought,' Roger answered. 'That's what I meant when I said that the exercise would be practical for some of us and academic for others.'

'But you've got so much more experience than us on the practical side, Mr Sheringham,' pouted Mrs Fielder-Flemming (yes, pouted).

'And the police have so much more than me,' Roger countered.

'It will depend whether we use deductive or inductive methods, no doubt,' observed Mr Morton Harrogate Bradley. 'Those who prefer the former will work from the police facts and won't need to make any investigations of their own, except perhaps to verify a conclusion or two. But the inductive method demands a good deal of inquiry.'

'Exactly,' said Roger.

'Police facts and the deductive method have solved plenty of serious mysteries in this country,' pronounced Sir Charles Wildman. 'I shall rely on them for this one.'

'There's one particular feature of this case,' murmured Mr Bradley to nobody, 'that ought to lead one straight to the criminal. I've thought so all the time. I shall concentrate on that.'

'I'm sure I haven't the remotest idea how one sets about investigating a point, if it becomes desirable,' observed Mr Chitterwick uneasily; but nobody heard him, so it did not matter.

'The only thing that struck me about this case,' said Alicia Dammers, very distinctly, 'regarded, I mean, as a pure case, was its complete absence of any psychological interest whatever.' And without actually saying so, Miss Dammers conveyed the impression that if that were so, she personally had no further use for it.

'I don't think you'll say that when you've heard what Moresby's got to tell us,' Roger said gently. 'We're going to hear a great deal more than has appeared in the newspaper, you know.'

'Then let's hear it,' suggested Sir Charles, bluntly.

'We're all agreed, then?' said Roger, looking round as happily as a child who has been given a new toy. 'Everybody is willing to try it out?'

Amid the ensuing chorus of enthusiasm, one voice alone was silent. Mr Ambrose Chitterwick was still wondering, quite unhappily, how, if it ever became to go a-detecting, one went. He had studied the reminiscences of a hundred ex-detectives, the real ones, with large black boots and bowler hats; but all he could remember at that moment, out of all those scores of fat books (published at eighteen and sixpence, and remaindered a few months later at eighteen pence), was that a real, *real* detective, if he means to attain results, never puts on a false moustache but simply shaves his eyebrows. As a mystery-solving formula, this seemed to Mr Chitterwick inadequate.

Fortunately in the buzz of chatter that preceded the very reluctant rising of Chief Inspector Moresby, Mr Chitterwick's poltroonery went unnoticed.

chapter two

Chief Inspector Moresby, having stood up and blushingly received his tribute of hand-claps, was invited to address the gathering from his chair and thankfully retired into that shelter. Consulting the sheaf of notes in his hand, he began to enlighten his very attentive audience as to the strange circumstances connected with Mrs Bendix's untimely death. Without reproducing his own words, and all the numerous supplementary questions which punctuated his story, the gist of what he had to tell was as follows:

On Friday morning, the fifteenth of November, Graham Bendix strolled into his club, the Rainbow, in Piccadilly, at about ten-thirty and asked if there were any letters for him. The porter handed him a letter and a couple of circulars, and he walked over to the fireplace in the hall to read them.

While he was doing so another member entered the club. This was a middle-aged baronet, Sir Eustace Pennefather, who had rooms just round the corner, in Berkeley Street, but spent most of his time at the Rainbow. The porter glanced up at the clock, as he did every morning when Sir Eustace came in, and, as always, it was exactly half-past ten. The time was thus definitely fixed by the porter beyond any doubt.

There were three letters and a small parcel for Sir Eustace, and he, too, took them over to the fireplace to open, nodding to Bendix as he joined him there. The two men knew each other only very slightly and had probably never exchanged more than half-a-dozen words in all. There were no other members in the hall just then.

Having glanced through his letters, Sir Eustace opened the parcel and snorted with disgust. Bendix looked at him enquiringly, and with a grunt Sir Eustace thrust out the letter which had been enclosed in the parcel, adding an uncomplimentary remark upon modern trade methods. Concealing a smile (Sir Eustace's habits and opinions were a matter of some amusement to his fellow members), Bendix read the letter. It was from the firm of Mason & Sons, the big chocolate manufacturers, and was to the effect that they had just put on the market a new brand of liqueur chocolates designed especially to appeal to the cultivated palates of Men of Taste. Sir Eustace being, presumably, a Man of Taste, would he be good enough to honour Mr Mason and his sons by accepting the enclosed one-pound box, and any criticisms or appreciation that he might have to make concerning them would be esteemed almost more than a favour.

'Do they think I'm a blasted chorus-girl,' fumed Sir Eustace, a choleric man, 'to write 'em testimonials about their blasted chocolates? Blast 'em! I'll complain to the blasted committee. That sort of blasted thing can't blasted well be allowed here.' For the Rainbow Club, as every one knows, is a very proud and exclusive club indeed, with an unbroken descent from the Rainbow Coffee-House, founded in 1734. Not even a family founded by a king's bastard can be quite so exclusive today as a club founded on a coffee-house.

'Well, it's an ill wind so far as I'm concerned,' Bendix soothed him. 'It's reminded me of something. I've got to get some chocolates myself, to pay an honourable debt. My wife and I had a box at the Imperial last night, and I bet her a box of chocolates to a hundred cigarettes that she wouldn't spot the villain by the end of the second act. She won. I must remember to get them. It's not a bad show. *The Creaking Skull*. Have you seen it?'

'Not blasted likely,' replied the other, unsoothed. 'Got something better to do than sit and watch a lot of blasted fools messing about with phosphorescent paint and pooping off blasted pop-guns at each other. Want a box of chocolates, did you say? Well, take this blasted one.'

The money saved by this offer had no weight with Bendix. He was a very wealthy man, and probably had enough on him in actual cash to buy a hundred such boxes. But trouble is always worth saving. 'Sure you don't want them?' he demurred politely.

In Sir Eustace's reply only one word, several times repeated, was clearly recognisable. But his meaning was plain. Bendix thanked him and, most unfortunately for himself, accepted the gift.

By an extraordinarily lucky chance the wrapper of the box was not thrown into the fire, either by Sir Eustace in his indignation or by Bendix himself when the whole collection, box, covering letter, wrapper and string, was shovelled into his hands by the almost apoplectic baronet. This was the more fortunate as both men had already tossed the envelopes of their letters into the flames.

Bendix however merely walked over to the porter's desk and deposited everything there, asking the man to keep the box for him. The porter put the box aside, and threw the wrapper into the waste-paper basket. The covering letter had fallen unnoticed from Bendix's hand as he walked across the floor. This the porter tidily picked up a few minutes later and put in the waste-paper basket too, whence, with the wrapper, it was retrieved later by the police.

These two articles, it may be said at once, constituted two of the only three tangible clues to the murder, the third of course being the chocolates themselves.

Of the three unconscious protagonists in the impending tragedy, Sir Eustace was by far the most remarkable. Still a year or two under fifty, he looked, with his flaming red face and thick-set figure, a typical country squire of the old school, and both his manners and his language were in accordance with tradition. There were other resemblances too, but they were equally on the surface. The voices of the country squires of the old school were often slightly husky towards late middle age, but it was not with the whisky. They hunted, and so did Sir Eustace, with avidity; but the country squires confined their hunting to foxes, and Sir Eustace was far more catholic in his predatory tastes. Sir Eustace in short, without doubt, was a thoroughly bad baronet. But his vices were all on the large scale, with the usual result that most other men, good or bad, liked him well enough (except perhaps a few husbands here and there, or a father or two), and women openly hung on his husky words.

In comparison with him Bendix was rather an ordinary man, a tall, dark, not unhandsome fellow of eight-and-twenty, quiet and somewhat reserved, popular in a way but neither inviting nor apparently reciprocating anything beyond a somewhat grave friendliness.

He had been left a rich man on the death five years ago of his father, who had made a fortune out of land-sites, which he had brought up in undeveloped areas with an uncanny foresight to sell later, at never less than ten times what he had given for them, when surrounded by houses and factories erected with other people's money. 'Just sit tight and let other people make you rich,' had been his motto, and a very sound one it proved. His son, though left with an income that precluded any necessity to work, had evidently inherited his father's tendencies, for he had a finger in a good many business pies just (as he explained a little apologetically) out of sheer love of the most exciting game in the world.

Money attracts money. Graham Bendix had inherited it, he made it, and inevitably he married it too. The orphaned daughter of a Liverpool ship-owner she was, with not far off half-a-million in her own right to bring to Bendix, who needed it not at all. But the money was incidental, for he needed her if not her fortune, and would have married her just as inevitably (said his friends) if she had not a farthing.

She was so exactly his type. A tall, rather serious-minded, highly cultured girl, not so young that her character had not had time to form (she was twenty-five when Bendix married her, three years ago), she was the ideal wife for him. A bit of a Puritan, perhaps, in some way, but Bendix himself was ready enough to be a Puritan by then if Joan Cullompton was.

For in spite of the way he developed later Bendix had sown as a youth a few wild oats in the normal way. Stage doors, that is to say, had not been entirely strange to him. His name had been mentioned in connection with that of more than one frail and fluffy lady. He had managed, in short, to amuse himself, discreetly but by no means clandestinely, in the usual manner of young men with too much money and too few years. But all that, again in the ordinary way, had stopped with his marriage.

He was openly devoted to his wife and did not care who knew it, while she too, if a trifle less obviously, was equally said to wear her heart on her sleeve. To make no bones about it, the Bendixes had apparently succeeded in achieving that eighth wonder of the modern world, a happy marriage.

And into the middle of it there dropped, like a clap of thunder, the box of chocolates.

'After depositing the box of chocolates with the porter,' Moresby continued, shuffling his papers to find the right one, 'Mr Bendix followed Sir Eustace into the lounge, where he was reading the *Morning Post.*'

Roger nodded approval. There was no other paper that Sir Eustace could possibly have been reading but the *Morning Post.*

Bendix himself proceeded to study *The Daily Telegraph.* He was rather at a loose end that morning. There were no board meetings for him, and none of the businesses in which he was interested called him out into the rain of a typical November day. He spent the rest of the morning in an aimless way, read the daily papers, glanced through the weeklies, and played a hundred up at billiards with another member equally idle. At about half-past twelve he went back to lunch to his house in Eaton Square, taking the chocolates with him.

Mrs Bendix had given orders that she would not be in to lunch that day, but her appointment had been cancelled and she too was lunching at home. Bendix gave her the box of chocolates after the meal as they were sitting over their coffee in the drawing-room, explaining how they had come into his possession. Mrs Bendix laughingly teased him about his meanness in not buying her a box, but approved the make and was interested to try the firm's new variety. Joan Bendix was not so serious-minded as not to have a healthy feminine interest in good chocolates.

Their appearance, however, did not seem to impress her very much.

'Kümmel, Kirsch, Maraschino,' she said, delving with her fingers among the silver-wrapped sweets, each bearing the name of its filling in neat blue lettering. 'Nothing else, apparently. I don't see anything new here, Graham: they've just taken those three kinds out of their ordinary liqueur chocolates.'

'Oh?' said Bendix, who was not particularly interested in chocolates. 'Well, I don't suppose it matters much. All liqueur chocolates taste the same to me.'

'Yes, and they've even packed them in their usual liqueur chocolate box,' complained his wife, examining the lid.

'They're only a sample,' Bendix pointed out. 'They may not have got the right boxes ready yet.'

'I don't believe there's the slightest difference,' Mrs Bendix pronounced, unwrapping a Kümmel. She held out the box to her husband. 'Have one?'

He shook his head. 'No, thank you, dear. You know I never eat the things.'

'Well, you've got to have one of these, as a penance for not buying me a proper box. Catch!' She threw him one. As he caught it she made a wry face. 'Oh! I was wrong. These are different. They're twenty times as strong.'

'Well, they can bear at least that,' Bendix smiled, thinking of the usual anaemic sweetmeat sold under the name of chocolate liqueur.

He put the one she had given him in his mouth and bit it up; a burning taste, not intolerable but far too pronounced to be pleasant, followed the release of the liquid. 'By Jove,' he exclaimed, 'I should think they are strong. I believe they've filled them with neat alcohol.'

'Oh, they wouldn't do that, surely,' said his wife, unwrapping another. 'But they are very strong. It must be the new mixture. Really, they almost burn. I'm not sure whether I like them or not. And that Kirsch one tasted far too strongly of almonds. This may be better. You try a Maraschino too.'

To humour her he swallowed another, and disliked it still more. 'Funny,' he remarked, touching the roof of his mouth with the tip of his tongue. 'My tongue feels quite numb.'

'So did mine at first,' she agreed. 'Now it's tingling rather. Well, I don't notice any difference between the Kirsch and the Maraschino. And they do burn! I can't make up my mind whether I like them or not.'

'I don't,' Bendix said with decision. 'I think there's something wrong with them. I shouldn't eat any more if I were you.'

'Well, they're only an experiment, I suppose,' said his wife.

A few minutes later Bendix went out, to keep an appointment in the city. He left his wife still trying to make up her mind whether she liked the chocolates or not, and still eating them to decide. Her last words to him were that they were making her mouth burn again so much that she was afraid she would not be able to manage any more.

'Mr Bendix remembers that conversation very clearly,' said Moresby, looking round at the intent faces, 'because it was the last time he saw his wife alive.'

The conversation in the drawing-room had taken place approximately between a quarter-past and half-past two. Bendix kept his appointment in the City at three, where he stayed for about half an hour, and then took a taxi back to his club for tea.

He had been feeling extremely ill during his business talk, and in the taxi he very nearly collapsed; the driver had to summon the porter to help to get him out and into the club. They both describe him as pale to the point of ghastliness, with staring eyes and livid lips, and his skin damp and clammy. His mind seemed unaffected, however, and once they had got him up the steps he was able to walk, with the help of the porter's arm, into the lounge.

The porter, alarmed by his appearance, wanted to send for a doctor at once, but Bendix, who was the last man to make a fuss, absolutely refused to let him, saying that it could only be a bad attack of indigestion and he would be all right in a few minutes; he must have eaten something that disagreed with him. The porter was doubtful, but left him.

Bendix repeated this diagnosis of his own condition a few minutes later to Sir Eustace Pennefather, who was in the lounge at the time, not having left the club at all. But this time Bendix added: 'And I believe it was those infernal chocolates you gave me, now I come to think of it. I thought there was something funny about them at the time. I'd better go and ring up my wife and find out if she's been taken like this too.'

Sir Eustace, a kind-hearted man, who was no less shocked than the porter at Bendix's appearance, was perturbed by the suggestion that he might in any way be responsible for it, and offered to go and ring up Mrs Bendix himself as the other was in no fit condition to move. Bendix was about to reply when a strange change came over him. His body, which had been leaning limply back in his chair, suddenly heaved rigidly upright; his jaws locked together, the livid lips drawn back in a hideous grin, and his hands clenched on the arms of the chair. At the same time Sir Eustace became aware of an unmistakable smell of bitter almonds.

Thoroughly alarmed now, believing indeed that Bendix was dying under his eyes, he raised a shout for the porter and a doctor. There were two or three other men at the further end of the big room (in which a shout had probably never been heard before in the whole course of its history) and these hurried up at once. Sir Eustace sent one off to tell the porter to get hold of the nearest doctor without a second's delay, and enlisted the others to try to make the convulsed body a little more comfortable. There was no doubt among them that Bendix had taken poison. They spoke to him, asking how he felt and what they could do for him, but he either would or could not answer. As a matter of fact, he was completely unconscious.

Before the doctor had arrived, a telephone message was received from an agitated butler asking if Mr Bendix was there, and if so would he come home at once as Mrs Bendix had been taken seriously ill.

At the house in Eaton Square matters had been taking much the same course with Mrs Bendix as with her husband, though a little more rapidly. She remained for half an hour or so in the drawing-room after the latter's departure, during which time she must have eaten about three more of the chocolates. She then went up to her bedroom and rang for her maid, to whom she said that she felt very ill and was going to lie down for a time. Like her husband, she ascribed her condition to a violent attack of indigestion.

The maid mixed her a draught from a bottle of indigestion-powder, which consisted mainly of bicarbonate of soda and bismuth, and brought her a hot-water bottle, leaving her lying on the bed. Her description of her mistress' appearance tallied exactly with the porter's and taxi-man's description of Bendix, but unlike them she did not seem to have been alarmed by it. She admitted later to the opinion that Mrs Bendix, though anything but a greedy woman, must have overeaten herself at lunch.

At a quarter-past three there was a violent ring from the bell in Mrs Bendix's room.

The girl hurried upstairs and found her mistress apparently in a cataleptic fit, unconscious and rigid. Thoroughly frightened now, she wasted some precious minutes in ineffectual attempts to bring her round, and then hurried downstairs to telephone for the doctor. The practitioner who regularly attended the house was not at home, and it was some time later before the butler, who had found the half-hysterical girl at the telephone and taken matters into his own hands, could get into communication with another. By the time the latter did get there, nearly half an hour after Mrs Bendix's bell had rung, she was past help. Coma had set in, and in spite of everything the doctor could do she died in less than ten minutes after his arrival.

She was, in fact, already dead when the butler telephoned to the Rainbow Club.

chapter three

Having reached this stage in his narrative Moresby paused, for effect, breath and refreshment. So far, in spite of the eager interest with which the story had been followed, no fact had been brought out of which his listeners were unaware. It was the police investigations that they wanted to hear, for not only had no details of these been published but not so much as a hint had been given even as to the theory that was officially held.

Perhaps Moresby had gathered something of this sentiment, for after a moment's rest he resumed with a slight smile. 'Well, ladies and gentlemen, I shan't keep you much longer with these preliminaries, but it's just as well to run through everything while we're on it, if we want to get a view of the case as a whole.

'As you know, then, Mr Bendix himself did not die. Luckily for himself he had eaten only two of the chocolates, as against his wife's seven, but still more luckily he had fallen into the hands of a clever doctor. By the time her doctor saw Mrs Bendix it was too late for him to do anything; but the smaller amount of poison that Mr Bendix had swallowed meant that its progress was not so rapid, and the doctor had time to save him.

'Not that the doctor knew what the poison was. He treated him chiefly for prussic acid poisoning, thinking from the symptoms and the smell that Mr Bendix must have taken oil of bitter almonds, but he wasn't sure and threw in one or two other things as well. Anyhow, it turned out in the end that he couldn't have had a fatal dose, and he was conscious again about eight o'clock that night. They'd put him into one of the club bedrooms, and by the next day he was convalescent.'

At first, Moresby went on to explain, it was thought at Scotland Yard that Mrs Bendix's death and her husband's narrow escape were due to a terrible accident. The police had, of course, taken the matter in hand as soon as the woman's death was reported to them and the fact of poison established. In due course a District Detective Inspector arrived at the Rainbow Club, and as soon as the doctor would permit after Bendix's recovery of consciousness held an interview with the still very sick man.

The fact of his wife's death was kept from him in his doubtful condition and he was questioned solely upon his own experience, for it was already clear that the two cases were bound up together and light on one would equally clarify the other. The Inspector told Bendix bluntly that he had been poisoned and pressed him as to how the stuff could have been taken; could he account for it in any way?

It was not long before the chocolates came into Bendix's mind. He mentioned their burning taste, and he mentioned having already spoken to Sir Eustace about them as the possible cause of his illness.

This the inspector already knew.

He had spent the time before Bendix came round in interviewing such people as had come into contact with him since his return to the club that afternoon. He had heard the porter's story and he had taken steps to trace the taxi-man; he had spoken with the members who had gathered round Bendix in the lounge, and Sir Eustace had reported to him the remark of Bendix about the chocolates.

The inspector had not attached very much importance to this at the moment, but simply as a matter of routine had questioned Sir Eustace closely as to the whole episode and, again as a matter of routine, had afterwards rummaged through the waste-paper basket and extricated the wrapper and the covering letter. Still as a matter of routine, and still not particularly impressed, he now proceeded to question Bendix on the same topic, and then at last began to realise its significance as he heard how the two had shared the chocolates after lunch and how, even before Bendix had left home, the wife had eaten more than the husband.

The doctor now intervened, and the inspector had to leave the sick-room. His first action was to telephone to his colleague at the Bendix home and tell him to take possession without delay of the box of chocolates which was probably still in the drawing-room; at the same time he asked for a rough idea of the number of chocolates that were missing. The other told him, nine or ten. The inspector, who on Bendix's information had only accounted for six or seven, rang off and telephoned what he had learnt to Scotland Yard.

Interest was now centred on the chocolates. They were taken to Scotland Yard that evening, and sent off at once to be analysed.

'Well, the doctor hadn't been far wrong,' said Moresby. 'The poison in those chocolates wasn't oil of bitter almonds as a matter of fact, it was nitrobenzene; but I understand that isn't so very different. If any of you ladies or gentlemen have a knowledge of chemicals, you'll know more about the stuff than I do, but I believe it's used occasionally in the cheaper sorts of confectionery (less than it is used to be, though) to give an almond flavour as a substitute for oil of bitter almonds, which I needn't tell you is a powerful poison too. But the most usual way of employing nitrobenzene commercially is in the manufacture of dyes.'

When the analyst's preliminary report came through Scotland Yard's initial theory of accidental death was strengthened. Here definitely was a poison used in the manufacture of chocolates and other sweets. A terrible mistake must have been made. The firm had been employing the stuff as a cheap substitute for genuine liqueurs and too much of it had been used. The fact that the only liqueurs named on the silver wrappings were Maraschino, Kümmel and Kirsch, all of which carry a greater or lesser flavour of almonds, supported this conception.

But before the firm was approached by the police for an explanation, other facts had come to light. It was found that only the top layer of chocolates contained any poison. Those in the lower layer were completely free from anything harmful. Moreover in the lower layer the fillings inside the chocolate cases corresponded with the description on the wrappings, whereas in the top layer, besides the poison, each sweet contained a blend of the three liqueurs mentioned and not, for instance, plain Maraschino and poison. It was further remarked that no Maraschino, Kirsch or Kümmel was to be found in the two lower layers.

The interesting fact also emerged, in the analyst's detailed report, that each chocolate in the top layer contained, in addition to its blend of the three liqueurs, exactly six minims of nitrobenzene, no more or less. The cases were a fair size and there was plenty of room for quite a considerable quantity of the liqueur blend besides this fixed quantity of poison. This was significant. Still more so was the further fact that in the bottom of each of the noxious chocolates there were distinct traces of a hole having been drilled in the case and subsequently plugged up with a piece of melted chocolate.

It was now plain to the police that foul play was in question.

A deliberate attempt had been made to murder Sir Eustace Pennefather. The would-be murderer had acquired a box of Mason's chocolate liqueurs; separated those in which a flavour of almonds would not come amiss; drilled a small hole in each and drained it of its contents; injected, probably with a fountain pen filler, the dose of poison; filled the cavity up from the mixture of former fillings; carefully stopped the hole, and rewrapped it in its silver-paper covering. A meticulous business, meticulously carried out.

The covering letter and wrapper which had arrived with the box of chocolates now became of paramount importance, and the inspector who had had the foresight to rescue these from destruction had occasion to pat himself on the back. Together with the box itself and the remaining chocolates, they formed the only material clues to this cold-blooded murder.

Taking them with him, the Chief Inspector now in charge of the case called on the managing director of Mason and Sons, and without informing him of the circumstances as to how it had come into his possession, laid the letter before him and invited him to explain certain points in connection with it. How many of these (the managing director was asked) had been sent out, who knew of this one, and who could have had a chance of handling the box that was sent to Sir Eustace?

If the police had hoped to surprise Mr Mason, the result was nothing compared with the way in which Mr Mason surprised the police.

'Well, sir?' prompted the Chief Inspector, when it seemed as if Mr Mason would go on examining the letter all day.

Mr Mason adjusted his glasses to the angle for examining Chief Inspectors instead of the letters. He was a small, rather fierce, elderly man who had begun life in a back street in Huddersfield, and did not intend any one to forget it.

'Where the devil did you get this?' he asked. The papers, it must be remembered, had not yet got hold of the sensational aspect of Mrs Bendix's death.

'I came,' replied the Chief Inspector with dignity, 'to ask you about your sending it out, sir, not tell you about my getting hold of it.'

'Then you can go to the devil,' replied Mr Mason with decision. 'And take Scotland Yard with you,' he added, by way of a comprehensive afterthought.

'I must warn you, sir,' said the Chief Inspector, somewhat taken aback but concealing the fact beneath his weightiest manner, 'I must warn you that it may be a serious matter for you to refuse to answer my questions.'

Mr Mason, it appeared, was exasperated rather than intimidated by this covert threat. 'Get out o' ma office,' he replied in his native tongue. 'Are ye druffen, man? Or do ye just think you're funny? Ye know as well as I do that that letter was never sent out from 'ere.'

It was then that the Chief Inspector became surprised. 'Not – not sent out by your firm at all?' he stammered. It was a possibility that had not occurred to him. 'It's – forged, then?'

'Isn't that what I'm telling ye?' growled the old man, regarding him fiercely from under bushy brows. But the

Chief Inspector's evident astonishment had mollified him somewhat.

'Sir,' said that official, 'I must ask you to be good enough to answer my questions as fully as possible. It's a case of murder I'm investigating, and' – he paused and thought cunningly – 'and the murderer seems to have been making free use of your business to cloak his operations.'

The cunning of the Chief Inspector prevailed.'The devil 'e 'as!' roared the old man. 'Damn the blackguard. Ask any question thou wants, lad; I'll answer right enough.'

Communication thus being established, the Chief Inspector proceeded to get to grips.

During the next five minutes his heart sank lower and lower. In place of the simple case he had anticipated it became rapidly plain to him that the affair was going to be very difficult indeed. Hitherto he had thought (and his superiors had agreed with him) that the case was going to prove one of sudden temptation. Somebody in the Mason firm had a grudge against Sir Eustace. Into his (or more probably, as the Chief Inspector had considered, her) hands had fallen the box and letter addressed to him. The opportunity had been obvious, the means, in the shape of nitrobenzene in use in the factory, ready to hand; the result had followed. Such a culprit would be easy enough to trace.

But now, it seemed, this pleasant theory must be abandoned, for in the first place no such letter as this had ever been sent out at all; the firm had produced no new brand of chocolates, if they had done so it was not their custom to dispense sample boxes among private individuals, the letter was a forgery. But the notepaper on the other hand (and this was the only remnant left to support the theory) was perfectly genuine, so far as the old man could tell. He could not say for certain, but was almost sure that this was a piece of old stock which had been finished up about six months ago. The heading might be forged, but he did not think so.

'Six months ago?' queried the Inspector unhappily.

'About that,' said the other, and plucked a piece of paper out of a stand in front of him. 'This is what we use now.' The Inspector examined it. There was no doubt of the difference. The new paper was thinner and more glossy. But the heading looked exactly the same. The Inspector took a note of the firm who had printed both.

Unfortunately no sample of the old paper was available. Mr Mason had a search made on the spot, but not a sheet was left.

'As a matter of fact,' Moresby now said, 'it had been noticed that the piece of paper on which the letter was written was an old one. It is distinctly yellow round the edges. I'll pass it round and you can see for yourselves. Please be careful of it.' The bit of paper, once handled by a murderer, passed slowly from each would-be detective to his neighbour.

'Well, to cut a long story shorter,' Moresby went on, 'we had it examined by the firm of printers, Webster's, in Frith Street, and they're prepared to swear that it's their work. That means the paper was genuine, worse luck.'

'You mean, of course,' put in Sir Charles Wildman impressively, 'that had the heading been a copy, the task of discovering the printers who executed it should have been comparatively simple?'

'That's correct, Sir Charles. Except if it had been done by somebody who owned a small press of their own; but that would have been traceable too. All we've actually got is that the murderer is someone who had access to Mason's note-paper up to six months ago; and that's pretty wide.'

'Do you think it was stolen with actual intention of putting it to the purpose for which it was used?' asked Alicia Dammers.

'It seems like it, madam. And something kept holding the murderer up.'

As regards the wrapper, Mr Mason had been unable to help at all. This consisted simply of a piece of ordinary, thin brown paper, such as could be bought anywhere, with Sir Eustace's name and address hand-printed on it in neat capitals. Apparently there was nothing to be learnt from it at all. The postmark showed that it had been despatched by the nine-thirty p.m. post from the post-office in Southampton Street, Strand.

'There is a collection at 8.30 and another at 9.30,' Moresby explained, 'so it must have been posted between these two times. The packet was quite small enough to go into the opening for letters. The stamps make up the right value. The post-office was shut by then, so it could not have been handed in over the counter. Perhaps you'd care to see it.' The piece of brown paper was handed gravely round.

'Have you brought the box too, and the other chocolates?' asked Mrs Fielder-Flemming.

'No, Madam. It was one of Mason's ordinary boxes, and the chocolates have all been used for analysis.'

'Oh!' Mrs Fielder-Flemming was plainly disappointed. 'I thought there might be fingerprints on it,' she explained.

'We have already looked for those,' replied Moresby without a flicker.

There was a pause while the wrapper passed from hand to hand.

'Naturally, we've made inquiries as to any one seen posting a packet in Southampton Street between half-past eight and half-past nine,' Moresby continued, 'but without result. We've also carefully interrogated Sir Eustace Pennefather to discover whether he could throw any light on the question why any one should wish to take his life, or who. Sir Eustace can't give us the faintest idea. Of course we followed up the usual line of inquiry as to who would benefit by his death, but without any helpful results. Most of his possessions go to his wife, who has a divorce suit pending against him; and she's out of the country. We've checked her movements and she's out of the question. Besides,' added Moresby unprofessionally, 'she's a very nice lady.

'And as to fact, all we know is that the murderer probably had some connection with Mason and Sons up to six months ago, and was almost certainly in Southampton Street at some time between eight-thirty and nine-thirty on that particular evening. I'm very much afraid we're up against a brick wall.' Moresby did not add that so were the amateur criminologists in front of him too, but he very distinctly implied it.

There was a silence.

'Is that all?' asked Roger.

'That's all, Mr Sheringham,' Moresby agreed.

There was another silence.

'Surely the police have a theory?' Mr Morton Harrogate Bradley threw out in a detached manner.

Moresby hesitated perceptibly.

'Come along, Moresby,' Roger encouraged him. 'It's quite a simple theory. I know it.'

'Well,' said Moresby, thus stimulated, 'we're inclined to believe that the crime was the work of a lunatic, or semi-lunatic, possibly quite unknown personally to Sir Eustace. You see…' Moresby looked a trifle embarrassed. 'You see,' he went on bravely, 'Sir Eustace's life was a bit, well, we might say hectic, if you'll excuse the word. We think at the

Yard that some religious or social maniac took it on himself to rid the world of him, so to speak. Some of his escapades had caused a bit of talk, as you may know.

'Or it might just be a plain homicidal lunatic, who likes killing people at a distance.

'There's the Horwood case, you see. Some lunatic sent poisoned chocolates to the Commissioner of Police himself. That caused a lot of attention. We think this case may be an echo of it. A case that creates a good deal of notice is quite often followed by another on exactly the same lines, as I needn't remind you.

'Well, that's our theory. And if it's the right one, we've got about as much chance of laying our hands on the murderer as – as – ' Chief Inspector Moresby cast about for something really scathing.

'As we have,' suggested Roger.

chapter four

The Circle sat for some time after Moresby had gone. There was a lot to discuss, and everybody had views to put forward, suggestions to make, and theories to advance.

One thing emerged with singular unanimity: the police had been working on the wrong lines. Their theory must be mistaken. This was not a casual murder by a chance lunatic. Somebody very definite had gone methodically about the business of helping Sir Eustace out of the world, and that somebody had behind him an equally definite motive. Like almost all murders, in fact, it was a matter of *cherchez le motif.*

On the exposition and discussion of theories Roger kept a firmly quelling hand. The whole object of the experiment, as he pointed out more than once, was that everybody should work independently, without bias from any other brain, form his or her own theory, and set about proving it in his or her own way.

'But oughtn't we to pool our facts, Sheringham?' boomed Sir Charles. 'I should suggest that though we pursue our investigations independently, any new facts we discover should be placed at once at the disposal of all. The exercise should be a mental one, not a competition in routine detection.'

'There's a lot to be said for that view, Sir Charles,' Roger agreed. 'In fact I've thought it over very carefully. But on the whole I think it would be better if we keep any new facts to ourselves after this evening. You see, we're already in possession of all the facts that the police have discovered, and anything else we may come across isn't likely to be so much a definite pointer to the murderer as some little thing, quite insignificant in itself, to support a particular theory.'

Sir Charles grunted, obviously unconvinced.

'I'm quite willing to have it put to the vote,' Roger said handsomely.

A vote was taken. Sir Charles and Mrs Fielder-Flemming voted for all facts being disclosed: Mr Bradley, Alicia Dammers, Mr Chitterwick (the last after considerable hesitation) and Roger voted against.

'We retain our own facts,' Roger said, and made a mental note of who had voted for each. He was inclined to guess that the voting indicated pretty correctly who was going to be content with general theorising, and who was ready to enter so far into the spirit of the game as to go out and work for it. Or it might simply show who already had a theory and who had not.

Sir Charles accepted the result with resignation. 'We start equal as from now, then,' he announced.

'As from the moment we leave this room,' amended Morton Harrogate Bradley, rearranging the set of his tie. 'But I agree so far with Sir Charles' proposition as to think that any one who can at this moment add anything to the Chief Inspector's statement should do so.'

'But can any one?' asked Mrs Fielder-Flemming.

'Sir Charles knows Mr and Mrs Bendix,' Alicia Dammers pointed out impartially. 'And Sir Eustace. And I know Sir Eustace too, of course.'

Roger smiled. This statement was a characteristic meiosis on the part of Miss Dammers. Everybody knew that Miss Dammers had been the only woman (so far as rumour recorded) who had ever turned the tables on Sir Eustace Pennefather. Sir Eustace had taken it into his head to add the scalp of an intellectual woman to those other rather unintellectual ones which already dangled at his belt. Alicia Dammers, with her good looks, her tall, slim figure, and her irreproachable sartorial taste, had satisfied his very fastidious requirements so far as feminine appearance was concerned. He had laid himself out to fascinate.

The results had been watched by the large circle of Miss Dammers' friends with considerable joy. Miss Dammers had apparently been only too ready to be fascinated. It seemed that she was living entirely on the point of succumbing to Sir Eustace's blandishments. They dined, visited, lunched, and made excursions together without respite. Sir Eustace, stimulated by the daily prospect of surrender on the following one, had exercised his ardour with every art he knew.

Miss Dammers had then retired serenely, and the next autumn published a book in which Sir Eustace Pennefather, dissected to the last ligament, was given to the world in all the naked unpleasingness of his psychological anatomy.

Miss Dammers never talked about her 'art,' because she was a really brilliant writer and not just pretending to be one, but she certainly held that everything had to be sacrificed (including the feelings of the Sir Eustace Pennefathers of this world) to whatever god she worshipped privately in place of it.

'Mr and Mrs Bendix are quite incidental to the crime, of course, from the murderer's point of view,' Mr Bradley now pointed out to her, in the gentle tones of one instructing a child that the letter A is followed in the alphabet by the letter B. 'So far as we know, their only connection with Sir Eustace is that he and Bendix both belonged to the Rainbow.'

'I needn't give you my opinion of Sir Eustace,' remarked Miss Dammers. 'Those of you who have read *Flesh and the Devil* know how I saw him, and I have no reason to suppose that he has changed since I was studying him. But I claim no infallibility. It would be interesting to hear whether Sir Charles' opinion coincides with mine or not.'

Sir Charles who had not read *Flesh and the Devil,* looked a little embarrassed. 'Well, I don't see that I can add much to the impression the Chief Inspector gave of him. I don't know the man well, and certainly have no wish to do so.'

Everybody looked extremely innocent. It was common gossip that there had been the possibility of an engagement between Sir Eustace and Sir Charles' only daughter, and that Sir Charles had not viewed the prospect with any perceptible joy. It was further known that the engagement had even been prematurely announced, and promptly denied the next day.

Sir Charles tried to look as innocent as everybody else. 'As the Chief Inspector hinted, he is something of a bad lot. Some people might go as far as to call him a blackguard. Women,' explained Sir Charles bluntly. 'And he drinks too much,' he added. It was plain that Sir Charles Wildman did not approve of Sir Eustace Pennefather.

'I can add one small point, of purely psychological value,' amplified Alicia Dammers. 'But it shows the dullness of his reactions. Even in the short time since the tragedy rumour has joined the name of Sir Eustace to that of a fresh woman. I was somewhat surprised to hear that,' added Miss Dammers drily. 'I should have been inclined to give him credit for being a little more upset by the terrible mistake, and its fortunate consequences to himself, even though Mrs Bendix was a total stranger to him.'

'Yes, by the way, I should have corrected that impression earlier,' observed Sir Charles. 'Mrs Bendix was not a total stranger to Sir Eustace, though he may probably have forgotten ever meeting her. But he did. I was talking to Mrs Bendix one evening at a first night (I forgot the play) and Sir Eustace came up to me. I introduced them, mentioning something about Bendix being a member of the Rainbow. I'd almost forgotten.'

'Then I'm afraid I was completely wrong about him,' said Miss Dammers, chagrined. 'I was far too kind.' To be too kind in the dissecting-room was evidently, in Miss Dammers' opinion, a far greater crime than being too unkind.

'As for Bendix,' said Sir Charles rather vaguely, 'I don't know that I can add anything to your knowledge of him. Quite a decent, steady fellow. Head not turned by his money in the least, rich as he is. His wife too, charming woman. A little serious perhaps. Sort of woman who likes sitting on committees. Not that that's anything against her though.'

'Rather the reverse, I should have said,' observed Miss Dammers, who liked sitting on committees herself.

'Quite, quite,' said Sir Charles hastily, remembering Miss Dammers' curious predilections. 'And she wasn't too serious to make a bet, evidently, although it was a trifling one.'

'She had another bet, that she knew nothing about,' chanted in solemn tones Mrs Fielder-Flemming, who was already pondering the dramatic possibilities of the situation. 'Not a trifling one: a grim one. It was with Death, and she lost it.' Mrs Fielder-Flemming was regrettably inclined to carry her dramatic sense into her ordinary life. It did not go at all well with her culinary aspect.

She eyed Alicia Dammers covertly, wondering whether she could get in with a play before that lady cut the ground away from under her with a book.

Roger, as chairman, took steps to bring the discussion back to relevancies. 'Yes, poor woman. But after all, we mustn't let ourselves confuse the issue. It's rather difficult to remember that the murdered person had no connection with the crime at all, so to speak, but there it is. Just by accident the wrong person died; it's on Sir Eustace that we have to concentrate. Now, does anybody else here know Sir Eustace, or anything about him, or any fact bearing on the crime?'

Nobody responded.

'Then we're all on the same footing. And now, about our next meeting. I suggest that we have a clear week for formulating our theories and carrying out any investigations we think necessary, that we then meet on consecutive evenings, beginning with next Monday, and that we now draw lots as to the order in which we are to read our several papers or give our conclusions. Or does any one think we should have more than one speaker each evening?'

After a little talk it was decided to meet again on Monday, that day week, and for purposes of fuller discussion allot one evening to each member. Lots were then drawn, with the result that members were to speak in the following order: (1) Sir Charles Wildman, (2) Mrs Fielder-Flemming, (3) Mr Morton Harrogate Bradley, (4) Roger Sheringham, (5) Alicia Dammers, and (6) Mr Ambrose Chitterwick.

Mr Chitterwick brightened considerably when his name was announced as last on the list. 'By that time,' he confided to Morton Harrogate, 'somebody is quite sure to have discovered the right solution, and I shall therefore not have to give my own conclusions. If indeed,' he added dubiously, 'I ever reach any. Tell me, how *does* a detective really set to work?'

Mr Bradley smiled kindly and promised to lend Mr Chitterwick one of his own books. Mr Chitterwick, who had read them all and possessed most of them, thanked him very gratefully.

Before the meeting finally broke up, Mrs Fielder-Flemming could not resist one or more opportunity of being mildly dramatic. 'How strange life is,' she sighed across the table to Sir Charles. 'I actually saw Mrs Bendix and her husband in their box at the Imperial the night before she died. (Oh, yes; I knew them by sight. They often came to my first nights.) I was in a stall almost directly under their box. Indeed life is certainly stranger than fiction. If I could have guessed for one minute at the dreadful fate hanging over her, I – '

'You'd have had the sense to warn her to steer clear of chocolates, I hope,' observed Sir Charles, who did not hold very much with Mrs Fielder-Flemming.

The meeting then broke up.

Roger returned to his rooms in the Albany feeling exceedingly pleased with himself. He had a suspicion that the various attempts at a solution were going to be almost as interesting to him as the problem itself.

Nevertheless he was on his mettle. He had not been very lucky in the draw and would have preferred the place of Mr Chitterwick, which would have meant that he would have the advantage of already knowing the results achieved by his rivals before having to disclose his own. Not that he intended to rely on others' brains in the least; like Mr Morton Harrogate Bradley he already had a theory of his own; but it would have been pleasant to be able to weigh up and criticise the efforts of Sir Charles, Mr Bradley and particularly Alicia Dammers (to these three he gave credit for possessing the best minds in the Circle) before irrevocably committing himself. And more than any other crime in which he had been interested, it seemed to him, he wanted to find the right solution of this one.

To his surprise when he got back to his rooms he found Moresby waiting in his sitting-room.

'Ah, Mr Sheringham,' said that cautious official. 'Thought you wouldn't mind me waiting here for a word with you. Not in a great hurry to go to bed, are you?'

'Not in the least,' said Roger, doing things with a decanter and syphon. 'It's early yet. Say when.'

Moresby looked discreetly the other way.

When they were settled in two huge leather armchairs before the fire Moresby explained himself. 'As a matter of fact, Mr Sheringham, the Chief's deputed me to keep a sort of unofficial eye on you and your friends over this business. Not that we don't trust you, or think you won't be discreet, or anything like that, but it's better for us to know just what's going on with a massed-detective attack like this.'

'So that if any of us finds out something really important, you can nip in first and make use of it,' Roger smiled. 'Yes, I quite see the official point.'

'So that we can take measures to prevent the bird from being scared,' Moresby corrected reproachfully. 'That's all, Mr Sheringham.'

'Is it?' said Roger, with unconcealed scepticism. 'But you don't think it very likely that your protecting hand will be required, eh, Moresby?'

'Frankly, sir, I don't. We're not in the habit of giving up a case so long as we think there's the least chance of finding the criminal; and Detective-Inspector Farrar, who's been in charge of this one, is a capable man.'

'And that's his theory, that it's the work of some criminal lunatic, quite untraceable?'

'That's the opinion he's been led to form, Mr Sheringham, sir. But there's no harm in your Circle amusing themselves,' added Moresby magnanimously, 'if they want to and they've got the time to waste.'

'Well, well,' said Roger, refusing to be drawn.

They smoked their pipes in silence for a few minutes.

'Come along, Moresby,' Roger said gently.

The chief inspector looked at him with an expression that indicated nothing but bland surprise. 'Sir?'

Roger shook his head. 'It won't wash, Moresby; it won't wash. Come along, now; out with it.'

'Out with what, Mr Sheringham?' queried Moresby, the picture of innocent bewilderment.

'Your real reason for coming round here,' Roger said nastily. 'Wanted to pump me, for the benefit of that effete institution you represent, I suppose? Well, I warn you, there's nothing doing this time. I know you better than I did eighteen months ago at Ludmouth, remember.'

'Well, what can have put such an idea as that into your head, Mr Sheringham, sir?' positively gasped that much misunderstood man, Chief Inspector Moresby of Scotland Yard. 'I came round because I thought you might like to ask me a few questions, to give you a leg up in finding the murderer before any of your friends could. That's all.'

Roger laughed. 'Moresby, I like you. You're a bright spot in a dull world. I expect you try to persuade the very criminals you arrest that it hurts you more than it does them. And I shouldn't be at all surprised if you don't somehow make them believe it. Very well, if that's all you came round for I'll ask you some questions, and thank you very much. Tell me this, then. Who do *you* think was trying to murder Sir Eustace Pennefather?'

Moresby sipped delicately at his whisky and soda. 'You know what I think, Mr Sheringham, sir.'

'Indeed I don't,' Roger retorted. 'I only know what you've told me you think.'

'I haven't been in charge of the case at all, Mr Sheringham,' Moresby hedged.

'Who do you really think was trying to murder Sir Eustace Pennefather?' Roger repeated patiently. 'Is it your opinion that the official police theory is right or wrong?'

Driven into a corner, Moresby allowed himself the novelty of speaking his unofficial mind. He smiled covertly, as if at a secret thought. 'Well, Mr Sheringham, sir,' he said with deliberation, 'our theory is a useful one, isn't it? I mean, it gives us every excuse for not finding the murderer. We can hardly be expected to be in touch with every half-baked creature in the country who may have homicidal impulses.

'Our theory will be put forward at the conclusion of the adjourned inquest, in about a fortnight's time, with reason and evidence to support it, and any evidence to the contrary not mentioned, and you'll see that the coroner will agree with it, and the jury will agree with it, and the papers will agree with it, and everyone will say that really, the police can't be blamed for not catching the murderer this time, and everybody will be happy.'

'Except Mr Bendix, who doesn't get his wife's murder avenged,' added Roger. 'Moresby, you're being positively sarcastic. And from all this I deduce that you personally will stand aside from this general and amicable agreement. Do you think the case has been badly handled by your people?'

Roger's last question followed so closely on the heels of his previous remarks that Moresby had answered it almost before he had time to reflect on the possible indiscretion of doing so. 'No, Mr Sheringham, I don't think that. Farrar's a capable man, and he'd leave no stone unturned – no stone, I mean, that he *could* turn.' Moresby paused significantly.

'Ah!' said Roger.

Having committed himself to this lamb, Moresby seemed disposed to look about for a sheep. He resettled himself in his chair and recklessly drank a gill from his tumbler. Roger, scarcely daring to breathe too audibly for fear of scaring the sheep, studiously examined the fire.

'You see, this is a very difficult case, Mr Sheringham,' Moresby pronounced. 'Farrar had an open mind, of course, when he took it up, and he kept an open mind even after he'd found out that Sir Eustace was even a bit more of a daisy than he'd imagined at first. That is to say, he never lost sight of the fact that it *might* have been some outside lunatic who sent those chocolates to Sir Eustace, just out of a general socialistic or religious feeling that he'd be doing a favour to society, or Heaven by putting him out of the world. A fanatic, you might say.'

'Murder from conviction,' Roger murmured. 'Yes?'

'But naturally what Farrar was concentrating on was Sir Eustace's private life. And that's where we police officers are handicapped. It's not easy for us to make enquiries into the private life of a baronet. Nobody wants to be helpful; everybody seems anxious to put a spoke in our wheel. Every line that looked hopeful to Farrar led to a dead end. Sir Eustace himself told him to go to the devil, and made no bones about it.'

'Naturally, from his point of view,' Roger said thoughtfully. 'The last thing he'd want would be a sheaf of his pecadilloes laid out for a harvest festival in court.'

'Yes, and Mrs Bendix lying in her grave on account of them,' retorted Moresby with asperity. 'No, he was responsible for her death, though indirectly enough I'll admit, and it was up to him to be as helpful as he could to the police officer investigating the case. But there Farrar was; couldn't get any further. He unearthed a scandal or two, it's true, but they led to nothing. So – well, he hasn't admitted this, Mr Sheringham, and you'll realise I ought not to be telling you; it's to go no further than this room, mind.'

'Good heavens, no,' Roger said eagerly.

'Well, then, it's my private opinion that Farrar was driven to the other conclusion in self-defence. And the chief had to agree with it in self-defence too. But if you want to get to the bottom of the business, Mr Sheringham (and nobody would be more pleased if you did than Farrar himself) my advice to you is to concentrate on Sir Eustace's private life. You've a better chance than any of us there: you're on his level, you'll know members of his club, you'll know his friends personally, and the friends of his friends. And that,' concluded Moresby, 'is the tip I really came round to give you.'

'That's very decent of you, Moresby,' Roger said with warmth. 'Very decent indeed. Have another spot.'

'Well, thank you, Mr Sheringham, sir,' said Chief Inspector Moresby. 'I don't mind if I do.'

Roger was meditating as he mixed the drinks. 'I believe you're right, Moresby,' he said slowly. 'In fact, I've been thinking along those lines ever since I read the first full account. The truth lies in Sir Eustace's private life, I feel sure. And if I were superstitious, which I'm not, do you know what I should believe? That the murderer's aim misfired and Sir Eustace escaped death for an express purpose of Providence: so that he, the destined victim, should be the ironical instrument of bringing his own intended murder to justice.'

'Well, Mr Sheringham, would you really?' said the sarcastic Chief Inspector, who was not superstitious either.

Roger seemed rather taken with the idea. '*Chance, the Avenger.* Make a good film title, wouldn't it? But there's a terrible lot of truth in it.'

'How often don't you people at the Yard stumble on some vital piece of evidence out of pure chance? How often isn't it that you're led to the right solution by what seems a series of mere coincidences? I'm not belittling your detective work; but just think how often a piece of brilliant detective work which has led you most of the way but not the last few vital inches, meets with some remarkable stroke of sheer luck (thoroughly well-deserved luck, no doubt, but *luck*), which just makes the case complete for you. I can think of scores of incidences. The Milsom and Fowler murder, for example. Don't you see what I mean? Is it chance every time, or is it Providence avenging the victim?'

'Well, Mr Sheringham,' said Chief Inspector Moresby, 'to tell you the truth, I don't mind what it is, so long as it lets me put my hands on the right man.'

'Moresby,' laughed Roger, 'you're hopeless.'

chapter five

Sir Charles Wildman, as he has said, cared more for honest facts than for psychological fiddle-faddle.

Facts were very dear to Sir Charles. More, they were meat and drink to him. His income of roughly thirty thousand pounds a year was derived entirely from the masterful way in which he was able to handle facts. There was no one at the bar who could so convincingly distort an honest but awkward fact into carrying an entirely different interpretation from that which any ordinary person (counsel for the prosecution, for instance) would have put upon it. He could take that fact, look it boldly in the face, twist it round, read a message from the back of its neck, turn it inside out and detect auguries in its entrails, dance triumphantly on its corpse, pulverise it completely, remould it if necessary into an utterly different shape, and finally, if the fact still had the temerity to retain any vestige of its primary aspect, bellow at it in the most terrifying manner. If that failed he was quite prepared to weep at it in open court.

No wonder that Sir Charles Wildman, KC, was paid that amount of money every year to transform facts of menacing appearance to his clients into so many sucking doves, each cooing those very clients' tender innocence. If the reader is interested in statistics it might be added that the number of murderers whom Sir Charles in the course of his career had saved from the gallows, if placed one on top of the other, would have reached to a very great height indeed.

Sir Charles Wildman had rarely appeared for the prosecution. It is not considered etiquette for prosecution counsel to bellow, and there is scant need for their tears. His bellowing and his public tears were Sir Charles Wildman's long suit. He was one of the old school, one of its very last representatives; and he found that the old school paid him handsomely.

When therefore he looked impressively round the Crimes Circle on its next meeting, one week after Roger had put forward his proposal, and adjusted the gold-rimmed pince-nez on his somewhat massive nose, the other members could feel no doubt as to the quality of the entertainment in store for them. After all, they were going to enjoy for nothing what amounted to a thousand-guinea brief for the prosecution.

Sir Charles glanced at the notepad in his hand and cleared his throat. No barrister could clear his throat quite so ominously as Sir Charles.

'Ladies and Gentlemen,' he began, in weighty tones, 'it is not unnatural that I should have been more interested in this murder than perhaps anyone else, for personal reasons which will no doubt have occurred to you already. Sir Eustace Pennefather's name, as you must know, has been mentioned in connection with that of my daughter; and though the report of their engagement was not merely premature, but utterly without foundation, it is inevitable that I should feel some personal connection, however slight, with this attempt to assassinate a man who has been mentioned as a possible son-in-law to myself.

'I do not wish to stress this personal aspect of the case, which otherwise I have tried to view as impersonally as any other with which I have been connected; but I put it forward more as an excuse than anything. For it has enabled me to approach the problem set us by our President with a more intimate knowledge of the person concerned than the rest of you could have, and with, too, I fear, information at my disposal which goes a long way towards indicating the truth of this mystery.

'I know that I should have placed this information at the disposal of my fellow members last week, and I apologise to them wholeheartedly for not having done so; but the truth is that I did not realise then that this knowledge of mine was in any way germane to the solution, or even remotely helpful, and it is only since I began to ponder over the case with a view to clearing up the tangle, that the vital import of this information has impressed itself upon me.' Sir Charles paused and allowed his resounding periods to echo round the room.

'Now, with its help,' he pronounced, looking severely from face to face, 'I am of opinion that I have read this riddle.'

A twitter of excitement, no less genuine because obviously awaited, ran round the faithful Circle.

Sir Charles whisked off his pince-nez and swung them, in a characteristic gesture, on their broad ribbon. 'Yes, I think, in fact I am sure, that I am about to elucidate this dark business to you. And for this reason I regret that the lot has fallen upon me to speak first. It would have been more interesting perhaps had we been permitted to examine some other theories first, and demonstrate their falsity, before we probed to the truth. That is, assuming that there are other theories to examine.

'It would not surprise me, however, to learn that you had all leapt to the conclusion to which I have been driven. Not in the least. I claim no extraordinary powers in allowing the facts to speak to me for themselves; I pride myself on no superhuman insight in having been able to see further into this dark business than our official solvers of mysteries and readers of strange riddles, the trained detective force. Very much the reverse. I am only an ordinary human being, endowed with no more powers than any of my fellow creatures. It would not astonish me for an instant to be apprised that I am only following in the footsteps of others of you in fixing the guilt on the individual who did, as I submit I am about to prove to you beyond any possibility of doubt, commit this foul crime.'

Having thus provided for the improbable contingency of some other member of the Circle having been so clever as himself, Sir Charles cut some of the cackle and got down to business.

'I set about this matter with one question in my mind and only one – the question to which the right answer has proved a sure guide to the criminal in almost every murder that has ever been committed, the question which hardly any criminal can avoid leaving behind him, damning though he knows the answer must be: the question – *cui bono?*' Sir Charles allowed a pregnant moment of silence. 'Who,' he translated obligingly, 'was the gainer? Who,' he paraphrased, for the benefit of any possible half-wits in his audience, 'would, to put it bluntly, *score* by the death of Sir Eustace Pennefather?' He darted looks of enquiry from under his tufted eyebrows, but his hearers dutifully played the game; nobody undertook to enlighten him prematurely.

Sir Charles was far too practised a rhetorician to enlighten them prematurely himself. Leaving the question as an immense query-mark in their minds, he veered off on another track.

'Now there were, as I saw it, only three definite clues in this crime,' he continued, in almost conversational tones. 'I refer, of course, to the forged letter, the wrapper, and the chocolates themselves. Of these the wrapper could only be helpful so far as its postmark. The hand-printed address I dismissed as useless. It could have been done by any one, at any time. It led, I felt, nowhere. And I could not see that the chocolates or the box that contained them were of the least use as evidence. I may be wrong, but I could not see it. They were specimens of a well-known brand, on sale at hundreds of shops; it would be fruitless to attempt to trace their purchaser. Moreover any possibilities in that direction would quite certainly have been explored already by the police. I was left, in short, with only two pieces of material evidence, the forged letter and the postmark on the wrapper, on which the whole structure of proof must be erected.'

Sir Charles paused again, to let the magnitude of this task sink into the minds of others; apparently he had overlooked the fact that this problem must have been common to all. Roger, who with difficulty had remained silent so long, interposed a gentle question.

'Had you already made up your mind as to the criminal, Sir Charles?'

'I had already answered to my own satisfaction the question I had posed to myself, to which I made reference a few minutes ago,' replied Sir Charles, with dignity but without explicitness.

'I see. You had made up your mind,' Roger pinned him down. 'It would be interesting to know, so that we can follow better your way of approaching the proof. You used inductive methods then?'

'Possibly, possibly,' said Sir Charles testily. Sir Charles strongly disliked being pinned down.

He glowered for a moment in silence, to recover from this indignity.

'The task, I saw at once,' he resumed, in a sterner voice, 'was not going to be an easy one. The period at my disposal was extremely limited, far-reaching enquiries were obviously necessary, my own time was far too closely engaged to permit me to make in person, any investigations I might find advisable. I thought the matter over and decided that the only possible way in which I could arrive at a conclusion was to consider the facts of the case for a sufficient length of time till I was enabled to formulate a theory which would stand every test I could apply to it out of such knowledge as was already at my disposal, and then make a careful list of further points which were outside my own knowledge but which must be facts if my theory were correct; these points could then be investigated by persons acting on my behalf and, if they were substantiated, my theory would be conclusively proved.' Sir Charles drew a breath.

'In other words,' Roger murmured with a smile to Alicia Dammers, turning a hundred words into six, ' "I decided to employ inductive methods." ' But he spoke so softly that nobody but Miss Dammers heard him.

She smiled back appreciatively. The art of the written word is not that of the spoken one.

'I formed my theory,' announced Sir Charles, with surprising simplicity. Perhaps he was still a little short of breath.

'I formed my theory. Of necessity much of it was guesswork. Let me give an example. The possession by the criminal of a sheet of Mason & Sons' notepaper had puzzled me more than anything. It was not an article which the individual I had in mind might be expected to possess, still less be able to acquire. I could not conceive any method by which, the plot already decided upon and the sheet of paper required for its accomplishment, such a thing could be deliberately acquired by the individual in question without suspicion being raised afterwards.

'I therefore formed the conclusion that it was the actual ability to obtain a piece of Mason's notepaper in a totally unsuspicious way, which was the reason of the notepaper of that particular firm being employed at all.' Sir Charles looked triumphantly round as if awaiting something.

Roger supplied it; no less readily for all that the point must have occurred to every one as being almost too obvious to need any comment. 'That's a very interesting point indeed, Sir Charles. Most ingenious.'

Sir Charles nodded his agreement. 'Sheer guesswork, I admit. Nothing but guesswork. But guesswork that was justified in the result.' Sir Charles was becoming so lost in admiration of his own perspicacity that he had forgotten all his love of long, winding sentences and smooth-rolling subordinate clauses. His massive head positively jerked on his shoulders.

'I considered how such a thing might come into one's possession, and whether the possession could be verified afterwards. It occurred to me at last that many firms insert a piece of notepaper with a receipted bill, with the words "With compliments" or some such phrase typed on it. That gave me three questions. Was this practice employed at Mason's? Had the individual in question an account at Mason's, or more particularly, to explain the yellowed edge of the paper, had there been such an account in the past? Were there any indications on the paper of such a phrase having been carefully erased?

'Ladies and gentlemen,' boomed Sir Charles, puce with excitement, 'you will see that the odds against those three questions being answered in the affirmative were enormous. Overwhelming. Before I posed them I knew that, should it prove to be the case, no mere chance could be held responsible.' Sir Charles dropped his voice. 'I knew,' he said slowly, 'that if those three questions of mine were answered in the affirmative, the individual I had in mind must be as guilty as if I had actually watched the poison being injected into those chocolates.'

He paused and looked impressively round him, riveting all eyes on his face.

'Ladies and gentlemen, those three questions *were* answered in the affirmative.'

Oratory is a powerful art. Roger knew perfectly well that Sir Charles, out of sheer force of habit, was employing on them all the usual and hackneyed forensic tricks. It was with difficulty, Roger felt that he refrained from adding 'of the jury' to his 'Ladies and gentlemen'. But really this was only what might have been expected. Sir Charles had a good story to tell, and a story in which he obviously sincerely believed, and was simply telling it in the way which, after these years of practice, came most naturally to him. That was not what was annoying Roger.

What did annoy him was that he himself had been plodding on the scent of quite a different hare and, convinced as he had been that his must be the right one, had at first been only mildly amused as Sir Charles flirted round the skirts of his own quarry. Now he had allowed himself to be influenced by mere rhetoric, cheap though he knew it to be, into wondering.

But was it only rhetoric that had made him begin to doubt? Sir Charles seemed to have some substantial facts to weave into the airy web of his oratory. And pompous old fellow though he might be, he was certainly no fool. Roger began to feel distinctly uneasy. For his own hare, he had to admit, was a very elusive one.

As Sir Charles proceeded to develop his thesis, Roger's uneasiness began to turn into downright unhappiness.

'There can be no doubt about it. I ascertained through an agent that Mason's, an old-fashioned firm, invariably paid such private customers as had an account with them (nine-tenths of their business of course is wholesale) the courtesy of including a statement of thanks, just two or three words typed in the middle of a sheet of notepaper. I ascertained that this individual had had an account with the firm, which was apparently closed five months ago; that is to say, a cheque was sent then in settlement and no goods have been ordered since.

'Moreover I found time to pay a special visit myself to Scotland Yard in order to examine that letter again. By looking at the back I could make out quite distinct though indecipherable traces of former typewritten words in the middle of the page. These latter cut halfway down one of the lines of the letter and so prove that they could not have been an erasure from that; they correspond in length to the statement I expected; and they show signs of the most careful attempts, by rubbing, rolling and re-roughening the smoothed paper, to eradicate not only the typewriter-ink but even the actual indentations caused by the metal letter-arms.

'This I held to be conclusive proof that my theory was correct, and at once I set about clearing up such other doubtful points as had occurred to me. Time was short, and I had recourse to no less than four firms of trustworthy inquiry-agents among whom I divided the task of providing the data I was seeking. This not only saved me considerable time, but had the advantage of not putting the sum-total of the information obtained into any hands but my own. Indeed I did my best so to split up my queries as to prevent any of the firms from even guessing what object I had in mind; and in this I am of the opinion that I have been successful.

'My next care was the postmark. It was necessary for my case that I should prove that my suspect had actually been in the neighbourhood of the Strand at the time in question. You will say,' suggested Sir Charles, searching the interested faces round him, and apparently picking upon Mr Morton Harrogate Bradley as the raiser of this futile objection. 'You will say,' said Sir Charles sternly to Mr Bradley, 'that this was not necessary. The parcel might have been posted quite innocently by an unwitting accomplice to whom it had been entrusted, so that the actual criminal had an unshakable alibi for that period; the more so as the individual to whom I refer was actually not in this country, so that it would be all the easier to request a friend who might be travelling to England to undertake the task of posting the parcel in this country and so saving the cost of the foreign postage, which on parcels is not considerable.

'I do not agree,' said Sir Charles to Mr Bradley, still more severely. 'I have considered that point, and I do not think the individual I had in mind would undertake such a very grave risk. For the friend would almost certainly remember the incident when she read of the affair in the papers, as would be almost inevitable.

'No,' concluded Sir Charles, finally crushing Mr Bradley once and for all, 'I am convinced that the individual I am thinking of would realise that nobody else must handle that parcel till it had passed into the keeping of the post-office.'

'Of course,' said Mr Bradley academically, 'Lady Pennefather may have had not an innocent accomplice but a guilty one. You've considered that, of course?' Mr Bradley managed to convey that the matter was of no real interest, but as Sir Charles had been addressing these remarks directly to him it was only courteous to comment on them.

Sir Charles purpled visibly. He had been priding himself on the skilful way in which he had been withholding his suspect's name, to bring it out with a lovely plump right at the end after proving his case, just like a real detective story. And now this wretched scribbler of the things had spoilt it all.

'Sir,' he intoned, in proper Johnsonian manner, 'I must call your attention to the fact that I have mentioned no names at all. To do such a thing is most imprudent. Do I need to remind you that there is such a thing as a law of libel?'

Morton Harrogate smiled his maddeningly superior smile (he really was a most insufferable young man). 'Really, Sir Charles!' he mocked, stroking his little sleek object he wore on his upper lip. 'I'm not going to write a story about Lady Pennefather trying to murder her husband, if that's what you're warning me against. Or could it possibly be that you were referring to the law of slander?'

Sir Charles who had meant slander, enveloped Mr Bradley in a crimson glare.

Roger sped to the rescue. The combatants reminded him of a bull and a gadfly, and that is a contest which is often good fun to watch. But the Crimes Circle had been founded to investigate the crimes of others, not to provide opportunities for new ones. Roger did not particularly like either the bull or the gadfly, but both amused him in their different ways; he certainly disliked neither. Mr Bradley on the other hand disliked both Roger and Sir Charles. He disliked Roger the more of the two because Roger was a gentleman and pretended not to be, whereas he himself was not a gentleman and pretended he was. And that surely is cause enough to dislike anyone.

'I'm glad you raised that point, Sir Charles,' Roger now said smoothly. 'It's one we must consider. Personally I don't see how we're to progress at all unless we come to some arrangement concerning the law of slander, do you?'

Sir Charles consented to be mollified. 'It is a difficult point,' he agreed, the lawyer in him immediately swamping the outraged human being. A born lawyer will turn aside from any other minor pursuit, even briefs, for a really knotty legal point, just as a born woman will put on her best set of underclothes and powder her nose before inserting the latter in the gas-oven.

'I think,' Roger said carefully, anxious not to wound legal susceptibilities (it was a bold proposition for a layman to make), 'that we should disregard that particular law. I mean,' he added hastily, observing the look of pain on Sir Charles' brow at being asked to condone this violation of a *lex intangenda*, 'I mean, we should come to some such arrangement as that anything said in this room should be without prejudice, or among friends, or – or not in the spirit of the adverb,' he plunged desperately, 'or whatever the legal wriggle is.' On the whole it was not a tactful speech.

But it is doubtful whether Sir Charles heard it. A dreamy look had come into his eyes, as of a Lord of Appeal crooning over a piece of red tape. 'Slander, as we all know,' he murmured, 'consists in the malicious speaking of such words as render the party who speaks them in the hearing of others liable to an action at the suit of the party to whom they apply. In this case, the imputation being of a crime or misdemeanour which is punishable corporeally, pecuniary damage would not have to be proved, and, the imputation being defamatory, its falsity would be presumed and the burden of proving its truth would be laid upon the defendant. We should therefore have the interesting situation of the defendant in a slander action becoming, in essence, the plaintiff in a civil suit for murder. And really,' said Sir Charles in much perplexity, 'I don't know what would happen then.'

'Er – what about privilege?' suggested Roger feebly.

'Of course,' Sir Charles disregarded him, 'there would have to be stated in the declaration the actual words used, not merely their meaning and general inference, and failure to prove them as stated would result in the plaintiff being nonsuited; so that unless notes were taken here and signed by a witness who had heard the defamation, I do not quite see how an action could lie.'

'Privilege?' murmured Roger despairingly.

'Moreover I should be of the opinion,' said Sir Charles, brightening, 'that this might be regarded as one of those proper occasions upon which statements, in themselves defamatory, and even false, may be made if from a perfectly proper motive and with an entire belief in their truth. In that case the presumption would be reversed and the burden would be on the plaintiff to prove, and that to the satisfaction of a jury, that the defendant was actuated by express malice. In that case I rather fancy that the court would be guided almost wholly by considerations of public expediency, which would probably mean that – '

'Privilege!' said Roger loudly.

Sir Charles turned on him the dull eye of a red-ink fiend. But this time the word had penetrated. 'I was coming to that,' he reproved. 'Now in our case I hardly think that a plea of public privilege would be accepted. As to private privilege, the limits are of course exceedingly difficult to define. It would be doubtful if we could plead successfully that all statements made here are matters of purely private communication, because it is a question whether this Circle does constitute, in actual fact, a private or a public gathering. One could,' said Sir Charles with much interest, 'argue either way. Or even, for the matter of that, that it is a private body meeting in public, or, *vice versa,* a public gathering held in private. The point is a very debatable one.' Sir Charles swung his glasses for a moment to emphasise the extreme debatability of the point.

'But I do feel inclined to venture the opinion,' he plunged at last, 'that on the whole we might be justified in taking up our stand upon the submission that the occasion *is* privileged in so far as it is concerned entirely with communications which are made with no *animus injuriandi* but solely in performance of a duty not necessarily legal but moral or social, and any statements so uttered are covered by a plea of *veritas convicii* being made within proper limits by persons in the *bona fide* prosecution of their own and the public interest. I am bound to say however,' Sir Charles immediately proceeded to hedge as if horrified at having committed himself at last, 'that this is not a matter of complete certainty, and a wiser policy might be to avoid the direct mention of any name, while holding ourselves free to indicate in some unmistakable manner, such as by signs, or possibly by some form of impersonation or acting, the individual to whom we severally refer.'

'Still,' pursued the President, faint but persistent, 'on the whole you do think that the occasion may be regarded as privileged, and we may go ahead and mention any name we like?'

Sir Charles' glasses described a complete and symbolical circle. 'I think,' said Sir Charles very weightily indeed (after all it was an opinion which would have cost the Circle such a surprisingly round sum had it been delivered in chambers that Sir Charles need not be grudged a little weight in the delivering of it). 'I think,' said Sir Charles, 'that we might take that risk.'

'Right-ho!' said the President with relief.

chapter six

'I dare say,' resumed Sir Charles, 'that many of you will have already reached the same conclusion as myself, with regard to the identity of the murderer. The case seems to me to afford so striking a parallel with one of the classical murders, that the similarity can hardly have passed unnoticed. I refer, of course, to the Marie Lafarge case.'

'Oh!' said Roger, surprised. So far as he was concerned the similarity had passed unnoticed. He wriggled uncomfortably. Now one came to consider it, of course the parallel was obvious.

'There too we have a wife, accused of sending a poisoned article to her husband. Whether the article was a cake or a box of chocolates is beside the point. It will not do perhaps to – '

'But nobody in their sane senses still believes that Marie Lafarge was guilty,' Alicia Dammers interrupted, with unusual warmth. 'It's been practically proved that the cake was sent by the foreman, or whatever he was. Wasn't his name Dennis? His motive was much bigger than hers, too.'

Sir Charles regarded her severely. 'I think I said, *accused* of sending. I was referring to a matter of fact, not of opinion.'

'Sorry,' nodded Miss Dammers, unabashed.

'In any case, I just mention the coincidence for what it is worth. Let us now go back to resume our argument at the point we left it. In that connection, the question was raised just now,' said Sir Charles, determinedly impersonal, 'as to whether Lady Pennefather may have had not an innocent accomplice but a guilty one. That doubt had already occurred to me. I have satisfied myself that it is not the case. She planned and carried through this affair alone.' He paused, inviting the obvious question.

Roger tactfully supplied it.

'How could she, Sir Charles? We know that she was in the South of France the whole time. The police investigated that very point. She has a complete alibi.'

Sir Charles positively beamed at him. 'She *had* a complete alibi. I have destroyed it.'

'This is what actually happened. Three days before the parcel was posted Lady Pennefather left Mentone and went, ostensibly, for a week to Avignon. At the end of the week she returned to Mentone. Her signature is in the hotel register at Avignon, she has the receipted bill, everything is quite in order. The only curious thing is that apparently she did not take her maid, a very superior young woman of smart appearance and good manners, to Avignon with her, for the hotel receipt is for one person only. And yet the maid did not stay at Mentone. Did the maid then vanish into thin air?' demanded Sir Charles indignantly.

'Oh!' nodded Mr Chitterwick, who had been listening intently. 'I see. How ingenious.'

'Highly ingenious,' agreed Sir Charles, complacently taking the credit for the erring lady's ingenuity. 'The maid took the mistress' place; the mistress paid a secret visit to England. And I have verified that beyond any doubt. An agent, acting on telegraphic instructions from me, showed the hotel proprietor at Avignon a photograph of Lady Pennefather and asked whether such a person had ever stayed in the hotel; the man averred that he had never seen her in his life. My agent showed him a snapshot which he had obtained of the maid; the proprietor recognised her instantly as Lady Pennefather. Another "guess" of mine had proved only too accurate.' Sir Charles leaned back in his chair and swung his glasses in silent tribute to his own astuteness.

'Then Lady Pennefather did have an accomplice?' murmured Mr Bradley, with the air of one discussing *The Three Bears* with a child of four.

'An innocent accomplice,' retorted Sir Charles. 'My agent questioned the maid tactfully, and learned that her mistress had told her that she had to go over to England on urgent business but, having already spent six months of the current year in that country, would have to pay British income-tax if she so much as set foot in England again that year. A considerable sum was in question, and Lady Pennefather suggested this plan as a means of getting around the difficulty with a handsome bribe to the girl. Not unnaturally the offer was accepted. Most ingenious; most ingenious.' He paused again and beamed round, inviting tributes.

'How very clever of you, Sir Charles,' murmured Alicia Dammers, stepping into the breach.

'I have no actual proof of her stay in this country,' regretted Sir Charles, 'so that from the legal point of view the case against her is incomplete in that respect, but that will be a matter for the police to discover. In all other respects, I submit, my case is complete. I regret, I regret exceedingly, having to say so, but I have no alternative: Lady Pennefather is Mrs Bendix's murderess.'

There was a thoughtful silence when Sir Charles had finished speaking. Questions were in the air, but nobody seemed to care to be the first to put one. Roger gazed into vacancy, as if looking longingly after the spoor of his own hare. There was no doubt that, as matters stood at present, Sir Charles seemed to have proved his case.

Mr Ambrose Chitterwick plucked up courage to break the silence. 'We must congratulate you, Sir Charles. Your solution is as brilliant as it is surprising. Only one question occurs to me and that is the one of motive. Why should Lady Pennefather desire her husband's death when she is actually in process of divorcing him? Had she any reason to suspect that a decree would not be granted?'

'None at all,' replied Sir Charles blandly. 'It was just because she was so certain that a decree would be granted that she desired his death.'

'I – I don't quite understand,' stammered Mr Chitterwick.

Sir Charles allowed the general bewilderment to continue for a few more moments before he condescended to dispel it. He had the orator's feeling for atmosphere.

'I referred at the beginning of my remarks to a piece of knowledge which had come into my possession and which had helped me materially towards my solution. I am now prepared to disclose, in strict confidence, what that piece of knowledge was.

'You already know that there was talk of an engagement between Sir Eustace and my daughter. I do not think I shall be violating the secrets of the confessional if I tell you that not many weeks ago, Sir Eustace came to me and formally asked me to sanction an engagement between them as soon as his wife's decree *nisi* had been pronounced.

'I need not tell you all that transpired at that interview. What is relevant is that Sir Eustace informed me categorically that his wife had been extremely unwilling to divorce him, and he had only succeeded in the end by making a will entirely in her favour, including his estate in Worcestershire. She had a small private income of her own, and he was going to make her such allowance in addition as he was able; but with the interest on the mortgage on his estate swallowing up nearly all the rent he was getting for it, and his other expenses, this could not be a large one. His life, however, was heavily insured in accordance with Lady Pennefather's marriage settlements, and the mortgage on the estate was in the nature of an endowment policy, and lapsed with his death. He had therefore, as he candidly admitted, very little to offer my daughter.

'Like myself,' said Sir Charles impressively, 'you cannot fail to grasp the significance of this. According to the will then in existence, Lady Pennefather from being not even comfortably off would become a comparatively rich woman on her husband's death. But rumours are reaching her ears of a possible marriage between that husband and another woman as soon as the divorce is complete. What is more probable than that when such an engagement is actually concluded, a new will will be made?

'Her character is already shown in a strong enough light by her willingness to accept the bribe of the will as an inducement to divorce. She is obviously a grasping woman, greedy for money. Murder is only another step for such a woman to take. And murder is her only hope. I do not think,' concluded Sir Charles, 'that I need to labour the point any further.' His glasses swung deliberately.

'It's uncommonly convincing,' Roger said, with a little sigh. 'Are you going to hand this information over to the police, Sir Charles?'

'I conceive that failure to do so would be a gross dereliction of my duty as a citizen,' Sir Charles replied, with a pomposity that in no way concealed how pleased he was with himself.

'Humph!' observed Mr Bradley, who evidently was not going to be so pleased with Sir Charles as Sir Charles was. 'What about the chocolates? Is it part of your case that she prepared them over here, or brought them with her?'

Sir Charles waved an airy hand. 'Is that material?'

'I should say that it would be very material to connect her at any rate with the poison.'

'Nitrobenzene? One might as well try to connect her with the purchase of the chocolates. She would have no difficulty in getting hold of that. I regard her choice of poison, in fact, as on a par with the ingenuity she has displayed in all the other particulars.'

'I see.' Mr Bradley stroked his little moustache and eyed Sir Charles combatively. 'Come to think of it, you know, Sir Charles, you haven't really proved a case against Lady Pennefather at all. All you've proved is motive and opportunity.'

An unexpected ally ranged herself beside Mr Bradley. 'Exactly!' cried Mrs Fielder-Flemming. 'That's just what I was about to point out myself. If you hand over the information you've collected to the police, Sir Charles, I don't think they'll thank you for it. As Mr Bradley says, you haven't proved that Lady Pennefather's guilty, or anything like it. I'm quite sure you're altogether mistaken.'

Sir Charles was so taken aback that for a moment he could only stare. '*Mistaken!*' he managed to ejaculate. It was clear that such a possibility had never entered Sir Charles' orbit.

'Well, perhaps I'd better say – wrong,' amended Mrs Fielder-Flemming, quite drily.

'But my dear madam – ' For once words did not come to Sir Charles. 'But why?' he fell back upon, feebly.

'Because I'm sure of it,' retorted Mrs Fielder-Flemming, most unsatisfactorily.

Roger had been watching this exchange with a gradual change of feeling. From being hypnotised by Sir Charles' persuasiveness and self-confidence into something like reluctant agreement, he was swinging round now in reaction to the other extreme. Dash it all, this fellow Bradley had kept a clearer head after all. And he was perfectly right. There were gaps in Sir Charles' case that Sir Charles himself, as counsel for Lady Pennefather's defence, could have driven a coach-and-six through.

'Of course,' he said thoughtfully, 'the fact that before she went abroad Lady Pennefather may have had an account at Mason's isn't surprising in the least. Nor is the fact that Mason's send out a complimentary chit with their receipts. As Sir Charles himself said, very many old-fashioned firms of good repute do. And the fact that the sheet of paper on which the letter was written had been used previously for some such purpose is not only not surprising, when one comes to consider; it's even obvious. Whoever the murderer, the same problem of getting hold of the piece of notepaper would arise. Yes, really, that Sir Charles' three initial questions should have happened to find affirmative answers, does seem little more than a coincidence.'

Sir Charles turned on this new antagonist like a wounded bull. 'But the odds were enormous against it!' he roared. 'If it was a coincidence, it was the most incredible one in the whole course of my experience.'

'Ah, Sir Charles, but you're prejudiced,' Mr Bradley told him gently. 'And you exaggerate dreadfully, you know. You seem to be putting the odds at somewhere round about a million to one. I should put them at six to one. Permutations and combinations, you know.'

'Damn your permutations, sir!' riposted Sir Charles with vigour. 'And your combinations too.'

Mr Bradley turned to Roger. 'Mr Chairman, is it within the rules of this club for one member to insult another member's underwear? Besides, Sir Charles,' he added to that fuming knight, 'I don't wear the things. Never have done, since I was an infant.'

For the dignity of the chair Roger could not join in the delighted titters that were escaping round the table; in the interests of the Circle's preservation he had to pour oil on these very seething waters.

'Bradley, you're losing sight of the point, aren't you? I don't want to destroy your theory necessarily, Sir Charles, or detract in any way from the really brilliant manner in which you've defended it; but if it's to stand its ground it must be able to resist any arguments we can bring against it. That's all. And I honestly do think that you're inclined to attach a little too much importance to the answers to those three questions. What do you say, Miss Dammers?'

'I agree,' Miss Dammers said crisply. 'The way Sir Charles emphasised their importance reminded me at the time of a favourite trick of detective-story writers. He said, if I remember rightly, that if those questions were answered in the affirmative he knew that his suspect was guilty just as much as if he'd seen her with his own eyes putting the poison into the chocolates, because the odds against a coincidental affirmative to all three of them were incalculable. In other words he simply made a strong assertion, unsupported by evidence or argument.'

'And that is what detective-story writers do, Miss Dammers?' queried Mr Bradley, with a tolerant smile.

'Invariably, Mr Bradley. I've often noticed it in your own books. You state a thing so emphatically that the reader does not think of questioning the assertion. "Here," says the detective, "is a bottle of red liquid and here is a bottle of blue. If these two liquids turn out to be ink, then we know that they were purchased to fill up the empty ink-pots in the library as surely as if we had read the dead man's very thoughts." Whereas the red ink might have been bought by one of the maids to dye a jumper, and the blue by the secretary for his fountain-pen; or a hundred other such explanations. But any possibilities of that kind are silently ignored. Isn't that so?'

'Perfectly,' agreed Bradley, unperturbed. 'Don't waste time on unessentials. Just tell the reader very loudly what he's to think, and he'll think it all right. You've got the technique perfectly. Why don't you try your hand at it? It's quite a paying game, you know.'

'I may one day. And anyhow I will say for you, Mr Bradley, that your detectives do detect. They don't just stand about and wait for somebody else to tell them who committed the murder, as the so-called detectives do in most of the so-called detective stories I read.'

'Thank you,' said Mr Bradley, 'Then you actually read detective-stories, Miss Dammers?'

'Certainly,' said Miss Dammers crisply. 'Why not?' She dismissed Mr Bradley as abruptly as she had answered his challenge. 'And the letter itself, Sir Charles? The typewriting. You don't attach any importance to that?'

'As a detail, of course it would have to be considered; I was only sketching out the broad lines of the case.' Sir Charles was no longer bull-like. 'I take it that the police would ferret out pieces of conclusive evidence of that nature.'

'I think they might have some difficulty in connecting Pauline Pennefather with the machine that typed that letter,' observed Mrs Fielder-Flemming, not without tartness.

The tide of feeling had obviously set in against Sir Charles.

'But the motive,' he pleaded, now pathetically on the defensive. 'You must admit that the motive is overwhelming.'

'You don't know Pauline, Sir Charles – Lady Pennefather?' Miss Dammers suggested.

'I do not.'

'Evidently,' commented Miss Dammers.

'You don't agree with Sir Charles' theory, Miss Dammers?' ventured Mr Chitterwick.

'I do not,' said Miss Dammers with emphasis.

'Might one enquire your reason?' ventured Mr Chitterwick further.

'Certainly you may. It's a conclusive one, I'm afraid, Sir Charles. I was in Paris at the time of the murder, and just about the very hour when the parcel was being posted I was talking to Pauline Pennefather in the foyer of the Opera.'

'What!' exclaimed the discomfited Sir Charles, the remnants of his beautiful theory crashing about his ears.

'I should apologise for not having given you this information before, I suppose,' said Miss Dammers with the utmost calmness, 'but I wanted to see what sort of a case you could put up against her. And I really do congratulate you. It was a remarkable piece of inductive reasoning. If I hadn't happened to know that it was built up on a complete fallacy you would have quite convinced me.'

'But – but why the secrecy, and – and the impersonation by the maid, if her visit was an innocent one?' stammered Sir Charles, his mind revolving wildly round private aeroplanes and the time they would take from the *Place de l'Opéra* to Trafalgar Square.

'Oh, I didn't say it was an innocent one,' retorted Miss Dammers carelessly. 'Sir Eustace isn't the only one who is waiting for the divorce to marry again. And in the interim Pauline, quite rightly, doesn't see why she should waste valuable time. After all, she isn't so young as she was. And there's always a strange creature called the King's Proctor, isn't there?'

Shortly after that the Chairman adjourned the meeting of the Circle. He did so because he did not wish one of the members to die of apoplexy on his hands.

chapter seven

Mrs Fielder-Flemming was nervous. Actually nervous.

She shuffled the pages of her notebook aimlessly, and seemed hardly able to sit through the few preliminaries which had to be settled before Roger asked her to give the solution which she had already affirmed, privately, to Alicia Dammers, to be indubitably the correct one of Mrs Bendix's murder. With such a weighty piece of knowledge in her mind one would have thought that for once in her life Mrs Fielder-Flemming had a really heaven-sent opportunity to be impressive, but for once in her life she made no use of it. If she had not been Mrs Fielder-Flemming, one might have gone so far as to say that she dithered.

'Are you ready, Mrs Fielder-Flemming?' Roger asked, gazing at this surprising manifestation.

Mrs Fielder-Flemming adjusted her very unbecoming hat, rubbed her nose (being innocent of powder, it did not suffer under this habitual treatment; just shone a little more brightly in pink embarrassment), and shot a covert glance round the table. Roger continued to gaze in astonishment. Mrs Fielder-Flemming was positively shrinking from the limelight. For some occult reason she was approaching her task with real distaste, and a distaste at that quite out of comparison with the task's significance.

She cleared her throat nervously. 'I have a very difficult duty to perform,' she began in a low voice. 'Last night I hardly slept. Anything more distasteful to a woman like myself it is impossible to imagine.' She paused, moistening her lips.

'Oh, come, Mrs Fielder-Flemming,' Roger felt himself impelled to encourage her. 'It's the same for all of us, you know. And I've heard you make a most excellent speech at one of your own first nights.'

Mrs Fielder-Flemming looked at him, not at all encouraged. 'I was not referring to that aspect of it, Mr Sheringham,' she retorted, rather more tartly. 'I was speaking of the burden which has been laid on me by the knowledge that has come into my possession, the terrible duty I have to perform in consequence of it.'

'You mean you've solved the little problem?' enquired Mr Bradley, without reverence.

Mrs Fielder-Flemming regarded him sombrely. 'With infinite regret,' she said, in low, womanly tones, 'I have.' Mrs Fielder-Flemming was recovering her poise.

She consulted her notes for a moment, and then began to speak in a firmer voice. 'Criminology I have always regarded with something of a professional eye. Its main interest has always been for me its immense potentialities for drama. The inevitability of murder; the predestined victim, struggling unconsciously and vainly against fate; the predestined killer, moving first unconsciously too and then with full and relentless realisation, towards the accomplishment of his doom; the hidden causes, unknown perhaps to both victim and killer, which are all the time urging on the fulfilment of destiny.

'Apart from the action and the horror of the deed itself, I have always felt that there are more possibilities of real drama in the most ordinary or sordid of murders than in any other situation that can occur to man. Ibsenish in the inevitable working out of certain circumstances in juxtaposition that we call fate, no less than Edgar-Wallacish in the καθαρσιζ undergone by the emotions of the onlooker at their climax.

'It was perhaps natural then that I should regard not only this particular case from something of the standpoint of my calling (and certainly no more dramatic twist could well be invented), but the task of solving it too. Anyhow, natural or not, this is what I did; and the result has terribly justified me. I considered the case in the light of one of the oldest dramatic situations, and very soon everything became only too clear. I am referring to the situation which the gentlemen who pass among us in these days for dramatic critics, invariably call the Eternal Triangle.

'I had to begin of course with only one of the triangle's three members, Sir Eustace Pennefather. Of the two unknown one must be a woman, the other might be woman or man. So I fell back on another very old and very sound maxim, and proceeded to *chercher la femme.* And,' said Mrs Fielder-Flemming, very solemnly, 'I found her.'

So far, it must be admitted, her audience was not particularly impressed. Even the promising opening had not stirred them, for it was only to be expected that Mrs Fielder-Flemming would feel it her duty to emphasise her feminine shrinkings from handing a criminal over to justice. Her somewhat laborious sentences too, obviously learned off by heart for the occasion, detracted if anything from the interest of what she had to convey.

But when she resumed, having waited in vain for a tributary gasp at her last momentous piece of information, the somewhat calculated tenseness of her style had given way to an unrehearsed earnestness which was very much more impressive.

'I wasn't expecting the triangle to be the hackneyed one,' she said, with a slight dig at the deflated remains of Sir Charles. 'Lady Pennefather I hardly considered for a moment. The subtlety of the crime, I felt sure, must be a reflection of an unusual situation. And after all a triangle need not necessarily include a husband and wife among its members; any three people, if the circumstances arrange them so, can form one. It is the circumstances, not the three protagonists, that make the triangle.

'Sir Charles has told us that this crime reminded him of the Marie Lafarge case, and in some respects (he might have added) the Mary Ansell case too. It reminded me of a case as well but it was neither of these. The Molineux case in New York, it seems to me, provides a much closer parallel than either.

'You all remember the details, of course. Mr Cornish, a director of the important Knickerbocker Athletic Club, received in his Christmas mail a small silver cup and a phial of bromo-seltzer, addressed to him at the club. He thought they had been sent by way of a joke, and kept the wrapper in order to identify the humorist. A few days later a woman who lived in the same boarding-house as Cornish complained of a headache and Cornish gave her some of the bromo-seltzer. In a very short time she was dead, and Cornish, who had taken just a sip because she complained of it being bitter, was violently ill but recovered later.

'In the end a man named Molineux, another member of the same club, was arrested and put on trial. There was quite a lot of evidence against him, and it was known that he hated Cornish bitterly, so much so that he had already assaulted him once. Moreover another member of the club, a man named Barnet, had been killed earlier in the year through taking what purported to be a sample of a well-known headache powder which had also been sent to him at the club and, shortly before the Cornish episode, Molineux married a girl who had actually been engaged to Barnet at the time of his death; he had always wanted her, but she had preferred Barnet. Molineux, as you remember, was convicted at his first trial and acquitted at his second; he afterwards became insane.

'Now this parallel seems to me complete. Our case is to all purposes a composite Cornish-cum-Barnet case. The resemblances are extraordinary. There is the poisoned article addressed to the man's club; there is, in the case of Cornish, the death of the wrong victim; there is the preservation of the wrapper; there is, in Barnet's case, the triangle element (and a triangle, you will notice, without husband and wife). It's quite startling. It is, in fact, more than startling; it's significant. Things don't happen like that quite by chance.'

Mrs Fielder-Flemming paused and blew her nose, delicately but with emotion. She was getting nicely worked up now, and so, in consequence, was her audience. If there were no gasps there was at any rate the tribute of complete silence till she was ready to go on.

'I said that this similarity was more than startling, that it was significant. I will explain its particular significance later; at present it is enough to say that I found it very helpful also. The realisation of the extreme closeness of the parallel came as quite a shock to me, but once I had grasped it I felt strangely convinced that it was in this very similarity that the clue to the solution of Mrs Bendix's murder was to be found. I felt this so strongly that I somehow actually *knew* it. These intuitions do come to me sometimes (explain them as you will) and I have never yet known them fail me. This one did not do so either.

'I began to examine this case in the light of the Molineux one. Would the latter help me to find the woman I was looking for in the former? What were the indications, so far as Barnet was concerned? Barnet received his fatal package because he was purposing to marry a girl whom the murderer was resolved he should not marry. With so many parallels between the two cases already, was there – ' Mrs Fielder-Flemming pushed back her unwieldy hat to a still more unbecoming angle and looked deliberately round the table with the air of an early Christian trying the power of the human eye on a doubtfully intimidated covey of lions – '*was there another here!*'

This time Mrs Fielder-Flemming was rewarded with several real and audible gasps. That of Sir Charles was quite the most audible, an outraged, indignant gasp that came perilously near to a snort. Mr Chitterwick gasped apprehensively, as if fearing something like a physical sequel to the sharp exchange of glances between Sir Charles and Mrs Fielder-Flemming, those of the former positively menacing in their warning, those of the lady almost vocal with her defiance of it.

The Chairman gasped too, wondering what a Chairman should do if two members of his circle, and of opposite sexes at that, should proceed to blows under his very nose.

Mr Bradley forgot himself so far as to gasp as well, in sheer, blissful ecstasy. Mrs Fielder-Flemming looked as if she were to prove a better hand at bull-baiting than himself, but Mr Bradley did not grudge her the honour so long as he was to be allowed to sit and hug himself in the audience. Not in his most daring toreador-like antics would Mr Bradley have ever dared to postulate the very daughter of his victim as the cause of the murder itself. Could this magnificent woman really bring forward a case to support so puncturing an idea? And what if it should actually turn out to be true? After all, such a thing was conceivable enough. Murders have been committed for the sake of lovely ladies often enough before; so why not for the lovely daughter of a pompous old silk? Oh God, oh Montreal.

Finally Mrs Fielder-Flemming gasped too, at herself.

Alone without a gasp sat Alicia Dammers, her face alight with nothing but an intellectual interest in the development of her fellow member's argument, determinedly impersonal. One was to gather that to Miss Dammers it was immaterial whether her own mother had been mixed up in the murder, so long as her part in it had provided opportunities for the sharpening of wits and the stimulation of intelligence. Without ever acknowledging her recognition that a personal element was being introduced into the Circle's investigations, she yet managed to radiate the idea that Sir Charles ought, if anything, to be detachedly delighted at the possibility of such enterprise on the part of his daughter.

Sir Charles however was far from delighted. From the red swelling of the veins on his forehead it was obvious that something was going to burst out of him in a very few seconds. Mrs Fielder-Flemming leapt, like an agitated but determined hen, for the gap.

'We have agreed to waive the law of slander here,' she almost squawked. 'Personalities don't exist for us. If the name crops up of any one personally known to us, we utter it as unflinchingly, in whatever connection, as if it were a complete stranger's. That is the definite arrangement we came to last night, Mr President, isn't it? We are to do what we conceive to be our duty to society quite irrespective of any personal considerations?'

For a moment Roger indulged his tremors. He did not want his beautiful Circle to explode in a cloud of dust, never again to be re-united. And though he could but admire the flurried but undaunted courage of Mrs Fielder-Flemming, he had to be content to envy it so far as Sir Charles was concerned, for he certainly did not possess anything like it himself. On the other hand there was no doubt that the lady had right on her side, and what can any President do but administer justice?

'Perfectly correct, Mrs Fielder-Flemming.' He had to admit, hoping his voice sounded as firm as he would have wished.

For a moment a blue glare, emanating from Sir Charles, enveloped him luridly. Then, as Mrs Fielder-Flemming, evidently heartened by this official support, took up her bomb again, the rays of the glare were switched again on to her. Roger, nervously watching the two of them, could not help reflecting that blue rays are things which should never be directed on to bombs.

Mrs Fielder-Flemming juggled featly with her bomb. Often though it seemed about to slip through her fingers, it never quite reached the ground or detonated. 'Very well, then. I will go on. My triangle now had the second of its members. On the analogy of the Barnet murder, where was the third to be found? Obviously with Molineux as the prototype, in some person who was anxious to prevent the first member from marrying the second.

'So far, you will see, I am not out of harmony with the conclusions Sir Charles gave us last night, though my method of arriving at them was perhaps somewhat different. He gave us a triangle also, without expressly defining it as such (perhaps even without recognising it as such). And the first two members of his triangle are precisely the same as the first two of mine.'

Here Mrs Fielder-Flemming made a notable effort to return something of Sir Charles' glare, in defiant challenge to contradiction. As she had simply stated a plain fact, however, which Sir Charles was quite unable to refute without explaining that he had not meant what he had meant the evening before, the challenge passed unanswered. Also the glare visibly diminished. But for all that (patently remarked Sir Charles' expression) a triangle by any other name does *not* smell so unsavoury.

'It is when we come to the third member,' pursued Mrs Fielder-Flemming with renewed poise, 'that we are at variance. Sir Charles suggested to us Lady Pennefather. I have not the pleasure of Lady Pennefather's acquaintance, but Miss Dammers who knows her well, tells me that in almost every particular the estimate given us by Sir Charles of her character was wrong. She is neither mean, grasping, greedy, nor in any imaginable way capable of the awful deed with which Sir Charles, perhaps a little rashly, was ready to credit her. Lady Pennefather, I understand, is a particularly sweet and kindly woman; somewhat broad-minded no doubt, but none the worse for that; indeed as some of us would think, a good deal the better.'

Mrs Fielder-Flemming encouraged the belief that she was not merely tolerant of a little harmless immorality, but actually ready to act as godmother to any particular instance of it. Indeed she went sometimes quite a long detour out of her way in order to propogate this belief among her friends. But unfortunately her friends would persist in remembering that she had refused to have anything more to do with one of her own nieces since the latter, on learning that her middle-aged husband kept, for purposes of convenience, a different mistress in each of the four quarters of England, and just to be on the safe side one in Scotland too, had run away with a young man of her own with whom she happened to be very devotedly in love.

'Just as I differ from Sir Charles over the identity of the third person in the triangle,' went on Mrs Fielder-Flemming, happily ignorant of her friends' memories, 'so I differ from him in the means by which that identity is to be established. We are at complete variance in our ideas regarding the very heart of the problem, the motive. Sir Charles would have us think that that this was a murder committed (or attempted, rather) for gain; I am convinced that the incentive was, at any rate, a less ignoble one than that. Murder, we are taught, can never be really justifiable; but there are occasions when it comes dangerously near it. This, in my opinion, was one of them.

'It is in the character of Sir Eustace himself that I see the clue to the identity of the third person. Let us consider it for a moment. We are not restricted by any considerations of slander, and we can say at once that, from certain points of view, Sir Eustace is a quite undesirable member of the community. From the point of view of a young man, for the sake of example, who is in love with a girl, Sir Eustace must be one of the very last persons with whom the young man would wish that girl to come into contact. He is not merely immoral, he is without excuse for his immorality, a far more serious thing. He is a rake, a spendthrift, without honour or scruples where women are concerned, and a man moreover who has already made a mess of marriage with a very charming woman and one by no means too narrow to overlook even a more than liberal allowance of the usual male peccadilloes and lapses. As a prospective husband for any young girl Sir Eustace Pennefather is a tragedy.

'And as a prospective husband for a young girl whom a man loves with all his heart,' intoned Mrs Fielder-Flemming very solemnly, 'it is easy to conceive that, in that particular man's regard, Sir Eustace Pennefather becomes nothing short of an impossibility.

'And a man who *is* a man,' added Mrs Fielder-Flemming, quite mauve with intensity, 'does not admit impossibilities.'

She paused, pregnantly.

'Curtain, Act I,' confided Mr Bradley behind his hand to Mr Ambrose Chitterwick.

Mr Chitterwick smiled nervously.

chapter eight

Sir Charles took the usual advantage of the first interval to rise from his seat. Like so many of us in these days by the time of the first interval (when it is not a play of Mrs Fielder-Flemming's that is in question) he felt almost physically unable to contain himself longer.

'Mr President,' he boomed, 'let us get this clear. Is Mrs Fielder-Flemming making the preposterous accusation that some friend of my daughter's is responsible for this crime, or is she not?'

The President looked somewhat helplessly up at the bulk towering wrathfully above him and wished he were anything but the President. 'I really don't know, Sir Charles,' he professed, which was not only feeble but untrue.

Mrs Fielder-Flemming however was by now quite able to speak up for herself. 'I have not yet specifically accused any one of the crime, Sir Charles,' she said, with a cold dignity that was only marred by the fact that her hat, which had apparently been sharing its mistress' emotions, was now perched rakishly over her left ear. 'So far I have been simply developing a thesis.'

To Mr Bradley Sir Charles would have replied, with Johnsonian scorn of evasion: 'Sir, damn your thesis.' Hampered now by the puerilities of civilised convention regarding polite intercourse between the sexes, he could only summon up once more the blue glare.

With the unfairness of her sex Mrs Fielder-Flemming promptly took advantage of his handicap. 'And,' she added pointedly, 'I have not yet finished doing so.'

Sir Charles sat down, the perfect allegory. But he grunted very naughtily to himself as he did so.

Mr Bradley restrained an impulse to clap Mr Chitterwick on the back and then chuck him under the chin.

Her serenity so natural as to be patently artificial, Mrs Fielder-Flemming proceeded to call the interval closed and ring up the curtain on her second act.

'Having given you my processes towards arriving at the identity of the third member of the triangle I postulated, in other words towards that of the murderer, I will go on to the actual evidence and show how that supports my conclusions. Did I say "supports"? I meant, confirms them beyond all doubt.'

'But what are your conclusions, Mrs Fielder-Flemming?' Bradley asked, with an air of bland interest. 'You haven't defined them yet. You only hinted that the murderer was a rival of Sir Eustace's for the hand of Miss Wildman.'

'Exactly,' agreed Alicia Dammers. 'Even if you don't want to tell us the man's name yet, Mabel, can't you narrow it down a little more for us?' Miss Dammers disliked vagueness. It savoured to her of the slipshod, which above all things in this world she detested. Moreover she really was extremely interested to know upon whom Mrs Fielder-Flemming's choice had alighted. Mabel, she knew, might look like one sort of fool, talk like another sort, and behave like a third; and yet really she was not a fool at all.

But Mabel was determined to be coy. 'Not yet, I'm afraid. For certain reasons I want to prove my case first. You'll understand later, I think.'

'Very well,' sighed Miss Dammers. 'But do let's keep away from the detective-story atmosphere. All we want to do is to solve this difficult case, not mystify each other.'

'I have my reasons, Alicia,' frowned Mrs Fielder-Flemming, and rather obviously proceeded to collect her thoughts. 'Where was I? Oh yes, the evidence. Now this is very interesting. I have succeeded in obtaining two pieces of quite vital evidence which I have never heard brought forward before.

'The first is that Sir Eustace was not in love with – ' Mrs Fielder-Flemming hesitated; then, as the plunge had already been taken for her, followed the intrepid Mr Bradley into the deeps of complete candour ' – with Miss Wildman at all. He intended to marry her simply for her money – or rather, for what he hoped to get of her father's money. I hope, Sir Charles,' added Mrs Fielder-Flemming frostily, 'that you will not consider me slanderous if I allude to the fact that you are an exceedingly rich man. It has a most important bearing on my case.'

Sir Charles inclined his massive, handsome head. 'It is hardly a matter of slander, madam. Simply one of taste, which is outside my professional orbit. I fear it would be a waste of time for me to attempt to advise you on it.'

'That is very interesting, Mrs Fielder-Flemming,' Roger hastily interposed on this exchange of pleasantries. 'How did you discover it?'

'From Sir Eustace's man, Mr Sheringham,' replied Mrs Fielder-Flemming not without pride. 'I interrogated him. Sir Eustace had made no secret of it. He seems to confide most freely in his man. He expected, apparently, to be able to pay off his debts, buy a racehorse or two, provide for the present Lady Pennefather, and generally make a fresh and no doubt discreditable start. He had actually promised Barker (that is his man's name) a present of a hundred pounds on the day he "led the little filly to the altar," as he phrased it. I am sorry to hurt your feelings, Sir Charles, but I have to deal with facts, and feelings must go down before them. A present of ten pounds bought me all the information I wanted. Quite remarkable information, as it turned out.' She looked round triumphantly.

'You don't think, perhaps,' ventured Mr Chitterwick with an apologetic smile, 'that information from such a tainted source might not be entirely reliable? The source seems so very tainted. Why, I don't think my own man would sell me for a ten-pound note.'

'Like master like man,' returned Mrs Fielder-Flemming shortly. 'His information was perfectly reliable. I was able to check nearly everything he told me, so that I think I am entitled to accept the small residue as correct too.

'I should like to quote another of Sir Eustace's confidences. It is not pretty, but it is very, very illuminating. He had made an attempt to seduce Miss Wildman in a private room at the Pug-Dog Restaurant (that, for instance, I checked later), apparently with the object of ensuring the certainty of the marriage he desired. (I am sorry again, Sir Charles, but these facts must be brought out.) I had better say at once that the attempt was unsuccessful. That night Sir Eustace remarked (and to his valet of all people, remember); "You can take a filly to the altar, but you can't make her drunk." That I think, will show you better than any words of mine just what manner of man Sir Eustace Pennefather is. And it will also show you how overwhelmingly strong was the incentive of the man who really loved her to put her for ever out of the reach of such a brute.

'And that brings me to the second piece of my evidence. This is really the foundation stone of the whole structure, the basis on which the necessity for murder (as the murderer saw it) rested, and the basis at the same time of my own reconstruction of the crime. Miss Wildman was hopelessly, unreasonably, irrevocably infatuated with Sir Eustace Pennefather.'

As an artist in dramatic effect, Mrs Fielder-Flemming was silent for a moment to allow the significance of this information to sink into the minds of her audience. But Sir Charles was far too personally preoccupied to be interested in significances.

'And may one ask how you found *that* out, madam?' he demanded, swelling with sarcasm. 'From my daughter's maid?'

'From your daughter's maid,' responded Mrs Fielder-Flemming sweetly. 'Detecting, I discover, is an expensive hobby, but one mustn't regret money spent in a good cause.'

Roger sighed. It was plain that, once this ill-fortuned child of his invention had died a painful death, the Circle (if it had not been completely squared by then) would be found to be without either Mrs Fielder-Flemming or Sir Charles Wildman; and he knew which of the two it would be. It was a pity. Sir Charles, besides being such an asset from the professional point of view, was the only leavening apart from Mr Ambrose Chitterwick of the literary element; and Roger, who had attended a few literary parties in his earlier days, was quite sure he would not be able to face a gathering that consisted of nothing but people who made their livings by their typewriters.

Besides, Mrs Fielder-Flemming really was being a little hard on the old man. After all, it was his daughter who was in question.

'I have now,' said Mrs Fielder-Flemming, 'established an overwhelming motive for the man who is in my mind to eliminate Sir Eustace. In fact it must have seemed to him the only possible way out of an intolerable situation. Let me now go on to connect him with the few facts allowed us by the anonymous murderer.

'When the Chief Inspector the other evening permitted us to examine the forged letter from Mason and Sons I examined it closely, because I know something about typewriters. That letter was typed on a Hamilton Machine. The man I have in mind has a Hamilton typewriter at his place of business. You may say that might be only a coincidence, the Hamilton being so generally used. So it might; but if you get enough coincidences lumped together, they cease to become coincidences at all and become certainties.

'In the same way we have the further coincidence of Mason's notepaper. This man has a definite connection with Mason's. Three years ago, as you may remember, Mason's were involved in a big lawsuit. I forget the details, but I think they brought an action against one of their rivals. You may remember, Sir Charles?'

Sir Charles nodded reluctantly, as if unwilling to help his antagonist even with this unimportant information. 'I ought to be,' he said shortly. 'It was against the Fearnley Chocolate Company for infringement of copyright in an advertisement figure. I led for Mason's.'

'Thank you. Yes, I thought it was something like that. Very well, then. This man was connected with that very case. He was helping Mason's, on the legal side. He must have been in and out of their office. His opportunities for possessing himself of a piece of their notepaper would have been legion. The chances by which he might have found himself three years later in possession of a piece would be innumerable. The paper had yellowed edges; it must have been quite three years old. It had an erasure. That erasure, I suggest, is the remains of a brief note on the case jotted down one day in Mason's office. The thing is obvious. Everything fits.

'Then there is the matter of the postmark. I agree with Sir Charles that we may take it for granted that the murderer, cunning though he is, and anxious though he might be to establish an alibi, would not entrust the posting of the fatal parcel to any one else. Apart from a confederate, which I am sure we may rule out of the question, it would be far too dangerous; the name of Sir Eustace Pennefather could hardly escape being seen, and the connection later established. The murderer, secure in his conviction that suspicion will never fall on himself of all people (just like all murderers that have ever been), gambles a possible alibi against a certain risk and posts the thing himself. It is therefore advisable, just to clinch the case against him, to connect the man with the neighbourhood of the Strand between the hours of eight-thirty and nine-thirty on that particular evening.

'Surprisingly enough I found this task, which I had expected to be the most difficult, the easiest of all. The man of whom I am thinking actually attended a public dinner that night at the Hotel Cecil, a reunion dinner to be exact of his old school. The Hotel Cecil, I need not remind you, is almost opposite Southampton Street. The Southampton Street post-office is the nearest one to the Hotel. What could be easier for him than to slip out of his seat for the five minutes which is all that would be required, and be back again almost before his neighbours had noticed his action?'

'What indeed?' murmured the rapt Mr Bradley.

'I have two final points to make. You remember that in pointing out the resemblance of this case to the Molineux affair, I remarked that this similarity was more than surprising, it was significant. I will explain what I meant by that. What I meant was that the parallel was far too close for it to be just a coincidence. This case is a deliberate *copy* of that one. And if it is, there is only one inference. This murder is the work of a man steeped in criminal history – of a criminologist. And the man I have in mind *is* a criminologist.

'My last point concerns the denial in the newspaper of the rumoured engagement between Sir Eustace Pennefather and Miss Wildman. I learnt from his valet that Sir Eustace did not send that denial himself. Nor did Miss Wildman. Sir Eustace was furiously angry about it. It was sent, on his own initiative without consulting either of them, by the man whom I am accusing of having committed this crime.'

Mr Bradley stopped hugging himself for a moment. 'And the nitrobenzene? Were you able to connect him with that too?'

'That is one of the very few points on which I agree with Sir Charles. I don't think it in the least necessary, or possible, to connect him with such a common commodity, which can be bought anywhere without the slightest difficulty or remark.'

Mrs Fielder-Flemming was holding herself in with a visible effort. Her words, so calm and judicial to read, had hitherto been spoken too with a strenuous attempt towards calm and judicial delivery. But with each sentence the attempt was obviously becoming more difficult. Mrs Fielder-Flemming was clearly getting so excited that a few more such sentences seemed likely to choke her, though to the others such intensity of feeling seemed a little unnecessary. She was approaching her climax, of course, but even that seemed hardly an excuse for such a very purple face and a hat that had now managed somehow to ride to the very back of her head where it trembled agitatedly in sympathy with its mistress.

'That is all,' she concluded jerkily. 'I submit that I have proved my case. This man is the murderer.'

There was complete silence.

'Well?' said Alicia Dammers impatiently. 'Who is he, then?'

Sir Charles, who had been regarding the orator with a frown that grew more and more lowering every minute, thumped quite menacingly on the table in front of him. 'Precisely,' he growled. 'Let us get out in the open. Against whom are these ridiculous insinuations of yours directed, madam?' One gathered that Sir Charles did not find himself in agreement with the lady's conclusions, even before knowing what they were.

'Accusations, Sir Charles,' Mrs Fielder-Flemming squeaked correction. 'You – you pretend you don't know?'

'Really, madam,' retorted Sir Charles, with massive dignity, 'I'm afraid I have no idea.'

And then Mrs Fielder-Flemming became regrettably dramatic. Rising slowly to her feet like a tragedy queen (except that tragedy queens do not wear their hats tremblingly on the very backs of their heads, and if faces are apt to go brilliant purple with emotion disguise the tint with appropriate grease paints), heedless of the chair overturning behind her with a dull, doom-like thud, her quivering finger pointing across the table, she confronted Sir Charles with every inch of her five-foot nothing.

'Thou!' shrilled Mrs Fielder-Flemming. 'Thou art the man!' Her outstretched finger shook like a ribbon on an electric fan. 'The brand of Cain is on your forehead! Murderer!'

In the silence of ecstatic horror that followed Mr Bradley clung deliriously to the arm of Mr Chitterwick.

Sir Charles succeeded in finding his voice, temporarily mislaid. 'The woman's mad,' he gasped.

Finding that she had not been shot on the spot, or even blasted by blue lightning from Sir Charles' eyes, either of which possibilities it seemed that she had been dreading, Mrs Fielder-Flemming proceeded rather less hysterically to amplify her charge.

'No, I am not mad, Sir Charles; I am very, very sane. You loved your daughter, and with the twofold love that a man who has lost his wife feels for the only feminine thing left to him. You considered that any lengths were justified to prevent her from falling into the hands of Sir Eustace Pennefather – from having her youth, her innocence, her trust exploited by such a scoundrel.

'Out of your own mouth I convict you. Already you've told us that it was not necessary to mention everything that took place at your interview with Sir Eustace. No; for then you would have had to give away the fact that you informed him you would rather kill him with your own hands than see your daughter married to him. And when matters reached such a pass, what with the poor girl's infatuation and obstinacy and Sir Eustace's determination to take advantage of them, that no means short of that very thing was left to you to prevent the catastrophe, you did not shrink from employing them. Sir Charles Wildman, may God be your judge, for I cannot.' Breathing heavily, Mrs Fielder-Flemming retrieved her inverted chair and sat down on it.

'Well, Sir Charles,' remarked Mr Bradley, whose swelling bosom was threatening to burst his waistcoat. 'Well, I wouldn't have thought it of you. Murder indeed. Very naughty; very, very naughty.'

For once Sir Charles took no notice of his faithful gadfly. It is doubtful whether he even heard him. Now that it had penetrated into his consciousness that Mrs Fielder-Flemming really intended her accusation in all seriousness and was not the victim of a temporary attack of insanity, his bosom was swelling just as tumultuously as Mr Bradley's. His face, adopting the purple tinge that Mrs Fielder-Flemming's was relinquishing, took on the aspect of the frog in the fable who failed to realise his own bursting-point. Roger, whose emotions on hearing Mrs Fielder-Flemming's outburst had been so mixed as to be almost scrambled, began to feel quite alarmed for him.

But Sir Charles found the safety-valve of speech just in time. 'Mr President,' he exploded through it, 'if I am not right in assuming this to be a jest on this lady's part, even though a jest in the worst possible taste, am I to be expected to take this preposterous nonsense seriously?'

Roger glanced at Mrs Fielder-Flemming's face, now set in flinty masses, and gulped. However, preposterous though Sir Charles might term it, his antagonist had certainly made out a case, and not a flimsy, unsupported case either. 'I think,' he said, as carefully as he could, 'that if it had been any one but yourself in question, Sir Charles, you would agree that a charge of this kind, when there is real evidence to support it, does at least require to be taken seriously so far as to need refuting.'

Sir Charles snorted and Mrs Fielder-Flemming nodded her head several times with vehemence.

'If refuting is possible,' observed Mr Bradley. 'But I must admit that, personally, I am impressed. Mrs Fielder-Flemming seems to me to have made out her case. Would you like me to go and telephone for the police, Mr President?' He spoke with an air of earnest endeavour to do his duty as a citizen, however distasteful it might be.

Sir Charles glared, but once more seemed bereft of words.

'Not yet, I think,' Roger said gently. 'We haven't heard yet what Sir Charles has to answer.'

'Well, I suppose we may as well *hear* him,' conceded Mr Bradley.

Five pairs of eyes glued themselves on Sir Charles, five pairs of ears were strained.

But Sir Charles, struggling mightily with himself, was silent.

'As I expected,' murmured Mr Bradley. 'There is no defence. Even Sir Charles, who has snatched so many murderers from the rope, can find nothing to say in such a glaring case. It's very sad.'

From the look he flashed at his tormentor it was to be deduced that Sir Charles might have found plenty to say had the two of them been alone together. As it was, he could only rumble.

'Mr President,' said Alicia Dammers, with her usual brisk efficiency, 'I have a proposal to make. Sir Charles appears to be admitting his guilt by default, and Mr Bradley, as a good citizen, wishes to hand him over to the police.'

'Hear, hear!' observed the good citizen.

'Personally I should be sorry to do that. I think there is a good deal to be said for Sir Charles. Murder, we are taught, is invariably anti-social. But is it? I am of the opinion that Sir Charles' intention, that of ridding the world (and incidentally his own daughter) of Sir Eustace Pennefather, was quite in the world's best interests. That his intention miscarried and an innocent victim was killed is quite beside the point. Even Mrs Fielder-Flemming seemed to be doubtful whether Sir Charles ought to be condemned, as a jury would certainly condemn him, though she added in conclusion that she did not feel competent to judge him.

'I differ from her. Being a person of, I hope, reasonable intelligence, I feel perfectly competent to judge him. And I consider further that all five of us are competent to judge him. I therefore suggest that we do in fact judge him ourselves. Mrs Fielder-Flemming could act as prosecutor; somebody (I propose Mr Bradley) could defend him; and all five of us constitute a jury, the finding to be by majority in favour or against. We would bind ourselves to abide by the result, and if it is against him we send for the police; if it is in his favour we agree never to breathe a word of his guilt outside this room. May this be put to the meeting?'

Roger smiled at her reprovingly. He knew quite well that Miss Dammers no more believed in Sir Charles' guilt than he, Roger, did himself, and he knew that she was only pulling that eminent counsel's leg; a little cruelly, but no doubt she thought it was good for him. Miss Dammers professed herself a strong believer in seeing the other side, and held that it would be a very good thing for the cat occasionally to find itself chased by the mouse; certainly therefore it was most salutory for a man who had prosecuted other men for their lives to find himself for once in the dock on just such a terrifying charge. Mr Bradley, on the other hand, though he, too, obviously did not believe that Sir Charles was the murderer, mocked not out of conviction but because only so could he get a little of his own back against Sir Charles for having made more of a success of his life than Mr Bradley was likely to do.

Nor, Roger thought, had Mr Chitterwick any serious doubt as to the possibility of Sir Charles being guilty, though he was still looking so alarmed at Mrs Fielder-Flemming's temerity in suggesting such a thing that it was not altogether possible to say what he did think. Indeed Roger was quite sure that nobody entertained the least suspicion of Sir Charles' innocence except Mrs Fielder-Flemming – and perhaps, from the look of him, Sir Charles himself. As that outraged gentleman had pointed out, such an idea, looked at in sober reflection, was plainly the most preposterous nonsense. Sir Charles could not be guilty because – well, because he was Sir Charles, and because such things don't happen, and because he obviously couldn't be.

On the other hand Mrs Fielder-Flemming had very neatly proved that he was. And Sir Charles had not even attempted yet to prove that he wasn't.

Not for the first time Roger wished, very sincerely, that anybody were sitting in the presidential chair but himself.

'I think,' he now repeated, 'that before we take any steps at all we ought to hear what Sir Charles has to say. I am sure,' added the President kindly, remembering the right phrase, 'that he will have a complete answer to all charges.' He looked expectantly towards the criminal.

Sir Charles appeared to jerk himself out of the haze of his wrath. 'I am really expected to defend myself against this – this hysteria?' he barked. 'Very well. I admit I am a criminologist, which Mrs Fielder-Flemming appears to think so damning. I admit that I attended a dinner at the Hotel Cecil on that night, which it seems is enough to put the rope round my neck. I admit, since it appears that my private affairs are to be dragged into public, regardless of taste or decency, that I would rather have strangled Sir Eustace with my own hands than see him married to my daughter.'

He paused, and passed his hand rather wearily over his high forehead. He was no longer formidable, but only a rather bewildered old man. Roger felt intensely sorry for him. But Mrs Fielder-Flemming had stated her case too well for it to be possible to spare him.

'I admit all this, but none of it is evidence that would have very much weight in a court of law. If you want me to prove that I did not actually send those chocolates, what am I to say? I could bring my two neighbours at the dinner, who would swear that I never left my seat till – well, it must have been after ten o'clock. I can prove by means of other witnesses that my daughter finally consented, on my representations, to give up the idea of marriage with Sir Eustace and has gone voluntarily to stay with relations of ours in Devonshire for a considerable time. But there again I have to admit that this has happened since the date of posting the chocolates.

'In short, Mrs Fielder-Flemming has managed, with considerable skill, to put together a *prima facie* case against me, though it was based on a mistaken assumption (I would point out to her that counsel is never constantly in and out of his client's premises, but meets him usually only in the presence of his solicitor, either at the former's place of business or in his own chambers), and I am quite ready, if this meeting thinks it advisable, for the matter to be investigated officially. More, I welcome such investigation in view of the slur that has been cast upon my name. Mr President, I ask you, as representing the members as a whole, to take such action as you think fit.'

Roger steered a wary course. 'Speaking for myself, Sir Charles, I am quite sure that Mrs Fielder-Flemming's reasoning, exceedingly clever though it was, has been based as you say upon an error, and really, as a matter of mere probability, I cannot see a father sending poisoned chocolates to the would-be fiancé of his own daughter. A moment's thought would show him the practical inevitability of the chocolates reaching eventually the daughter herself. I have my own opinion about this crime, but even apart from that I feel quite certain in my own mind that the case against Sir Charles has not really been proved.'

'Mr President,' cut in Mrs Fielder-Flemming, not without heat, 'you may say what you like, but in the interests of – '

'I agree, Mr President,' Miss Dammers interrupted incisively. 'It is unthinkable that Sir Charles could have sent those chocolates.'

'Humph!' said Mr Bradley, unwilling to have his sport spoiled quite so soon.

'Hear, hear!' Mr Chitterwick said, with surprising decision.

'On the other hand,' Roger pursued, 'I quite see that Mrs Fielder-Flemming is entitled to the official investigation which Sir Charles asks for, no less than is Sir Charles himself on behalf of his good name. And I agree with Sir Charles that she has certainly made out a *prima facie* case for investigation. But what I should like to stress is that so far only two members out of six have spoken, and it is not outside possibility that such startling developments may have been traced out by the time we have all had our turn, that the one we are discussing now may (I do not say that it will, but it *may*) have faded into insignificance.'

'Oho!' murmured Mr Bradley. 'What has our worthy President got up his sleeve?'

'I therefore propose, as a formal motion,' Roger concluded, disregarding the somewhat sour looks cast on him by Mrs Fielder-Flemming, 'that we shelve the question regarding Sir Charles entirely, for discussion or report either inside or outside this room, for one week from today, when any member who wishes may bring it up again for decision, failing which it passes into oblivion for good and all. Shall we vote on that? Those in favour?'

The motion was carried unanimously. Mrs Fielder-Flemming would have liked to vote against it, but she never yet belonged to any committee where all motions were not carried unanimously and habit was too strong for her.

The meeting then adjourned, rather oppressed.

chapter nine

Roger sat on the table in Moresby's room at Scotland Yard and swung his legs moodily. Moresby was being no help at all.

'I've told you, Mr Sheringham,' said the Chief Inspector, with a patient air. 'It's not a bit of good you trying to pump me. I've told you all we know here. I'd help you if I could, as you know' – Roger snorted incredulously – 'but we're simply at a dead end.'

'So am I,' Roger grunted. 'And I don't like it.'

'You'll soon get used to it, Mr Sheringham,' consoled Moresby, 'if you take on this sort of job often.'

'I simply can't get any further,' Roger lamented. 'In fact I don't think I want to. I'm practically sure I've been working on the wrong tack altogether. If the clue really does lie in Sir Eustace's private life, he's shielding it like the very devil. But I don't think it does.'

'Humph!' said Moresby, who did.

'I've cross-examined his friends, till they're tired of the sight of me. I've cadged introductions to the friends of his friends, and the friends of his friends of his friends, and cross-examined them too. I've haunted his club. And what have I discovered? That Sir Eustace was not only a daisy, as you'd told me already, but a perfectly indiscreet daisy at that; the quite unpleasant type, fortunately very much rarer than women suppose, that talks of his feminine successes, with names – though I think that in Sir Eustace's case this was simply through lack of imagination and not any natural caddishness. But you see what I mean. I've collected the names of scores of women, and they all lead – nowhere! If there is a woman at the bottom of it, I should have been sure to have heard of her by this time. And I haven't.'

'And what about that American case, which we thought such an extraordinary parallel, Mr Sheringham?'

'That was cited last night by one of our members,' said Roger gloomily. 'And a very pretty little deduction she drew from it.'

'Ah, yes,' nodded the chief inspector. 'That would be Mrs Fielder-Flemming, I suppose. She thinks Sir Charles Wildman is the guilty party, doesn't she?'

Roger stared at him. 'How the devil did you know that? Oh! The unscrupulous old hag. She passed you the wink, did she?'

'Certainly not, sir,' retorted Moresby with a virtuous air, as if half the difficult cases Scotland Yard solves are not edged in the first place along the right path by means of 'information received'. 'She hasn't said a word to us, though I'm not saying it wouldn't have been her duty to do so. But there isn't much that your members are doing which we don't know about, and thinking too for that matter.'

'We're being shadowed,' said Roger, pleased. 'Yes, you told me at the beginning that we were to have an eye kept on us. Well, well. So in that case, are you going to arrest Sir Charles?'

'Not yet, I think, Mr Sheringham,' Moresby returned gravely.

'What do you think of the theory, then? She made out a very striking case for it.'

'I should be very surprised,' said Moresby, with care, 'to be convinced that Sir Charles Wildman had taken to murdering people himself instead of preventing us from hanging other murderers.'

'Less paying, certainly,' Roger agreed. 'Yes, of course there can't be anything in it really, but it's a nice idea.'

'And what theory are you going to put forward, Mr Sheringham?'

'Moresby, I haven't the faintest idea. And I've got to speak tomorrow night, too. I suppose I can fake up something to pass muster, but it's a disappointment.' Roger reflected for a moment. 'I think the real trouble is that my interest in this case is simply academic. In all the others it has been personal, and that not only gives one such a much bigger incentive to get to the bottom of a case but somehow actually helps one to do so. Bigger gleanings in the way of information, I suppose. And more intimate sidelights on the people concerned.'

'Well, Mr Sheringham,' remarked Moresby, a little maliciously, 'perhaps you'll admit now that we people here, whose interest is never personal (if you mean by that looking at a case from the inside instead of from the outside), have a bit of an excuse when we do come to grief over a case. Which, by the way,' Moresby added with professional pride, 'is precious seldom.'

'I certainly do,' Roger agreed feelingly. 'Well, Moresby, I've got to go through the distressing business of buying a new hat before lunch. Do you feel like shadowing me to Bond Street? I might afterwards walk into a neighbouring hostelry, and it would be nice for you to be able to shadow me in there too.'

'Sorry, Mr Sheringham,' said Chief Inspector Moresby pointedly, 'but *I* have some work to do.'

Roger removed himself.

He was feeling so depressed that he took a taxi to Bond Street instead of a bus, to cheer himself up. Roger, having been in London occasionally during the war-years and remembering the interesting habits cultivated by taxi-drivers during that period, had never taken one since when a bus would do as well. The public memory is notoriously short, but the public prejudices are equally notoriously long.

Roger had reason for his depression. He was, as he told Moresby, not only at a dead end, but the conviction was beginning to grow in him that he had actually been working completely on the wrong lines; and the possibility that all the labour he had put into the case had simply been time wasted was a sad one. His initial interest in the affair, though great, had been as he had just realised only an academic one, such as he would feel in any cleverly planned murder; and in spite of the contacts established with persons who were acquainted with various of the protagonists he still felt himself awkwardly outside the case. There was no personal connection somehow to enable him really to get to grips with it. He was beginning to suspect that it was the sort of case, necessitating endless inquiries such as a private individual has neither the skill, the patience nor the time to prosecute, which can really only be handled by the official police.

It was hazard, two chance encounters that same day and almost within an hour, which put an entirely different complexion on the case to Roger's eyes, and translated at last his interest in it from the academic into the personal.

The first was in Bond Street.

Emerging from his hat-shop, the new hat at just the right angle on his head, he saw bearing down on him Mrs Verreker-le-Mesurer. Mrs Verreker-le-Mesurer was small, exquisite, rich, comparatively young, and a widow, and she coveted Roger. Why, even Roger, who had his share of proper conceit, could not understand, but whenever he gave her the opportunity she would sit at his feet (metaphorically of course; he had no intention of giving her the opportunity to do so literally) and gaze up at him with her big brown eyes melting in earnest uplift. But she talked. She talked, in short, and talked, and talked. And Roger, who rather liked talking himself, could not bear it.

He tried to dart across the road, but there was no opening in the traffic stream. He was cornered. With a gay smile that masked a vituperative mind he spoilt the angle of his beautiful new hat.

Mrs Verreker-le-Mesurer fastened on him gladly. 'Oh, Mr Sheringham! Just the very person I wanted to see. Mr Sheringham, *do* tell me. In the strictest confidence of course. *Are* you taking up this dreadful business of *poor* Joan Bendix's death? Oh, don't – *don't* tell me you're not.' Roger tried to tell her that he had hoped to do so, but she gave him no chance. 'Oh, aren't you really? But it's too dreadful. You ought, you know, you really *ought* to try and find out who sent those chocolates to Sir Eustace Pennefather. I do think it's naughty of you not to.'

Roger, the frozen grin of civilised intercourse on his face, again tried to edge a word in; without result.

'I was horrified when I heard of it. Simply horrified.' Mrs Verreker-le-Mesurer registered horror. 'You see, Joan and I were such *very* close friends. Quite intimate. In fact we were at school together. – Did you say anything, Mr Sheringham?'

Roger, who had allowed a faintly incredulous groan to escape him, hastily shook his head.

'And the awful thing, the truly *terrible* thing is that Joan brought the whole thing on herself. Isn't that appalling, Mr Sheringham?'

Roger no longer wanted to escape. 'What did you say?' he managed to insert, again incredulously.

'I suppose it's what they call tragic irony.' Mrs Verreker-le-Mesurer chattered happily. 'Certainly it was tragic enough and I've never heard of anything so terribly ironical. You know about that bet she made with her husband, of course, so that he had to get her a box of chocolates and if he hadn't Sir Eustace would never have given him the poisoned ones but would have eaten them and died himself, and from all I hear about him good riddance? Well, Mr Sheringham – ' Mrs Verreker-le-Mesurer lowered her voice to a conspirator-like whisper and glanced about her in the approved manner. 'I've never told any one else this, but I'm telling you because I know you'll appreciate it. You *are* interested in irony aren't you?'

'I adore it,' Roger said mechanically. 'Yes?'

'Well – *Joan wasn't playing fair!*'

'How do you mean?' Roger asked, bewildered.

Mrs Verreker-le-Mesurer was artlessly pleased with her sensation. 'Why, she ought not to have made that bet at all. It was a judgment on her. A terrible judgment of course, but the appalling thing is that she did bring it on herself, in a way. I'm so terribly distressed about it. Really, Mr Sheringham, I can hardly bear to turn the light out when I go to bed. I see Joan's face simply looking at me in the dark. It's awful.' And for a fleeting instant Mrs Verreker-le-Mesurer's face did for once really mirror the emotion she professed: it looked quite haggard.

'Why oughtn't Mrs Bendix to have made the bet?' Roger asked patiently.

'Oh! Why, because she'd seen the play before. We went together, the very first week it was on. She *knew* who the villain was all the time.'

'By Jove!' Roger was as impressed as Mrs Verreker-le-Mesurer could have wished. 'The Avenging Chance again, eh? We're none of us immune from it.'

'Poetic justice, you mean?' twittered Mrs Verreker-le-Mesurer, to whom these remarks had been a trifle obscure. 'Yes it was, in a way, wasn't it? Though really, the punishment was out of all proportion to the crime. Good gracious, if every woman who cheats over a bet is to be killed for it, where would any of us be?' demanded Mrs Verreker-le-Mesurer with unconscious frankness.

'Umph!' said Roger tactfully.

Mrs Verreker-le-Mesurer glanced rapidly up and down the pavement, and moistened her lips. Roger had an odd impression that she was talking not as usual just for the sake of talking, but in some recondite way to escape from not talking. It was as if she was more distressed over her friend's death than she cared to show and found some relief in babbling. It interested Roger also to notice that fond though she had probably been of the dead woman, she now found herself driven as if against her will to hint at blame even while praising her. It was as though she was able thus to extract some subtle consolation for the actual death.

'But Joan Bendix of all people! That's what I can't get over, Mr Sheringham. I should never have thought Joan *would* do a thing like that. Joan was such a nice girl. A little close with money perhaps, considering how well-off she was, but that isn't anything. Of course I know it was only fun, and pulling her husband's leg, but I always used to think Joan was such a *serious* girl, if you know what I mean.'

'Quite,' said Roger, who could understand plain English as well as most people.

'I mean, ordinary people don't talk about honour, and truth, and playing the game, and all those things one takes for granted. But Joan did. She was always saying that this wasn't honourable, or that wouldn't be playing the game. Well, she paid herself for not playing the game, poor girl, didn't she? Still, I suppose it all goes to prove the truth of the old saying.'

'What old saying?' asked Roger, almost hypnotised by this flow.

'Why, that still waters run deep. Joan must have been deep after all, I'm afraid.' Mrs Verreker-le-Mesurer sighed. It was evidently a grave social error to be deep. 'Not that I want to say anything against her now she's dead, poor darling, but – well, what I mean is, I do think psychology is so very interesting, don't you, Mr Sheringham?'

'Quite fascinating,' Roger agreed gravely. 'Well, I'm afraid I must be – '

'And what does that man, Sir Eustace Pennefather, think about it all?' demanded Mrs Verreker-le-Mesurer, with an expression of positive vindictiveness. 'After all, he's as responsible for Joan's death as anybody.'

'Oh, really.' Roger had not conceived any particular love for Sir Eustace, but he felt constrained to defend him against this charge. 'Really, I don't think you can say that, Mrs Verreker-le-Mesurer.'

'I can, and I do,' affirmed that lady. 'Have you ever met him, Mr Sheringham? I hear he's a horrible creature. Always running after some woman or other, and when he's tired of her just drops her – biff! – like that. Is it true?'

'I'm afraid I can't tell you,' Roger said coldly. 'I don't know him at all.'

'Well, it's common talk who he's taken up with now,' retorted Mrs Verreker-le-Mesurer, perhaps a trifle more pink than the delicate aids to nature on her cheeks would have warranted. 'Half-a-dozen people have told me. That Bryce woman, of all people. You know, the wife of the oil man, or petrol, or whatever he made his money in.'

'I've never heard of her,' Roger said, quite untruthfully.

'It began about a week ago, they say,' rattled on this red-hot gossiper. 'To console himself for not getting Dora Wildman, I suppose. Well, thank goodness Sir Charles had the sense to put his foot down there. He did, didn't he? I heard so the other day. Horrible man! You'd have thought that such a dreadful thing as being practically responsible for poor Joan's death would have sobered him up a little, wouldn't you? But not a bit of it. As a matter of fact I believe he – '

'Have you seen any shows lately?' Roger asked in a loud voice.

Mrs Verreker-le-Mesurer stared at him, for a moment nonplussed. 'Shows? Yes, I've seen almost everything, I think. Why, Mr Sheringham?'

'I just wondered. The new revue at the Pavilion's quite good, isn't it? Well, I'm afraid I must – '

'Oh, don't!' Mrs Verreker-le-Mesurer shuddered delicately. 'I was there the night before Joan's death.' (Can no subject take us away from that for a moment? thought Roger.) 'Lady Cavelstoke had a box and asked me to join her party.'

'Yes?' Roger was wondering if it would be considered rude if he simply handed the lady off, as at rugger, and dived for the nearest opening in the traffic. 'Quite a good show,' he said at random, edging restlessly towards the curb. 'I liked that sketch, *The Sempiternal Triangle,* particularly.'

'*The Sempiternal Triangle*?' repeated Mrs Verreker-le-Mesurer vaguely.

'Yes, quite near the beginning.'

'Oh! Then I may not have seen it. I got there a few minutes late, I'm afraid. But then,' said Mrs Verreker-le-Mesurer with pathos, 'I always do seem to be late for everything.' Roger noted mentally that the few minutes was by way of a euphemism, as were most of Mrs Verreker-le-Mesurer's statements regarding herself. *The Sempiternal Triangle* had certainly not been in the first half-hour of the performance.

'Ah!' Roger looked fixedly at an oncoming bus. 'I'm afraid you'll have to excuse me, Mrs Verreker-le-Mesurer. There's a man on that bus who wants to speak to me. *Scotland Yard!*' he hissed, in an impressive whisper.

'Oh! Then – then does that mean you *are* looking into poor Joan's death, Mr Sheringham? *Do* tell me! I won't breathe it to a soul.'

Roger looked round him with a mysterious air and frowned in the approved manner. 'Yes!' he nodded, his finger to his lips. 'But not a word, Mrs Verreker-le-Mesurer.'

'Of course not, I promise.' But Roger was disappointed to notice that the lady did not seem quite so impressed as he had hoped. From her expression he was almost ready to believe that she suspected how unavailing his efforts had been, and was a little sorry that he had taken on more than he could manage.

But the bus had now reached them, and with a hasty 'Goodbye' Roger swung himself onto the step as it lumbered past. With awful stealth, feeling those big brown eyes fixed in awe on his back, he climbed the steps and took his seat, after an exaggerated scrutiny of the other passengers, beside a perfectly inoffensive little man in a bowler-hat. The little man, who happened to be a clerk in the employment of a monumental mason at Tooting, looked at him resentfully. There were plenty of quite empty seats all round them.

The bus swung into Piccadilly, and Roger got off at the Rainbow Club. He was lunching once again with a member. Roger had spent most of the last ten days asking such members of the Rainbow Club as he knew, however remotely, out to lunch in order to be asked to the club in return. So far nothing helpful had arisen out of all this wasted labour, and he anticipated nothing more today.

Not that the member was at all reluctant to talk about the tragedy. He had been at school with Bendix, it appeared, and was as ready to adopt responsibility on the strengtth of this tie as Mrs Verreker-le-Mesurer had been for Mrs Bendix. He plumed himself more than a little therefore on having a more intimate connection with the business than his fellow members. Indeed one gathered that the connection was even a trifle closer than that of Sir Eustace himself. Roger's host was that kind of man.

As they were talking a man entered the dining-room and walked past their table. Roger's host became abruptly silent. The newcomer threw him an abrupt nod and passed on.

Roger's host leaned forward across the table and spoke in the hushed tones of one to whom a revelation had been vouchsafed. 'Talk of the devil! That was Bendix himself. First time I've seen him in here since it happened. Poor devil! It knocked him all to pieces, you know. I've never seen a man so devoted to his wife. It was a byword. Did you see how ghastly he looked?' All this in a tactful whisper that must have been far more obvious to the subject of it had he happened to be looking their way than the loudest bellowing.

Roger nodded shortly. He had caught a glimpse of Bendix's face and had been shocked by it even before he learned his identity. It was haggard and pale and seamed with lines of bitterness, prematurely old. 'Hang it all,' he now thought, much moved, 'somebody really must make an effort. If the murderer isn't found soon it will kill that chap too.'

Aloud he said, somewhat at random and certainly without tact: 'He didn't exactly fall on your neck. I thought you two were such bosom friends?'

His host looked uncomfortable. 'Oh, well, you must make allowances just at present,' he judged. 'Besides, we weren't *bosom* friends exactly. As a matter of fact he was a year or two senior to me. Or it might have been three even. We were in different houses too. And he was on the modern side of course (can you imagine the son of his father being anything else?), while I was a classical bird.'

'I see,' said Roger quite gravely, realising that his host's actual contact with Bendix at school had been limited, at most, to that of the latter's toe with the former's hinder parts.

He left it at that.

For the rest of the lunch he was a little inattentive. Something was nagging at his brain, and he could not identify it. Somewhere, somehow, during the last hour, he felt, a vital piece of information had been conveyed to him and he had never grasped its importance.

It was not until he was putting on his coat half-an-hour later, and for the moment had given up trying to worry his mind into giving up its booty, that the realisation suddenly came to him unbidden, in accordance with its usual and maddening way. He stopped dead, one arm in his coat-sleeve, the other in act to fumble.

'*By Jove!*' he said softly.

'Anything the matter, old man?' asked his host now mellowed by much port.

'No, thanks; nothing,' said Roger hastily, coming to earth again.

Outside the club he hailed a taxi.

For probably the first time in her life Mrs Verreker-le-Mesurer had given somebody a constructive idea.

For the rest of the day Roger was very busy indeed.

chapter ten

The president called on Mr Bradley to hold forth.

Mr Bradley stroked his moustache and mentally shot his cuffs.

He had begun his career (when still Percy Robinson) as a motor-salesman, and had discovered that there is more money in manufacturing. Now he manufactured detective stories, and found his former experience of the public's gullibility not unhelpful. He was still his own salesman, but occasionally had difficulty in remembering that he was no longer mounted on a stand at Olympia. Everything and everybody in this world, including Morton Harrogate Bradley, he heartily despised, except only Percy Robinson. He sold, in tens of thousands.

'This is rather unfortunate for me,' he began, in the correct gentlemanly drawl, as if addressing an audience of morons. 'I had rather been under the impression that I should be expected to produce as a murderer the most unlikely person, in the usual tradition; and Mrs Fielder-Flemming has cut the ground away from under my feet. I don't see how I can possibly find you a more unlikely murderer than Sir Charles here. All of us who have the misfortune to speak after Mrs Fielder-Flemming will have to be content to pile up so many anti-climaxes.

'Not that I haven't done my best. I studied the case according to my own lights, and it led me to a conclusion which certainly surprised myself quite a lot. But as I said, after the last speaker it will probably seem to everybody else a dismal anti-climax. Let me see now, where did I begin? Oh, yes; with the poison.

'Now the use of nitrobenzene as the poisoning agent interested me quite a lot. I find it extremely significant. Nitrobenzene is the last thing one would expect inside those chocolates. I've made something of a study of poisons, in connection with my work, and I've never heard of nitrobenzene being employed in a criminal case before. There are cases on record of its use in suicide, and in accidental poisoning, but not more than three or four all told.

'I'm surprised that this point doesn't seem to have struck either of my predecessors. The really interesting thing is that so few people know nitrobenzene as a poison at all. Even the experts don't. I was speaking to a man who got a Science Scholarship at Cambridge and specialised in chemistry, and he had actually never heard of it as a poison. As a matter of fact I found I knew a good deal more about it than he did. A commercial chemist would certainly never think of it among the ordinary poisons. It isn't even listed as such, and the list is comprehensive enough. Well, all this seems most significant to me.

'Then there are other points about it. It's used most extensively in commerce. In fact it's the kind of thing that might be used in almost any manufacture. It's a solvent, of quite a universal kind. We've been told that its chief use is in making aniline dyes. That may be the most important one, but it certainly isn't the most extensive. It's used a lot in confectionery, as we were also told, and in perfumery as well. But really I can't attempt to give you a list of its uses.

They range from chocolates to motor-car tyres. The important thing is that it's perfectly easy to get hold of.

'For that matter it's perfectly easy to make too. Any schoolboy knows how to treat benzol with nitric acid to get nitrobenzene. I've done it myself a hundred times. The veriest smattering of chemical knowledge is all that's wanted, and nothing in the way of expensive apparatus. Or, so far as that goes, it could be done equally by somebody without any chemical knowledge at all; that is, the actual process of making it. Oh, and it could be made quite secretly by the way. Nobody need even guess. But I think just a little chemical knowledge at any rate would be wanted, ever to set one about making it at all. At least, for this particular purpose.

'Well, so far as the case as a whole was concerned, this use of nitrobenzene seemed to me not only the sole original feature but by far the most important piece of evidence. Not in the way that prussic acid is valuable evidence for the reason that prussic acid is so hard to obtain, because once its use was determined anybody could get hold of or make nitrobenzene, and that of course is a tremendous point in favour of it from the would-be murderer's point of view. No, what I mean is that the sort of person who would ever think of employing the stuff at all ought to be definable within surprisingly narrow limits.'

Mr Bradley stopped a moment to light a cigarette, and if he was secretly pleased that his fellow members showed the extent to which he had engaged their interest by not uttering a word until he was ready to go on, he did not divulge the fact. Surveying them for a moment as if inspecting a class composed entirely of half-wits, he took up his argument again.

'First of all, then, we can credit this user of nitrobenzene with a minimum at any rate of chemical knowledge. Or perhaps I ought to qualify that. Either chemical knowledge, or specialised knowledge. A chemist's assistant, for instance, who was interested enough in his job to read it up after shop-hours would fit the bill for the first case, and a woman employed in a factory where nitrobenzene was used and where the employees had been warned against its poisonous properties would do for an example of the second. There are two kinds of person, it seems to me, who might think of using the stuff as a poison at all, and the first kind is subdivided into the two classes I've mentioned.

'But it's the second kind that I think we are much more probably dealing with in this crime. This is a more intelligent sort of person altogether.

'In this category the chemist's assistant becomes an amateur dabbler in chemistry, the girl in the factory a woman-doctor, let us say, with an interest in toxicology, or, to get away from the specialist, a highly intelligent lady with a strong interest in criminology particularly on its toxicological side – just, in fact, like Mrs Fielder-Flemming here.' Mrs Fielder-Flemming gasped indignantly and Sir Charles, though momentarily startled at the unexpected quarter from which was dealt this tit for the tats he had suffered at the gasping lady's hands, emitted the next instant a sound which from anybody else could only have been described as a guffaw. 'All of them, you understand,' continued Mr Bradley with complete serenity, 'the kind of people who might be expected not only to keep a Taylor's Medical Jurisprudence on their shelves but to consult it frequently.

'I agree with you, you see, Mrs Fielder-Flemming, that the method of this crime does show traces of criminological knowledge. You cited one case which was certainly a remarkable parallel, Sir Charles cited another, and I am going to cite yet a third. It is a regular jumble of old cases, and I am quite sure, as you are, that this is something more than a mere coincidence. I'd arrived at this conclusion myself, of criminological knowledge, before you mentioned it at all, and I was helped to it as well by the strong feeling that whoever sent those chocolates to Sir Eustace possesses a Taylor. That is a pure guess, I admit, but in my copy of Taylor the article on nitrobenzene occurs on the very next page after cyanide of potassium; and there seems to me food for thought there.' The speaker paused a moment.

Mr Chitterwick nodded. 'I think I see. You mean, anybody deliberately searching the pages for a poison that would fulfil certain requirements...?'

'Exactly,' Mr Bradley concurred.

'You lay great stress on this matter of the poison,' Sir Charles remarked, almost genial. 'Do you tell us that you think you've identified the murderer by deductions drawn from this one point alone?'

'No, Sir Charles, I don't think I can go quite so far as that. I lay so much stress on it because, as I said, it's the only really original feature of the crime. By itself it won't solve the problem, but considered in conjunction with other features I do think it should go a long way towards doing so – or at any rate provide such a check on a person suspected for other reasons as to turn suspicion into certainty.

'Let's look at it for instance in the light of the crime as a whole. I think the first thing one realises is that this crime is the work not only of an intelligent person but of a well-educated one too. Well, you see, that rules out at once the first division of people who might be expected to think of using nitrobenzene as the poisoning agent. Gone are our chemist's assistant and our factory-girl. We can concentrate on our intelligent, well-educated person, with an interest in criminology, some knowledge of toxicology, and, if I'm not very much mistaken (and I very seldom am), a copy of Taylor or some similar book on his or her shelves.

'That, my dear Watsons, is what the criminal's singular choice of nitrobenzene has to tell me.' And Mr Bradley stroked the growth on his upper lip with an offensive complacency that was not wholly assumed. Mr Bradley took some pains to impress on the world how pleased he was with himself, but the pose was not without its foundation in fact.

'Most ingenious, certainly,' murmured Mr Chitterwick, duly impressed.

'So now let's get on with it,' observed Miss Dammers, not at all impressed. 'What's your theory? That is, if you've really got one.'

'Oh, I've got one all right.' Mr Bradley smiled in a superior manner. This was the first time he had succeeded in provoking Miss Dammers to snap at him, and he was rather pleased. 'But let's take things in their proper order. I want to show you how inevitably I was led to my conclusion, and I can only do that by tracing out my own footsteps, so to speak. Having made my deductions from the poison itself, then, I set about examining the other clues to see if they would lead me to a result that I could check by the other. First of all I concentrated on the notepaper of the forged letter, the only really valuable clue apart from the poison.

'Now this piece of notepaper puzzled me. For some reason which I couldn't identify, the name of Mason's seemed to strike a reminiscent note to me. I felt sure that I'd heard of Mason's in some other connection than just through their excellent chocolates. At last I remembered.

'I'm afraid I must touch here on the personal, and I apologise in advance, Sir Charles, for the lapse of taste. My sister, before she married, was a shorthand typist.' Mr Bradley's extreme languor all of a sudden indicated that he felt this connection needed some defence and was determined not to give it. The next instant he gave it. 'That is to say, her education put her on rather a different level from the usual shorthand-typist, and she was, in point of fact, a trained secretary.

'She had joined an establishment run by a lady who supplied secretaries to business firms to take the places temporarily of girls in responsible positions who were ill, or away on holiday, or anything like that. Including my sister there were only two or three girls at the place, and the posts they went to only lasted as a rule for two or three weeks. Each girl would therefore have a good many such posts in the course of a year. However, I did remember distinctly that one of the firms to which my sister went while she was there was Mason's, as temporary secretary to one of the directors.

'This seemed to me possibly useful. It wouldn't be likely that she could throw a sidelight on the murder, but at any rate she might be able to give me introductions to one or two members of Mason's staff if necessary. So I went down to see her about it.

'She remembered quite well. It was between three and four years ago, and she liked being there so much that she had thought quite seriously of putting in for a permanent secretaryship with the firm, should one be available. Naturally she hadn't got to know any of the staff really well, but quite enough to give me the introductions if I wanted them.

'"By the way," I happened to say to her casually, "I saw the letter that was sent to Sir Eustace with the chocolates, and not only Mason's name but the actual paper itself struck me as familiar. I suppose you wrote to me on it while you were there?"

'"I don't know that I ever did that," she said, "but, of course, the paper was familiar to you. You've played paper games here often enough, haven't you? You know we always use it. It's such a convenient size." Paper games, I should explain, have always been a favourite thing in our family.

'It's funny how a connection will stick in the mind, but not the actual circumstances of it. Of course I remembered then at once. There was quite a pile of the paper, in one of the drawers of my sister's writing table. I'd often torn it into strips for our paper games myself.

'"But how did you get hold of it?" I asked her.

'It seemed to me that she answered rather evasively, just saying that she'd got it from the office when she was working there. I pressed her, and at last she told me that one evening she was just on the point of leaving the office when she remembered that some friends were coming in after dinner at home. We should almost certainly play a paper game of some kind, and we had run out of suitable paper. She hurried up the stairs again back to the office, dumped her attaché-case on the table and opened it, hastily snatched up some paper from the pile beside her typewriter, and threw it into the case. In her hurry she didn't realise how much she'd taken, and that supply, which was supposed to tide us over one evening, had actually lasted for four years. She must have taken something like half a ream.

'Well, I went away from my sister's house rather startled. Before I left I examined the remaining sheets, and so far as I could see they were exactly like the one on which the letter was typed. Even the edges were a little discoloured too. I was more than startled: I was alarmed. Because I ought to tell you that it had already occurred to me that of all the ways of going about the search for the person who had sent that letter to Sir Eustace, the one that seemed most hopeful was to look for its writer among the actual employees, or ex-employees, of the firm itself.

'As a matter of fact this discovery of mine had a more discerning side still. On thinking over the case the idea had struck me that in the two matters of the notepaper and the method itself of the crime it was quite possible that the police, and everyone else had been putting the cart before the horse. It had been taken for granted apparently that the murderer had first of all decided on the method, and then set about getting hold of the notepaper to carry it out.

'But isn't it more feasible that the notepaper should have been already there, in the criminal's ownership, and that it was the chance possession of it which actually suggested the method of the crime? In that case, of course, the likelihood of the notepaper being traced to the murderer would be very small indeed, whereas in the other case there is always that possibility. Had that occurred to you for instance, Mr President?'

'I must admit that it hadn't,' Roger confessed. 'And yet, like Holmes' tricks, the possibility's evident enough now it's brought forward. I must say, it strikes me as being a very sound point, Bradley.'

'Psychologically, of course,' agreed Miss Dammers, 'it's perfect.'

'Thank you,' murmured Mr Bradley. 'Then you'll be able to understand just how disconcerting that discovery of mine was. Because if there was anything in that point at all, anybody who had in his or her possession some old notepaper of Mason's, with slightly discoloured edges, immediately became suspect.'

'Hr-r-r-mph!' Sir Charles cleared his throat forcibly by way of comment. The implication was obvious. Gentlemen don't suspect their own sisters.

'Dear, dear,' clucked Mr Chitterwick, more humanly.

Mr Bradley went on to pile up the agony. 'And there was another thing, which I could not overlook. My sister before she went in for her training as a secretary, had played with the idea of becoming a hospital nurse. She went through a short course in nursing as a young girl, and was always thoroughly interested in it. She would read not only books on nursing itself, but medical books too. Several times,' said Mr Bradley solemnly, 'I've seen her studying my own copy of Taylor, apparently quite absorbed in it.'

He paused again, but this time nobody commented. The general feeling was that this was getting really too much of a good thing.

'Well, I went home and thought it over. Of course it seemed absurd to put my own sister on the list of suspects, and at the very head of it too. One doesn't connect one's own circle with the idea of murder. The two things don't mix at all. Yet I couldn't fail to realise that if it had been anybody else in question but my sister I should be feeling quite jubilant over the prospect of solving the case. But as things were, what was I to do?

'In the end,' said Mr Bradley smugly, 'I did what I thought my duty and faced the situation. I went back to my sister's house the next day and asked her squarely whether she had ever had any kind of relations with Sir Eustace Pennefather, and if so what. She looked at me blankly and said that up till the time of the murder she had never heard of the man. I believed her. I asked her if she could remember what she had been doing on the evening before the murder. She looked at me still more blankly and said that she had been in Manchester with her husband at that time, they had stayed at the Peacock Hotel, and in the evening had been to a cinema where they had seen a film called, so far as she could recall, *Fires of Fate*. Again I believed her.

'As a matter of routine precaution however I checked her statements later and found them perfectly correct; for the time of the posting of the parcel she had an unshakable alibi. I felt more relieved than I can say.' Mr Bradley spoke in a low voice, with pathos and restraint, but Roger caught his eye as he looked up and there was a mocking glint in it which made the President feel vaguely uneasy. The trouble with Mr Bradley was that one never quite knew with him.

'Having drawn a blank with my first ticket, then, I tabulated the conclusions I'd formed to date and set about considering the other points in the case.

'It then struck me that the Chief Inspector from Scotland Yard had been somewhat reticent about the evidence that night he addressed us. So I rang him up and asked him a few questions that had occurred to me. From him I learnt that the typewriter was a Hamilton No. 4, that is, the ordinary Hamilton model; that the hand-printed address on the cover was written with a fountain-pen, almost certainly an Onyx fitted with a medium-broad nib; that the ink was Harfield's Fountain-Pen Ink; and that there was nothing to be learned from the wrapping-paper (ordinary brown) or the string. That there were no fingerprints anywhere we had been told.

'Well, I suppose I ought not to admit it, considering how I earn my living, but upon my soul I haven't the faintest idea how a professional detective goes about a job of work,' said Mr Bradley with candour. 'It's easy enough in a book, of course, because there are a certain number of things which the author wants found out and these he lets his detective discover, and no others. In real life, no doubt, it doesn't pan out quite like that.

'Anyhow, what I did was to copy my own detective's methods and set about the business in as systematic a way as I could. That is to say, I made a careful list of all the available evidence, both as to fact and to character (and it was surprising how much there was when one came to tabulate it), and drew as many deductions as I could from each piece, at the same time trying to keep a perfectly open mind as to the identity of the person who was to hatch out from my nest of completed conclusions.

'In other words,' said Mr Bradley, not without severity, 'I did *not* decide that Lady A or Sir Somebody B had such a good motive for the crime that she or he must undoubtedly have done it, and then twist my evidence to fit this convenient theory.'

'Hear, hear!' Roger felt constrained to approve.

'Hear, hear!' echoed in turn both Alicia Dammers and Mr Ambrose Chitterwick.

Sir Charles and Mrs Fielder-Flemming glanced at each other and then hastily away again, for all the world like two children in a Sunday school who have been caught doing quite the wrong thing together.

'Dear me,' murmured Mr Bradley, 'this is all very exhausting. May I have five minutes' rest, Mr President, and half a cigarette?'

The President kindly gave Mr Bradley an interval in which to restore himself.

chapter eleven

'I have always thought,' resumed Mr Bradley, restored, 'I have always thought that murders may be divided into two classes, closed or open. By a closed murder I mean one committed in a certain closed circle of persons, such as a house-party, in which it is known that the murder is limited to membership of that actual group. This is by far the commoner form in fiction. An open murder I call one in which the criminal is not limited to any particular group but might be almost any one in the whole world. This, of course, is almost invariably what happens in real life.

'The case with which we're dealing has this peculiarity, that one can't place it quite definitely in either category. The police say that it's an open murder; both our previous speakers here seem to regard it as a closed one.

'It's a question of the motive. If one agrees with the police that it is the work of some fanatic or criminal lunatic, then it certainly is an open murder; anybody without an alibi in London that night might have posted the parcel. If one's of the opinion that the motive was a personal one, connected with Sir Eustace himself, then the murderer is confined to the closed circle of people who have had relations of one sort or another with Sir Eustace.

'And talking of posting that parcel, I must just make a diversion to tell you something really interesting. For all I know to the contrary, I might have seen the murderer with my own eyes, in the very act of posting it! As it happened, I was passing through Southampton Street that evening at just about a quarter to nine. Little did I guess, as Mr Edgar Wallace would say, that the first act of this tragic drama was possibly being unfolded at that very minute under my unsuspecting nose. Not even a premonition of disaster caused me to falter in my stride. Providence was evidently being somewhat close with premonitions that night. But if only my sluggish instincts had warned me, how much trouble I might have saved us all. Alas,' said Mr Bradley sadly, 'such is life.

'However, that's neither here nor there. We were discussing closed and open murders.

'I was determined to form no definite opinions either way, so to be on the safe side I treated this as an open murder. I then had the position that every one in the whole world was under suspicion. To narrow down the field a little, I set to work to build up the one individual who really did it, out of the very meagre indications he or she had given us.

'I had the conclusions drawn already from the choice of nitrobenzene, which I've explained to you. But as a corollary to the good education, I added the very significant postscript: but not public school or university. Don't you agree, Sir Charles? It simply wouldn't be done.'

'Public-school men have been known to commit murders before now,' pointed out Sir Charles, somewhere at sea.

'Oh, granted. But not in such an underhand way as this. The public-school code does stand for something, surely, even in murder. So, I am sure, any public-school man would tell me. This isn't a gentlemanly murder at all. A public-school man, if he could ever bring himself to anything so unconventional as murder, would use an axe or a revolver or something which would bring him and his victim face to face. He would never murder a man behind his back, so to speak. I'm quite sure of that.

'Then another obvious conclusion is that he's exceptionally neat with his fingers. To unwrap those chocolates, drain them, refill them, plug up the holes with melted chocolate, and wrap them up in their silver paper again to look as if they've never been tampered with – I can tell you, that's no easy job. And all in gloves too, remember.

'I thought at first that the beautiful way it was done pointed strongly to a woman. However, I carried out an experiment and got a dozen or so of my friends to try their hands at it, men and women, and out of the whole lot I was the only one (I say it without any particular pride) who made a really good job of it. So it wasn't necessarily a woman. But manual dexterity's a good point to establish.

'Then there was the matter of the exact six-minim dose in each chocolate. That's very illuminating, I think. It argues a methodical turn of mind amounting to a real passion for symmetry. There are such people. They can't bear that the pictures on a wall don't balance each other exactly. I know, because I'm rather that way myself. Symmetry is synonymous with order, to my mind. I can quite see how the murderer came to fill the chocolates in that way. I should probably have done so myself. Unconsciously.

'Then I think we can credit him or her with a creative mind. A crime like this isn't done on the spur of the moment. It's deliberately created, bit by bit, scene by scene, built up exactly as a play is built up. Don't you agree, Mrs Fielder-Flemming?'

'It wouldn't have occurred to me, but it may be true.'

'Oh, yes; a lot of thought must have gone to the carrying of it through. I don't think we need worry about the plagiarism from other crimes. The greatest creative minds aren't above adapting the ideas of other people to their own uses. I do myself. So do you, I expect, Sheringham; so do you, no doubt, Miss Dammers; so do you at times, I should imagine, Mrs Fielder-Flemming. Be honest now, all of you.'

A subdued murmur of honesty acknowledged occasional lapses in this direction.

'Of course. Look how Sullivan used to adapt old church music, and turn a Gregorian chant into *A Pair of Sparkling Eyes,* or something equally unchantlike. It's permissible. Well, there's all that to help with the portrait of our unknown and, lastly, there must be present in his or her mental make-up the particular cold, relentless inhumanity of the poisoner. That's all I think. But it's something isn't it? One ought to be able to go a fair way towards recognising our criminal if one ever ran across a person with these varied characteristics.

'Oh, and there's one other point I mustn't forget. The parallel crime. I'm surprised nobody's mentioned this. To my mind it's a closer parallel than any we've ever had yet. It isn't a well-known case, but you've all probably heard of it. The murder of Dr Wilson, at Philadelphia, just twenty years ago.

'I'll run through it briefly. This man Wilson received one morning what purported to be a sample bottle of ale, sent to him by a well-known brewery. There was a letter with it, written apparently on their official notepaper, and the address-label had the firm's name printed on it. Wilson drank the beer at lunch, and died immediately. The stuff was saturated with cyanide of potassium.

'It was soon established that the beer hadn't come from the brewery at all, which had sent out no samples. It had been delivered through the local express company, but all they could say was that it had been sent to them for delivery by a man. The printed label and the letter paper had been forged, printed specially for the occasion.

'The mystery was never solved. The printing press used to print the letter-heading and label couldn't be traced, though the police visited every printing-works in the whole of America. The very motive for the murder was never satisfactorily ascertained. A typical open murder. The bottle arrived out of the blue, and the murderer remained in it.

'You see the close resemblance to this case, particularly in the supposed sample. As Mrs Fielder-Flemming has pointed out, it's almost too good to be a coincidence. Our murderer *must* have had that case in mind, with its (for the murderer) most successful outcome. As a matter of fact there was a possible motive. Wilson was a notorious abortionist, and somebody may have wanted to stop his activities. Conscience, I suppose. There are people who have such a thing. That's another parallel with this affair, you see. Sir Eustace is a notorious evil-liver. And that goes to support the police view, of an anonymous fanatic. There's a good deal to be said for that view, I think.

'But I must get on with my own exposition.

'Well, having reached this stage I tabulated my conclusions and drew up a list of conditions which this criminal of ours must fulfil. Now I should like to point out that these conditions of mine were so many and so varied that if anybody could be found to fit them the chances, Sir Charles, would not be a mere million to one but several million to one that he or she must be the guilty person. This isn't just haphazard statement, it's cold mathematical fact.

'I have twelve conditions, and the mathematical odds against their all being fulfilled in one person are actually (if my arithmetic stands the test) four hundred and seventy nine million, one thousand and six hundred to one. And that, mark you, is if all the chances were even ones. But they're not. That he should have some knowledge of criminology is at least a ten to one chance. That he should be able to get hold of Mason's notepaper must be more than a hundred to one against.

'Well, taking it all in all,' opined Mr Bradley, 'I should think the real odds must be somewhere about four billion, seven hundred and ninety thousand million, five hundred and sixteen thousand, four hundred and fifty-eight to one. In other words, it's a snip. Does everyone agree?'

Everyone was far too stunned to disagree.

'Right; then we're all of one mind,' said Mr Bradley cheerfully. 'So I'll read you my list.'

He shuffled the pages of a little pocket-book and began to read:

CONDITIONS TO BE FILLED BY THE CRIMINAL

1. Must have at least an elementary amount of chemical knowledge.
2. Must have at least an elementary knowledge of criminology.
3. Must have had a reasonably good education, but not public school or university.
4. Must have possession of, or access to, Mason's notepaper.
5. Must have possession of, or access to, a Hamilton No. 4 typewriter.
6. Must have been in the neighbourhood of Southampton Street, Strand, during the critical hour, 8.30–9.30, on the evening before the murder.

7. Must be in possession of, or had access to, an Onyx fountain-pen, fitted with a medium-broad nib.
8. Must be in possession of, or had access to, Harfield's Fountain-Pen Ink.
9. Must have something of a creative mind, but not above adapting the creations of others.
10. Must be more than ordinarily neat with the fingers.
11. Must be a person of methodical habits, probably with a strong feeling for symmetry.
12. Must have the cold inhumanity of the poisoner.

'By the way,' said Mr Bradley, stowing away his pocket-book again, 'you see that I've agreed with you too, Sir Charles, that the murderer would never have entrusted the posting of the parcel to another person. Oh, and one other point. For purposes of reference. If anybody wants to see an Onyx pen, and fitted with a medium-broad nib as well, take a look at mine. And curiously enough it's filled with Harfield's Fountain-Pen Ink too.' The pen circulated slowly round the table while Mr Bradley, leaning back in his chair, surveyed its progress with a fatherly smile.

'And that,' said Mr Bradley, when the pen had been restored to him, 'is that.'

Roger thought he saw the explanation of the glint that had appeared from time to time in Mr Bradley's eye. 'You mean, the problem's still to solve. The four billion chances were too much for you. You couldn't find any one to fit your own conditions?'

'Well,' said Mr Bradley, apparently most reluctant all of a sudden, 'if you must know, I have found some one who does.'

'You have? Good man! Who?'

'Hang it all, you know,' said the coy Mr Bradley. 'I hardly like to tell you. It's really too ridiculous.'

A chorus of expostulation, cajolement, and encouragement was immediately directed at him. Never had Mr Bradley found himself so popular.

'You'll laugh at me if I do tell you.'

It appeared that everybody would rather suffer the tortures of the Inquisition than laugh at Mr Bradley. Never can five people less disposed to mirth at Mr Bradley's expense have been gathered together.

Mr Bradley seemed to take heart. 'Well, it's very awkward. Upon my soul I don't know what to do about it. If I can show you that the person I have in mind not only fulfils each of my conditions exactly, but also had a certain interest (remote I admit, but capable of proof) in sending those chocolates to Sir Eustace, have I your assurance, Mr President, that the meeting will give me its serious advice as to what my duty is in the matter?'

'Good gracious, yes,' at once agreed Roger, much excited. Roger had thought that he might be on the verge of solving the problem himself, but he was quite sure that he and Bradley had not hit upon the same solution. And if the fellow really had got some one... 'Good Lord, yes!' said Roger.

Mr Bradley looked round the table in a worried way. 'Well, can't you see who I mean? Dear me, I thought I'd told you in almost every other sentence.'

Nobody had seen whom he meant.

'The only possible person, so far as I can see, who could ever be expected to fulfil all those twelve conditions?' said this harassed version of Mr Bradley, dishevelling his carefully flattened hair. 'Why, dash it, not my sister at all, but – but – but *me*, of course!'

There was a stupefied silence.

'D-did you say, *you?*' finally ventured Mr Chitterwick.

Mr Bradley turned gloomy eyes on him. 'Obviously, I'm afraid. *I* have more than an elementary knowledge of chemistry. *I* can make nitrobenzene and often have. *I*'m a criminologist. *I*'ve had a reasonably good education, but not public school or university. *I* had access to Mason's notepaper. *I* possess a Hamilton No. 4 typewriter. *I* was in Southampton Street itself during the critical hour. *I* possess an Onyx pen, fitted with a medium-broad nib and filled with Harfield's ink. *I* have something of a creative mind, but I'm not above adapting the ideas of other people. *I*'m far more than ordinarily neat with my fingers. *I*'m a person of methodical habits, with a strong feeling for symmetry. And apparently *I* have the cold inhumanity of the poisoner.

'Yes,' sighed Mr Bradley, 'there's simply no getting away from it. *I* sent those chocolates to Sir Eustace.

'I must have done. I've proved it conclusively. And the extraordinary thing is that I don't remember a single jot about it. I suppose I did it when I was thinking about something else. I've noticed I'm getting a little absent-minded at times.'

Roger was struggling with an inordinate wish to laugh. However he managed to ask gravely enough; 'And what do you imagine was your motive, Bradley?'

Mr Bradley brightened a little. 'Yes, that was a difficulty. For quite a time I couldn't establish my motive at all. I couldn't even connect myself with Sir Eustace Pennefather. I'd heard of him of course, as anybody who's ever been to the Rainbow must. And I'd gathered he was somewhat savoury. But I'd no grudge against the man. He could be as savoury as he liked so far as I cared. I don't think I'd ever even seen him. Yes, the motive was a real stumbling-block, because of course there must be one. What should I have tried to kill him for otherwise?'

'And you've found it?'

'I think I've managed to ferret out what must be the real cause,' said Mr Bradley, not without pride. 'After puzzling for a long time I remembered that I had heard myself once say to a friend, in a discussion on detective-work, that the ambition of my life was to commit a murder, because I was perfectly certain that I could do so without ever being found out. And the excitement, I pointed out, must be stupendous; no gambling game ever invented can come anywhere near it. A murderer is really making a magnificent bet with the police, I demonstrated, with the lives of himself and his victim as the stakes; if he gets away with it, he wins both; if he's caught he loses both. For a man like myself, who has the misfortune to be extremely bored by the usual type of popular recreation, murder should be the hobby *par excellence*.'

'Ah!' Roger nodded portentously.

'This conversation, when I recalled it,' pursued Mr Bradley very seriously, 'seemed to me significant in the extreme. I at once went to see my friend and asked him if he remembered it and was prepared to swear that it took place at all. He was. In fact he was able to add further details, more damning still. I was so impressed that I took a statement from him.

'Amplifying my notion (according to his statement), I had gone on to consider how it could best be carried out. The obvious thing, I had decided, was to select some figure of whom the world would be well rid, not necessarily a politician (I was at some pains to avoid the obvious, apparently), and simply murder him at a distance. To play the game, one should leave a clue or two, more or less obscure. Apparently I left rather more than I intended.

'My friend concluded by saying that I went away from him that evening expressing the firmest intention of carrying out my first murder at the earliest opportunity. Not only would the practice make such an admirable hobby, I told him, but the experience would be invaluable to a writer of detective stories such as myself.

'That, I think,' said Mr Bradley with dignity, 'establishes my motive only too certainly.'

'Murder for experiment,' remarked Roger. 'A new category. Most interesting.'

'Murder for jaded pleasure-seekers,' Mr Bradley corrected him. 'There is a precedent, you know. Loeb and Leopold. Well, there you have it. Have I proved my case, Mr President?'

'Completely, so far as I can see. I can't detect a flaw in your argument.'

'I've been at some pains to make it a good deal more watertight than I ever bother to do in my books. You could argue a very nasty case against me in court on those lines, couldn't you, Sir Charles?'

'Well, I should want to go into it a little more closely, but at first sight, Bradley, I admit that so far as circumstantial evidence is worth (and in my opinion, as you know, it is worth everything), I can't see room for very much doubt that you sent those chocolates to Sir Eustace.'

'And if I said here and now that in sober truth I *did* send them?' persisted Mr Bradley.

'I couldn't disbelieve you.'

'And yet I didn't. But given time, I'm quite prepared to prove to you just as convincingly that the person who really sent them was the Archbishop of Canterbury, or Sybil Thorndike, or Mrs Robinson-Smythe of The Laurels, Acacia

Road, Upper Tooting, or the President of the United States, or anybody else in this world you like to name.

'So much for proof. I built that whole case up against myself out of the one coincidence of my sister having a few sheets of Mason's notepaper. I told you nothing but the truth. But I didn't tell you the whole truth. Artistic proof is, like artistic anything else, simply a matter of selection. If you know what to put in and what to leave out you can prove anything you like, quite conclusively. I do it in every book I write, and no reviewer has ever hauled me over the coals for slipshod argument yet. But then,' said Mr Bradley modestly, 'I don't suppose any reviewer has ever read one of my books.'

'Well, it was a very ingenious piece of work,' Miss Dammers summed up. 'And most instructive.'

'Thank you,' murmured Mr Bradley, with gratitude.

'And what it all amounts to,' Mrs Fielder-Flemming delivered a somewhat tart verdict, 'is that you haven't the faintest idea who is the real criminal.'

'Oh, I know *that*, of course,' said Mr Bradley languidly. 'But I can't prove it. So it's not much good telling you.'

Everybody sat up.

'You've found some one else, in spite of the odds, to fit those conditions of yours?' demanded Sir Charles.

'I suppose she must,' admitted Mr Bradley, 'as she did it. But unfortunately I haven't been able to check them all.'

'She!' Mr Chitterwick caught him up.

'Oh, yes, it was a woman. That was the most obvious thing about the whole case – and incidentally one of the things I was careful to leave out just now. Really, I wonder that's never been mentioned before. Surely if there's anything evident about this affair at all it is that it's a woman's crime. It would never occur to a man to send poisoned chocolates to another man. He'd send a poisoned sample razor-blade, or whisky, or beer like the unfortunate Dr Wilson's friend. Quite obviously it's a woman's crime.'

'I wonder,' Roger said softly.

Mr Bradley threw him a sharp glance. 'You don't agree, Sheringham?'

'I only wondered,' said Roger. 'But it's a very defendable point.'

'Impregnable, I should have said,' drawled Mr Bradley.

'Well,' said Miss Dammers, impatient of these minor matters, 'aren't you going to tell us who did it, Mr Bradley?'

Mr Bradley looked at her quizzically. 'But I said that it wasn't any good, as I can't prove it. Besides, there's a small matter of the lady's honour involved.'

'Are you resuscitating the law of slander, to get you out of a difficulty?'

'Oh, dear me, no. I wouldn't in the least mind giving her away as a murderess. It's a much more important thing than that. She happens to have been Sir Eustace's mistress at one time, you see, and there's a code governing that sort of thing.'

'Ah!' said Mr Chitterwick.

Mr Bradley turned to him politely. 'You were going to say something?'

'No, no. I was just wondering whether you'd been thinking on the same lines as I have. That's all.'

'You mean the discarded mistress theory?'

'Well,' said Mr Chitterwick uncomfortably, 'yes.'

'Of course. You'd hit on that line of research, too?' Mr Bradley's tone was that of a benevolent headmaster patting a promising pupil on the head. 'It's the right one, obviously. Viewing the crime as a whole, and in the light of Sir Eustace's character, a discarded mistress, radiating jealousy, stands out like a beacon in the middle of it. That's one of the things I conveniently omitted too from my list of conditions – No. 13, the criminal must be a woman. And touching on artistic proof again, both Sir Charles and Mrs Fielder-Flemming practised it, didn't they? Both of them omitted to establish any connection of nitrobenzene with their respective criminals, though such a connection is vital to both their cases.'

'Then you really think jealousy is the motive?' Mr Chitterwick suggested.

'I'm absolutely convinced of it,' Mr Bradley assured him. 'But I'll tell you something else of which I'm not by any means convinced, and that is that the intended victim really was Sir Eustace Pennefather.'

'Not the intended victim?' queried Roger, very uneasily. 'How do you make that out?'

'Why, I've discovered,' said Mr Bradley, dissembling his pride, 'that Sir Eustace had had an engagement for lunch on the day of the murder. He seems to have been very secretive about it, and it was certainly with a woman; and not only with a woman, but with a woman in whom Sir Eustace was more than a little interested. I think probably not Miss Wildman, but somebody of whom he was anxious that Miss Wildman shouldn't know. But in my opinion the woman who sent the chocolates knew. The appointment was cancelled, but the other woman might not have known that.

'My suggestion (it's only a suggestion, and I can't substantiate it in any way at all except that it makes chocolates still more reasonable) is that those chocolates were intended not for Sir Eustace at all but for the sender's rival.'

'Ah!' breathed Mrs Fielder-Flemming.

'This is quite a new idea,' complained Sir Charles.

Roger had been hastily conning over the names of Sir Eustace's various ladies. He had been unable to fit one before into the crime, and he was unable now; yet he did not think that any had escaped him. 'If the woman you're thinking of, Bradley, the sender,' he said tentatively, 'really was a mistress of Sir Eustace, I don't think you need worry about being too punctilious. Her name is almost certainly on the lips of the whole Rainbow Club in that connection, if not of every club in London. Sir Eustace is not a reticent man.'

'I can assure Mr Bradley,' said Miss Dammers with irony, 'that Sir Eustace's standard of honour falls a good deal short of his own.'

'In this case,' Mr Bradley told them, unmoved, 'I think not.'

'How is that?'

'Because I'm quite sure that apart from my unconscious informant, and Sir Eustace, and myself, there is nobody who knows of the connection at all. Except the lady, of course,' added Mr Bradley punctiliously. 'Naturally it would not have escaped her.'

'Then how did you find out?' demanded Miss Dammers.

'That,' Mr Bradley informed her equably, 'I regret that I'm not at liberty to say.'

Roger stroked his chin. Could there be another one of whom he had never heard? In that case, how would this new theory of his continue to stand up?

'Your so close parallel falls to the ground, then?' Mrs Fielder-Flemming was stating.

'Not altogether. But if it does I've got another just as good. Christina Edmunds. Almost the same case, with the insanity left out. Jealousy-mania. Poisoned chocolates. What could be better?'

'Humph! The mainstay of your last case, I gathered,' observed Charles, 'or at any rate the starting-point, was the choice of nitrobenzene. I suppose that, and the deductions you drew from it, are equally important to this one. Are we to take it that this lady is an amateur chemist, with a copy of Taylor on her shelves?'

Mr Bradley smiled gently. 'That, as you rightly point out, was the mainstay of my *last* case, Sir Charles. It isn't of this one. I'm afraid my remarks on the choice of poison were rather special pleading. I was leading up to a certain person, you see, and therefore only drew the deductions which suited that particular person. However, there was a good deal of possible truth in them for all that, though I wouldn't rate their probability quite as high as I pretended to do then. I'm quite prepared to believe that nitrobenzene was used simply because it's so easy to get hold of. But it's perfectly true that the stuff's hardly known as a poison at all.'

'Then you make no use of it in your present case?'

'Oh, yes, I do. I still think the point that the criminal not so much used it as knew of it to use, is a perfectly sound one. The reason for that knowledge should be capable of being established. I stuck out before for a copy of some such book as Taylor as the reason, and still do. As it happens this good lady *has* got a copy of Taylor.'

'She *is* a criminologist, then?' Mrs Fielder-Flemming pounced.

Mr Bradley leaned back in his chair and gazed at the ceiling. 'That, I should think, is very much open to question. Frankly I'm puzzled over the matter of criminology. Myself, I don't see that lady as an '-ist' of any description. Her function in life is perfectly obvious, the one she fulfilled for Sir Eustace, and I shouldn't have thought her capable of any other. Except to powder her nose rather charmingly, and look extremely decorative, but all that's part and parcel of her real *raison d'être*. No, I don't think she could possibly be a criminologist, any more than a canary-bird could. But she certainly has a smattering of criminology, because in her flat there's a whole bookshelf filled with works on the subject.'

'She's a personal friend of yours, then?' queried Mrs Fielder-Flemming, very casually.

'Oh, no. I've only met her once. That was when I called her flat with a brand-new copy of a recently published book of popular murders under my arm, and represented myself as a traveller for the publisher soliciting orders for the book; might I have the pleasure of putting her name down? The book had only been out four days, but she proudly showed me a copy of it on her shelves already. Was she interested in criminology, then. Oh, yes, she simply adored it; the murder was *too* fascinating, wasn't it? Conclusive, I think.'

'She sounds a bit of a fool,' commented Sir Charles.

'She looks like a bit of a fool,' agreed Mr Bradley. 'She talks like a bit of a fool. Meeting her at a tea-fight I should have said she *is* a bit of a fool. And yet she carried through a really cleverly planned murder, so I don't see how she can be a bit of a fool.'

'It doesn't occur to you,' remarked Miss Dammers, 'that perhaps she never did anything of the sort?'

'Well, no,' Mr Bradley had to confess. 'I'm afraid it doesn't. I mean, a comparatively recent discarded mistress of Sir Eustace's (well, not more than three years ago, and hope dies hard), who thinks no small champagne of herself and considers murder too fascinating for words. Well, really!

'By the way, if you want any confirmatory evidence that she had been one of Sir Eustace's lady-loves, I might add that I saw a photograph of him in her flat. It was in a frame that had a very wide border. The border showed the word

'Your' and conveniently cut off the rest. Not 'Yours,' notice, but 'Your'. I think it's a reasonable assumption that something quite affectionate lies under that discreet border.'

'I have it from his own lips that Sir Eustace changes his mistress as often as his hats,' Miss Dammers said briskly. 'Isn't it possible that more than one may have suffered from a jealousy complex?'

'But not, I think, have possessed a copy of Taylor as well,' Mr Bradley insisted.

'The criminological-knowledge factor seems to have taken the place in this case of the nitrobenzene factor in the last,' meditated Mr Chitterwick. 'Am I right in thinking that?'

'Quite,' Mr Bradley assured him kindly. 'That, in my opinion, is the really important clue. It's so emphasised, you see. We get it from two entirely different angles, the choice of poison and the reminiscent feature of the case. In fact we're coming up against it all the time.'

'Well, well,' muttered Mr Chitterwick, reproving himself as one might who had been coming up against a thing all the time and never even noticed it.

There was a short silence, which Mr Chitterwick imputed (quite wrongly) to a general condemnation of his own obtuseness.

'Your list of conditions,' Miss Dammers resumed the charge. 'You said you hadn't been able to check all of them. Which does this woman definitely fulfil, and which haven't you been able to check?'

Mr Bradley assumed an air of alertness. 'No. 1, I don't know whether she has any chemical knowledge. No. 2, I do know that she has at least an elementary knowledge of criminology. No. 3, she is almost certain to have had a reasonably good education (though whether she ever learnt anything is quite a different matter), and I think we may assume that she was never at a public school. No. 4, I haven't been able to connect her with Mason's notepaper, except in so far as she has an account at Mason's; and if that is good enough for Sir Charles, it's good enough for me. No. 5, I haven't been able to connect her with a Hamilton typewriter, but that ought to be quite easy; one of her friends is sure to have one.

'No. 6, she could have been in the neighbourhood of Southampton Street. She tried to establish an alibi, but bungled it badly; it's full of holes. She's supposed to have been in a theatre, but she didn't even get there till well past nine. No. 7, I saw an Onyx fountain-pen on her bureau. No. 8, I saw a bottle of Harfield's Fountain-Pen Ink in one of the pigeon-holes of the bureau.

'No. 9, I shouldn't have said she had a creative mind; I shouldn't have said that she had a mind at all; but apparently we must give her the benefit of any doubt there is. No. 10, judging from her face, I should say she was very neat with her fingers. No. 11, if she is a person of methodical habits she must feel it an incriminating point, for she certainly disguises it very well. No. 12, this I think might be amended, to "must have the poisoner's complete lack of imagination". That's the lot.'

'I see,' said Miss Dammers. 'There are gaps.'

'There are,' Mr Bradley agreed blandly. 'To tell the truth, I know this woman must have done it because really, you know, she must. But I can't believe it.'

'Ah!' said Mrs Fielder-Flemming, putting a neat sentence into one word.

'By the way, Sheringham,' remarked Mr Bradley, 'you know the bad lady.'

'I do, do I?' said Roger, apparently coming out of a trance. 'I thought I might. Look here, if I write a name down on a piece of paper, do you mind telling me if I'm right or wrong?'

'Not in the least,' replied the equable Mr Bradley. 'As a matter of fact I was going to suggest something like that myself. I think as President you ought to know who I mean, in case there is anything in it.'

Roger folded his piece of paper in two and tossed it down the table. 'That's the person, I suppose.'

'You're quite right,' said Mr Bradley.

'And you base most of your case on her reasons for interesting herself in criminology?'

'You might put it like that,' conceded Mr Bradley.

In spite of himself Roger blushed faintly. He had the best of reasons for knowing why Mrs Verreker-le-Mesurer professed such an interest in criminology. Not to put too fine a point on it, the reasons had been almost forced on him.

'Then you're absolutely wrong, Bradley,' he said without hesitation. 'Absolutely.'

'You know definitely?'

Roger suppressed an involuntary shudder. 'Quite definitely.'

'You know, I never believed she did it,' said the philosophical Mr Bradley.

chapter twelve

Roger was very busy.

Flitting in taxis hither and thither, utterly regardless of what the clocks had to tell him, he was trying to get his case completed before the evening. His activities might have seemed to that artless criminologist, Mrs Verreker-le-Mesurer, not only baffling but pointless.

On the previous afternoon, for instance, he had taken his first taxi to the Holborn Public Library and there consulted a work of reference of the most uninspiring description. After that he had driven to the offices of Messrs Weall and Wilson, the well-known firm which exists to protect the trade interests of individuals and supply subscribers with highly confidential information regarding the stability of any business in which it is intended to invest money.

Roger, glibly representing himself as a potential investor of large sums, had entered his name as a subscriber, filled up a number of the special enquiry forms which are headed Strictly Confidential, and not consented to go away until Messrs Weall and Wilson had promised, in consideration of certain extra moneys, to have the required information in his hands within twenty-seven hours.

He had then bought a newspaper and gone to Scotland Yard. There he sought out Moresby.

'Moresby,' he said without preamble, 'I want you to do something important for me. Can you find me a taxi-man who took up a fare in Piccadilly Circus or its neighbourhood at about ten minutes past nine on the night before the Bendix murder, and deposited same at or near the Strand end of Southampton Street? And/or another taxi who took up a fare in the Strand near Southampton Street at about a quarter-past nine, and deposited same in the neighbourhood of Piccadilly Circus? The second is the more likely of the two; I'm not quite sure about the first. Or one taxi might have been used for the double journey, but I doubt that very much. Do you think you can do this for me?'

'We may not get any results, after all this time,' said Moresby doubtfully. 'It's really important, is it?'

'Quite important.'

'Well, I'll try of course, seeing it's you, Mr Sheringham, and I know I can take your word for it that it is important. But I wouldn't for any one else.'

'That's fine,' said Roger with much heartiness. 'Make it pretty urgent, will you? And you might give me a ring at the Albany at about tea-time tomorrow, if you think you've got hold of my man.'

'What's the idea, then, Mr Sheringham?'

'I'm trying to break down a rather interesting alibi,' said Roger.

He went back to his rooms to dine.

After the meal his head was buzzing far too busily for him to be able to do anything else but take it for a walk. Restlessly he wandered out of the Albany and turned down Piccadilly. He ambled round the Circus thinking hard, and paused for a moment out of habit to inspect with unseeing eyes the photographs of the new revue hanging outside the Pavilion. The next thing he realised was that he must have turned down the Haymarket and swung round in a wide circle into Jermyn Street, for he was standing outside the Imperial Theatre in that fascinating thoroughfare, idly watching the last of the audience crowding in.

Glancing at the advertisements of *The Creaking Skull,* he saw that the terrible thing began at half-past eight. Glancing at his watch, he saw that the time was twenty-nine minutes past the hour.

There was an evening to be got through somehow.

He went inside.

The night passed somehow, too.

Early the next morning (or early, that is, for Roger; say half-past ten), in a bleak spot somewhere beyond the bounds of civilisation, in short in Acton, Roger found himself parleying with a young woman in the offices of the Anglo-Eastern Perfumery Company. The young woman was entrenched behind a partition just inside the main entrance, her only means of communication with the outer world being through a small window fitted with frosted glass. This window she would open (if summoned long and loudly enough) to address a few curt replies to important callers, and this window she would close with a bang by way of a hint that the interview, in her opinion, should now be closed.

'Good morning,' said Roger blandly, when his third rap had summoned this maiden from the depths of her fastness. 'I've called to – '

'Travellers, Tuesday and Friday mornings, ten to eleven,' said the maiden surprisingly, and closed the window with one of her best bangs. That'll teach him to try to do business with a respectable English firm on a Thursday morning, good gracious me, said the bang.

Roger stared blankly at the closed window. Then it dawned on him that a mistake had been made. He rapped again. And again.

At the fourth rap the window flew open as if something had exploded behind it. 'I've told you already,' snapped the maiden, righteously indignant, 'that we only see – '

'I'm not a traveller,' said Roger hastily. 'At least,' he added with meticulousness, thinking of the dreary deserts he had explored before finding this inhospitable oasis, 'at least, not a commercial one.'

'You don't want to sell anything?' asked the maiden suspiciously. Impregnated with all that is best in the go-ahead spirit of English business methods, she naturally looked with the deepest distrust on anybody who might possibly wish to do such an unbusinesslike thing as *sell* her firm something.

'Nothing,' Roger assured her with the utmost earnestness, impressed in his turn with the revolting vulgarity of such a proceeding.

On these conditions it appeared that the maiden, though by no means ready to take him to her bosom, was prepared to tolerate him for a few seconds. 'Well, what *do* you want then?' she asked, with an air of weariness patiently, even nobly borne. From her tone it was to be gathered that very few people penetrated as far as that door unless with the discreditable intention of trying to do business with her firm. Just fancy – business!

'I'm a solicitor,' Roger told her now, without truth, 'and I'm enquiring into the matter of a certain Mr Joseph Lea Hardwick, who was employed here. I regret to say that – '

'Sorry, never heard of the gentleman,' said the maiden shortly, and intimated in her usual way that the interview had lasted quite long enough.

Once more Roger got busy with his stick. After the seventh application he was rewarded with another view of indignant young English girlhood.

'I've told you already – '

But Roger had had about enough of this. 'And now, young woman, let me tell *you* something. If you refuse to answer my questions, let me warn you that you may find yourself in very serious trouble. Haven't you ever heard of contempt of court?' There are times when some slight juggling with the truth is permissable. There are times, too, when even a shrewd blow with a bludgeon may be excused. This time was one of both.

The maiden, though far from cowed, was at last impressed. 'Well, what do you want to know then?' she asked resignedly.

'This man, Joseph Lea Hardwick – '

'I've told you, I've never heard of him.'

As the gentleman in question had enjoyed an existence of only two or three minutes, and that solely in Roger's brain, his creator was not unprepared for this. 'It is possible that he was known to you under a different name,' he said darkly.

The maiden's interest was engaged. More, she looked positively alarmed. She spoke shrilly. 'If it's divorce, let me tell you you can't hang anything on *me*. I never even knew he was married. Besides, it isn't as if there was a cause. I mean to say – well, at least – anyhow, it's a pack of lies. I never – '

'It isn't divorce,' Roger hastened to stem the tide, himself scarcely less alarmed at these quite unmaidenly revelations. 'It's – it's nothing to do with your private life at all. It's about a man who was employed here.'

'Oh!' The late maiden's relief turned rapidly into indignation. 'Well, why couldn't you say so?'

'Employed here,' pursued Roger firmly, 'in the nitrobenzene department. You have a nitrobenzene department haven't you?'

'Not that I'm aware of, I'm sure.'

Roger made the noise that is usually spelt 'Tchah!' 'You know perfectly well what I mean. The department which handles the nitrobenzene used here. You are hardly prepared to deny that nitrobenzene *is* used here, I hope? And extensively?'

'Well, and what if it is?'

'It has been reported to my firm that this man met his death through insufficient warning having been issued to the employees here about the dangerous nature of this substance. I should like – '

'What? One of our men died? I don't believe it. I should have been the first to know if – '

'It's been hushed up,' Roger inserted quickly. 'I should like you to show me a copy of the warning that is hung up in the factory about nitrobenzene.'

'Well, I'm sorry then, but I'm afraid I can't oblige you.'

'Do you mean to tell me,' said Roger, much shocked, 'that no warning is issued at all to your employees about this most dangerous substance? They're not even told that it is a deadly poison?'

'I didn't say that, did I? Of course they're warned that it's poisonous. Everybody is. And they're most careful about the way it's handled, I'm sure. It just happens that there isn't a warning hung up. And if you want to know any more about it, you'd better see one of the directors. I'll – '

'Thank you,' said Roger, speaking the truth at last, 'I've learned all I wanted. Good morning.' He retreated jubilantly.

He retreated to Webster's, the printers, in a taxi.

Webster's of course are to printing what Monte Carlo is to the Riviera. Webster's, practically speaking, *are* printing. So where more naturally should Roger go if he wanted some new notepaper printed in a very special and particular way, as apparently he did?

To the young woman behind the counter who took him in charge he specified at great length and in the most meticulous detail exactly what he did want. The young woman handed him her book of specimen pieces and asked him to see if he could find a style there which would suit him. While he looked through it she turned to another customer. Not to palter with the truth, that young woman had been getting a little weary of Roger and his wants.

Apparently Roger could not find a style to suit him, for he closed the book and edged a little along the counter till he was within the territory of the next young woman. To her in turn he embarked on the epic of his needs, and in turn too she presented him with her book of specimens and asked him to choose one. As the book was only another copy of the same edition, it is not surprising that Roger found himself no further forward.

Once more he edged along the counter, and once more he recited his saga to the third, and last, young woman. Knowing the game, she handed him her book of specimens. But this time Roger had his reward. This book was one of the same edition, but it was not an exact copy.

'Of course I'm sure you'll have what I want,' he remarked garrulously as he flicked over the pages, 'because I was recommended here by a friend who is really most particular. *Most* particular.'

'Is that so?' said the young woman, doing her best to appear extremely interested. She was a very young woman indeed, young enough to study the technique of salesmanship in her spare time; and one of the first rules of salesmanship, she had learned, was to receive a customer's remarks that it is a fine day with the same eager and respectful admiration of the penetrating powers of his observation as she would accord to a fortune-teller who informed her that she would receive a letter from a dark stranger across the water containing an offer of money, on her note of hand alone. 'Well,' she said, trying hard, 'some people are particular, and that's a fact.'

'Dear me!' Roger seemed much struck. 'Do you know, I believe I've got my friend's photograph on me this very minute. Isn't that an extraordinary coincidence?'

'Well, I never,' said the dutiful young woman.

Roger produced the coincidental photograph and handed it across the counter. 'There! Recognise it?'

The young woman took the photograph and studied it closely. 'So that's your friend! Well, isn't that extraordinary? Yes, of course I recognise it. It's a small world, isn't it?'

'About a fortnight ago, I think my friend was in here last,' Roger persisted. 'Is that right?'

The young woman pondered. 'Yes, it would be about a fortnight ago, I suppose. Yes, just about. Now this is a line we're selling a good deal of just at present.'

Roger bought an inordinate quantity of notepaper he didn't want in the least, out of sheer lightness of heart. And because she really was a very nice young woman, and it was a shame to take advantage of her.

Then he went back to his rooms for lunch.

Most of the afternoon he spent in trying apparently to buy a second-hand typewriter.

Roger was very particular that his typewriter should be a Hamilton No. 4. When the salesman tried to induce him to consider other makes he refused to look at them, saying that he had had the Hamilton No. 4 so strongly recommended to him by a friend, who had bought a second-hand one just about three weeks ago. Perhaps it was at this very shop? No? They hadn't sold a Hamilton No. 4 for the last two months? How very odd.

But at one shop they had; and that was odder still. The obliging salesman looked up the exact date, and found that it was just a month ago. Roger described his friend, and the salesman at once agreed that Roger's friend and his own customer were one and the same.

'Good gracious, and now I come to think of it,' Roger cried, 'I actually believe I've got my friend's photograph on me at this very minute. Let me see!' He rummaged in his pockets, and to his great astonishment produced the photograph in question.

The salesman most obligingly proceeded to identify his customer without hesitation. He then went on, just as obligingly, to sell Roger the second-hand Hamilton No. 4 which that enthusiastic detective felt he had not the face to refuse to buy. Detecting, Roger was discovering, is for the person without official authority to back him, a singularly expensive business. But like Mrs Fielder-Flemming, he did not grudge money spent in a good cause.

He went back to his rooms to tea. There was nothing more to be done except await the call from Moresby.

It came sooner than expected.

'Is that you, Mr Sheringham? There are fourteen taxi-drivers here, littering up my office,' said Moresby offensively. 'They all took fares from Piccadilly Circus to the Strand, or *vice versa*, at your time. What do you want me to do with 'em?'

'Kindly keep them till I come, Chief Inspector,' returned Roger with dignity, and grabbed his hat. He had not expected more than three at the most, but he was not going to let Moresby know that.

The interview with the fourteen was brief enough however. To each grinning man in turn (Roger deduced a little heavy humour on the part of Moresby before he arrived) Roger showed the photograph, taking some pains to hold it so that Moresby could not see it, and asked if he could recognise his fare. Not a single one could.

Moresby dismissed the men with a broad grin. 'That's a pity, Mr Sheringham. Puts a bit of a spoke in the case you're trying to work up, no doubt?'

Roger smiled at him in a superior manner. 'On the contrary, my dear Moresby, it just about clinches it.'

'It what did you say?' asked Moresby, startled out of his grammar. 'What are you up to, Mr Sheringham, eh?'

'I thought you knew all that. Aren't we being sleuthed?'

'Well!' Moresby actually looked a shade out of countenance. 'To tell you the truth, Mr Sheringham, all your people seemed to be going so far off the lines that I called my men off; it didn't seem worth while keeping 'em on.'

'Dear, dear,' said Roger gently. 'Fancy that. Well, it's a small world, isn't it?'

'So what have you been doing, Mr Sheringham? You've no objection to telling me that, I suppose?'

'None in the least, Moresby. Your work for you. Does it interest you to know that I've found out who sent those chocolates to Sir Eustace?'

Moresby eyed him for a moment. 'It certainly does, Mr Sheringham. If you really have.'

'Oh, I have, yes,' said Roger very nonchalantly; even Mr Bradley himself could not have spoken more so. 'I'll give you a report on it as soon as I've got my evidence in order. – It was an interesting case,' he added. And suppressed a yawn.

'Was it now, Mr Sheringham?' said Moresby, in a choked voice.

'Oh, yes; in its way. But absurdly simple once one had grasped the really essential factor. Quite ridiculously so. I'll let you have that report some time. So long, then.' And he strolled out.

One cannot conceal the fact that Roger had his annoying moments.

chapter thirteen

Roger called on himself.

'Ladies and gentlemen, as the one responsible for this experiment, I think I can congratulate myself. The three members who have spoken so far have shown an ingenuity of observation and argument which I think could have been called forth by no other agency. Each was convinced before beginning to speak that he or she had solved the problem and could produce positive proof in support of such solution, and each, I think, is still entitled to say that his or her reading of the puzzle has not yet been definitely disproved.

'Even Sir Charles' choice of Lady Pennefather is perfectly arguable, in spite of the positive alibi that Miss Dammers is able to give to Lady Pennefather herself; Sir Charles is quite entitled to say that Lady Pennefather has an accomplice, and to adduce in support of that the rather dubious circumstances attending her stay in Paris.

'And in this connection I should like to take the opportunity of retracting what I said to Bradley last night. I said that I knew definitely that the woman he had in mind could not have committed the murder. That was a misstatement. I didn't know definitely at all. I found the idea, from what I personally know of her, to be quite incredible.

'Moreover,' said Roger bravely, 'I have some reason to suspect the origin of her interest in criminology, and I'm pretty sure it's quite a different one from that postulated by Bradley. What I should have said was, that her guilt of this crime was a psychological impossibility. But so far as facts go, one can't prove psychological impossibilities. Bradley is still perfectly entitled to believe her the criminal. And in any case she must certainly remain on the list of suspects.'

'I agree with you, Sheringham, you know, about the psychological impossibility,' remarked Mr Bradley. 'I said as much. The trouble is that I consider I proved the case against her.'

'But you proved the case against yourself too,' pointed out Mrs Fielder-Flemming sweetly.

'Oh, yes; but that doesn't worry me with its inconsistency. That involves no psychological impossibility, you see.'

'No,' said Mrs Fielder-Flemming. 'Perhaps not.'

'Psychological impossibility!' contributed Sir Charles robustly. 'Oh, you novelists. You're all so tied up with Freud nowadays that you've lost sight of human nature altogether. When I was a young man nobody talked about psychological impossibilities. And why? Because we knew very well that there's no such thing.'

'In other words, the most improbable person may, in certain circumstances, do the most unlikely things,' amplified Mrs Fielder-Flemming. 'Well, I may be old-fashioned, but I'm inclined to agree with that.'

'Constance Kent,' led Sir Charles.

'Lizzie Borden,' Mrs Fielder-Flemming covered.

'The entire Adelaide Bartlett case,' Sir Charles brought out the ace of trumps.

Mrs Fielder-Flemming gathered the cards up into a neat pack. 'In my opinion, people who talk of psychological impossibilities are treating their subjects as characters in one of their own novels – they're infusing a certain percentage of their own mental make-up into them and consequently never see clearly that what they think may be the impossible for themselves may quite well be the possible (however improbable) in somebody else.'

'Then there is something to be said after all for the detective story merchant's axiom of the most unlikely person,' murmured Mr Bradley. 'Good!'

'Shall we hear what Mr Sheringham's got to say about the case now?' suggested Miss Dammers.

Roger took the hint.

'I was going on to say how interestingly the experiment had turned out, too, in that the three people who have already spoken happen each to have hit on a different person for the criminal. I, by the way, am going to suggest another, or even if Miss Dammers and Mr Chitterwick each agree with one of us, that gives us four entirely different possibilities. I don't mind confessing that I'd hoped something like that would happen, though I hardly looked for such an excellent result.

'Still, as Bradley has pointed out in his remarks about closed and open murders, the possibilities in this case really are most infinite. That, of course, makes it so much more interesting from our point of view. For instance, I began my own investigations from the point of view of Sir Eustace's private life. It was there, I felt convinced, that the clue to the murder was to be found. Just as Bradley did. And like him, I thought that this clue would be in the form of a discarded mistress; jealousy or revenge, I was sure, would turn out to be the mainspring of the crime. Lastly, like him I was convinced from the very first glance at the business that the crime was the work of a woman.

'The consequence was that I began work entirely from the angle of Sir Eustace's women. I spent a good many not too savoury days collecting data, until I was convinced that I had a complete list of all his affairs during the past five years. It was not difficult. Sir Eustace, as I said last night, is not a reticent man. Apparently I had not got the full list, for mine hadn't included the lady whose name was not mentioned last night, and if there was one omission it's possible there may be more. At any rate, it seems that Sir Eustace, to do him justice, did have his moments of discretion.

'But now all that is really beside the point. What matters is that at first I was certain that the crime was the work not only of a woman, but of a woman who had comparatively recently been Sir Eustace's mistress.

'I have now changed all my opinions, *in toto*.'

'Oh, really!' moaned Mr Bradley. 'Don't tell me I was wrong all along the line.'

'I'm afraid so,' said Roger, trying to keep the triumph out of his voice. It is a difficult thing, when one has really and truly solved a problem which has baffled so many excellent brains, to appear entirely indifferent about it.

'I regret to have to say,' he went on, hoping he appeared humbler than he felt, 'I regret to have to say that I can't claim all credit for this change of view for my own perspicacity. To be quite honest, it was sheer luck. A chance meeting with a silly woman in Bond Street put me in possession of a piece of information, trivial in itself (my informant never for one moment saw its possible significance), but which immediately altered the whole case for me. I saw in a flash that I'd been working from the beginning on mistaken premises. That I'd been making, in fact, the particular fundamental mistake which the murderer had intended the police and everybody else to make.

'It's a curious business, this element of luck in the solution of crime puzzles,' Roger ruminated. 'As it happens I was discussing it with Moresby, in connection with this very case. I pointed out to him the number of impossible problems which Scotland Yard solves eventually through sheer luck – a vital piece of evidence turning up of its own accord so to speak, or a piece of information brought in by an angry woman because her husband happened to have given her grounds for jealousy just before the crime. That sort of thing is happening all the time. *The Avenging Chance*, I suggested as a title, if Moresby ever wanted to make a film out of such a story.

'Well, The Avenging Chance has worked again. By means of that lucky encounter in Bond Street, in one moment of enlightenment it showed me who really had sent those chocolates to Sir Eustace Pennefather.'

'Well, well, well!' Mr Bradley kindly expressed the feelings of the Circle.

'And who was it, then?' queried Miss Dammers, who had an unfortunate lack of dramatic feeling. For that matter Miss Dammers was inclined to plume herself on the fact that she had no sense of construction, and that none of her books ever had a plot. Novelists who use words like 'values' and 'reflexes' and 'Oedipus complex' simply won't have anything to do with plots. 'Who appeared to you in this interesting revelation, Mr Sheringham?'

'Oh, let me work my story up a little first,' Roger pleaded.

Miss Dammers sighed. Stories, as Roger as a fellow craftsman ought to have known, simply weren't done nowadays. But then Roger was a best-seller, and anything is possible with a creature like that.

Unconscious of these reflections, Roger was leaning back in his chair in an easy attitude, meditating gently. When he began to speak again it was in a more conversational tone than he had used before.

'You know, this really was a very remarkable case. You and Bradley, Mrs Fielder-Flemming, didn't do the criminal justice when you described it as a hotch-potch of other cases. Any ideas of real merit in previous cases may have been borrowed, perhaps; but as Fielding says, in *Tom Jones*, to borrow from the classics, even without acknowledgment, is quite legitimate for the purposes of an original work. And this *is* an original work. It has one feature which not only absolves it from all charge to the contrary, but which puts its head and shoulders above all its prototypes.

'It's bound to become one of the classical cases itself. And but for the merest accident, which the criminal for all his ingenuity couldn't possibly have foreseen, I think it would have become one of the classical mysteries. On the whole I'm inclined to consider it the most perfectly-planned murder I've ever heard of (because of course one doesn't hear of the even more perfectly-planned ones that are never known to be murders at all.) It's so exactly right – ingenious, utterly simple, and as near as possible infallible.'

'Humph! Not so very infallible, as it turned out, Sheringham, eh?' grunted Sir Charles.

Roger smiled at him.

'The motive's so obvious, when you know where to look for it; but you didn't know. The method's so significant, once you've grasped its real essentials; but you didn't grasp them. The traces are so thinly covered, when you've realised just what is covering them; but you didn't realise. Everything was anticipated. The soap was left lying about in chunks, and we all hurried to stuff our eyes with it. No wonder we couldn't see clearly. It really was beautifully planned. The police, the public, the press – everybody completely taken in. It seems almost a pity to have to give the murderer away.'

'Really, Mr Sheringham,' remarked Mrs Fielder-Flemming. 'You're getting quite lyrical.'

'A perfect murder makes me feel lyrical. If I was this particular criminal I should have been writing odes to myself for the last fortnight.'

'And as it is,' suggested Miss Dammers, 'you feel like writing odes to yourself for having solved the thing.'

'I do rather,' Roger agreed.

'Well, I'll begin with the evidence. As to that, I won't say that I've got such a collection of details as Bradley was able to amass to prove his first theory, but I think you'll agree that I've got quite enough. Perhaps I can't do better than run through his list of twelve conditions which the murderer must fulfil, though as you'll see I don't by any means agree with all of them.

'I grant and can prove the first two, that the murderer must have at least an elementary knowledge of chemistry and criminology, but I disagree with both parts of the third; I don't think a good education is really essential, and I should certainly not rule out any one with a public school or university education, for reasons which I'll explain later. Nor do I agree with the fourth, that he or she must have had possession of or access to Mason's notepaper. It was an ingenious idea of Bradley's that the possession of the notepaper suggested the method of the crime, but I think it mistaken; a previous case suggested the method, chocolates were decided on (for a very good reason indeed, as I'll show later) as the vehicle, and Mason's as being the most important firm of chocolate manufacturers. It then became necessary to procure a piece of their notepaper, and I'm in a position to show how this was done.

'The fifth condition I would qualify. I don't agree that the criminal must have possession of or access to a Hamilton No. 4 typewriter, but I do agree that such possession must have existed. In other words, I would put that condition in the past tense. Remember that we have to deal with a very astute criminal, and a very carefully planned crime. I thought it most unlikely that such an incriminating piece of evidence as the actual typewriter would be allowed to lie about for anyone to discover. Much more probably that a machine had been bought specially for the occasion. It was clear from the letter that it wasn't a new machine which had been used. With the courage of my deduction, therefore, I spent a whole afternoon making inquiries at second-hand typewriter-shops till I ran down the place where it had been bought, and proved the buying. The shopman was able to identify my murderer from a photograph I had with me.'

'And where's the machine now?' asked Mrs Fielder-Flemming eagerly.

'I expect at the bottom of the Thames. That's my point. This criminal of mine leaves nothing to chance at all.

'With the sixth condition, about being near the post-office during the critical hour, of course I agree. My murderer has a mild alibi, but it doesn't hold water. As to the next two, the fountain-pen and the ink, I haven't been able to check them at all, and while I agree that their possessions would be rather pleasing confirmation I don't attach great importance to them; Onyx pens are so universal, and so is Harfield's ink, that there isn't much argument either way. Besides, it would be just like my criminal not to own either of them but to have borrowed the pen unobtrusively. Lastly, I agree about the creative mind, and the neatness with the fingers, and of course with the prisoner's peculiar mentality, but not with the necessity for methodical habits.'

'Oh, come,' said Mr Bradley, pained. 'That was rather a sound deduction, I thought. And it stands to reason, too.'

'Not to my reason,' Roger retorted.

Mr Bradley shrugged his shoulders.

'It's the notepaper I'm interested in,' said Sir Charles. 'In my opinion that's the point on which the case against anyone must hang. How do you prove possession of the notepaper, Sheringham?'

'The notepaper,' said Roger, 'was extracted about three weeks ago from one of Webster's books of sample notepaper headings. The erasure would be some private mark of Webster's, the price, for instance: "This style, 5s. 9d." There are three books at Webster's, containing exactly the same samples. Two of them include a piece of Mason's paper; from the third it's missing. I can prove contact of my suspect with the book about three weeks ago.'

'You can, can you?' Sir Charles was impressed. 'That sounds pretty conclusive. What put you on the idea of the sample books?'

'The yellowed edges of the letter,' Roger said, not a little pleased with himself. 'I didn't see how a bit of paper that had been kept in a pile could get its edges quite so discoloured as all that, so concluded that it must have been an isolated piece. Then it struck me that walking about London, one does see isolated pieces of notepaper stuck on a board in the windows of printing firms. But this piece showed no drawing-pin holes or any other signs of having been fixed to a board. Besides, it would be difficult to remove it from a board. What was the next best thing? Obviously, a sample book, such as one usually finds inside the same shops. So to the printers of Mason's notepaper I went, and there, so to speak, my piece wasn't.'

'Yes,' muttered Sir Charles, 'certainly that sounds pretty conclusive.' He sighed. One gathered that he was gazing wistfully in his mind's eye at the diminishing figure of Lady Pennefather, and the beautiful case he had built up around her. Then he brightened. This time one had gathered that he had switched his vision to the figure, equally diminishing, of Sir Charles Wildman, and the beautiful case that had been built up around him too.

'So now,' Roger, feeling he could really put it off no longer, 'we come to the fundamental mistake to which I referred just now, the trap the murderer laid for us and into which we all so neatly fell.'

Everybody sat up.

Roger surveyed them benignly.

'You got very near seeing it, Bradley, last night, with your casual suggestion that Sir Eustace himself might not have been the intended victim after all. That's right enough. But I go further than that.'

'I fell in the trap, though, did I?' said Mr Bradley, pained. 'Well, what is this trap? What's the fundamental mistake we all side-slipped into?'

'Why,' Roger brought out in triumph, 'that the plan had miscarried – that the wrong person had been killed!'

He got his reward.

'What!' said everyone at once. 'Good heavens, you don't mean…?'

'Exactly,' Roger crowed. 'That was just the beauty of it. The plan had *not* miscarried. It had been brilliantly successful. The wrong person had *not* been killed. Very much the right person was.'

'What's all this?' positively gaped Sir Charles. 'How on earth do you make that out?'

'Mrs Bendix was the objective all the time,' Roger went on more soberly. 'That's why the plot was so ingenious. Every single thing was anticipated. It was forseen that, if Bendix could be brought naturally into Sir Eustace's presence when the parcel was being opened, the latter would hand the chocolates over to him. It was foreseen that the police would look for the criminal among Sir Eustace's associates, and not the dead woman's. It was probably even foreseen, Bradley, that the crime would be considered the work of a woman, whereas really, of course, chocolates were employed because it was a woman who was the objective.'

'Well, well, well!' said Mr Bradley.

'Then it's your theory,' pursued Sir Charles, 'that the murderer was an associate of the dead woman's, and had nothing to do with Sir Eustace at all?' He spoke as if not altogether averse from such a theory.

'It is,' Roger confirmed. 'But first let me tell you what finally opened my eyes to the trap. The vital piece of information I got in Bond Street was this: *that Mrs Bendix had seen that Play, The Creaking Skull, before.* There's no doubt about it; she actually went with my informant herself. You see the extraordinary significance, of course. That means that she already knew the answer to that bet she made with her husband about the identity of the villain.'

A little intake of breath testified to a general appreciation of this information.

'Oh! What a marvellous piece of divine irony.' Miss Dammers was exercising her usual faculty of viewing things from the impersonal aspect. 'Then she actually brought her own retribution on herself. The bet she won virtually killed her.'

'Yes,' said Roger. 'The irony hadn't failed to strike even my informant. The punishment, as she pointed out, was so much greater than the crime. But I don't think,' – Roger spoke very gently, in a mighty effort to curb this elation – 'I don't think that even now you quite see my point.'

Everybody looked inquiringly.

'You've all heard Mrs Bendix quite minutely described. You must all have formed a tolerably close mental picture of her. She was a straightforward, honest girl, making if anything (also according to my informant) almost too much of a fetish of straight dealing and playing the game. Does the making of a bet to which she already knew the answer, fit into that picture or does it not?'

'Ah!' Nodded Mr Bradley. 'Oh, very pretty.'

'Just so. It is (with apologies to Sir Charles) a psychological impossibility. It really is, you know, Sir Charles; one simply can't see her doing such a thing, in fun or out of it; and I gather that fun wasn't her strong suit, by any means.

'*Ergo*,' concluded Roger briskly, 'she didn't. *Ergo*, that bet was never made. *Ergo*, Bendix was lying. *Ergo*, Bendix wanted to get hold of those chocolates for some reason other than he stated. And the chocolates being what they were, there was only one other reason.

'That's my case.'

chapter fourteen

When the excitement that greeted this revolutionary reading of the case had died down, Roger went on to defend his theory in more detail.

'It *is* something of a shock, of course, to find oneself contemplating Bendix as the very cunning murderer of his own wife, but really, once one has been able to rid one's mind of all prejudice, I don't see how the conclusion can possibly be avoided. Every item of evidence, however minute, goes to support it.'

'But the motive!' ejaculated Mrs Fielder-Flemming.

'Motive? Good heavens, he'd motive enough. In the first place he was frankly – no, not frankly; secretly! – tired of her. Remember what we were told of his character. He'd sown his wild oats. But apparently he hadn't finished sowing them, because his name has been mentioned in connection with more than one woman even since his marriage, usually, in the good old-fashioned way, actresses. So Bendix wasn't such a solemn stick by any means. He liked his fun. And his wife, I should imagine, was just about the last person in the world to sympathise with such feelings.

'Not that he hadn't liked her well enough when he married her, quite possibly, though it was her money he was after all the time. But she must have bored him dreadfully very soon. And really,' said Roger impartially, 'I think one can hardly blame him there. Any woman, however charming otherwise, is bound to bore a normal man if she does nothing but prate continually about honour and duty and playing the game; and that, I have on good authority, was Mrs Bendix's habit.

'Just look at the *ménage* in this light. The wife would never overlook the smallest peccadillo. Every tiny lapse would be thrown up at him for years. Everything she did would be right and everything he did wrong. Her sanctimonious righteousness would be forever being contrasted with his vileness. She might even work herself into the state of those half-mad creatures who spend the whole of their married lives reviling their husbands for having been attracted by other women before they even met the girl it was their misfortune to marry. Don't think I'm trying to blacken Mrs Bendix. I'm just showing you how intolerable life with her might have been.

'But that's only the incidental motive. The real trouble was that she was too close with her money, and that too I know for a fact. That's where she sentenced herself to death. He wanted it, or some of it, badly (it's what he married her for), and she wouldn't part.

'One of the first things I did was to consult a Directory of Directors and make a list of the firms he's interested in, with a view to getting a confidential report on their financial condition. The report reached me just before I left my rooms. It told me exactly what I expected – that every single one of those firms is rocky, some only a little but some within sight of a crash. They all need money to save them. It's obvious, isn't it? He's run through all his own money, and he had to get more. I found time to run down to Somerset House and again it was as I expected: her will was entirely in his favour.

The really important point (which no one seems to have suspected) is that he isn't a good businessman at all; he's a rotten one. And half-a-million... Well!

'Oh, yes. There's motive enough.'

'Motive allowed,' said Mr Bradley. 'And the nitrobenzene? You said, I think, that Bendix has some knowledge of chemistry.'

Roger laughed. 'You remind me of a Wagner opera, Bradley. The nitrobenzene *motif* crops up regularly from you whenever a possible criminal is mentioned. However, I think I can satisfy even you in this instance. Nitrobenzene as you know, is used in perfumery. In the list of Bendix's businesses is the Anglo-Eastern Perfumery Company. I made a special, and dreadful, journey out to Acton for the express purpose of finding out whether the Anglo-Eastern Company used nitrobenzene at all, and, if so, whether its poisonous qualities were thoroughly recognised. The answer to both questions was in the affirmative. So there can be no doubt that Bendix is thoroughly acquainted with the stuff.

'He might easily enough have got his supply from the factory, but I'm inclined to doubt that. I think he'd be cleverer than that. He probably made the stuff himself, if the process is as easy as Bradley told us. Because I happen to know that he was on the modern side at Selchester (that I heard quite by chance too), which presupposes at any rate an elementary knowledge of chemistry. Do you pass that, Bradley?'

'Pass, friend nitrobenzene,' conceded Mr Bradley.

Roger drummed thoughtfully on the table with his fingertips. 'It was a well-planned affair, wasn't it?' he meditated. 'And so extremely easy to reconstruct. Bendix must have thought he'd provided against every possible contingency. And so he very nearly had. It was just that little bit of unlucky grit that gets into the smooth machinery of so many clever crimes: he didn't know that his wife had seen the play before. He'd decided on the mild alibi of his presence at the theatre, you see, just in case suspicion should ever impossibly arise, and no doubt he stressed his desire to see the play and take her with him. Not to spoil his pleasure, she would have unselfishly concealed from him the fact that she had seen the play before and didn't much want to see it again. That unselfishness let him down. Because it's inconceivable that she would have turned it to her own advantage to win the bet he pretends to have made with her.

'He left the theatre of course during the first interval, and hurried as far as he dare go in the ten minutes at his disposal, to post the parcel. I sat through the dreadful thing myself last night just to see when the intervals came. The first one fits excellently. I'd hoped he might have taken a taxi one way, as time was short, but if he did no driver of such taxis as did make a similar journey that evening can identify him. Or possibly the right driver hasn't come forward yet. I got Scotland Yard to look into that point for me. But it really fits much better with the cleverness he's shown all through, that he should have gone by bus or underground. Taxis, he'd know, are traceable. But if so he'd run it very fine indeed, and I shouldn't be surprised if he got back to his box a few minutes late. The police may be able to establish that.'

'It seems to me,' observed Mr Bradley, 'that we made something of a mistake in turning the man down from membership here. We thought his criminology wasn't up to standard, didn't we? Well, well.'

'But we could hardly be expected to know that he was a practical criminologist rather than a mere theoretical one,' Roger smiled. 'It was a mistake, though. It would have been pleasant to include a practical criminologist among our members.'

'I must confess that I thought at one time that we did,' said Mrs Fielder-Flemming, making her peace. 'Sir Charles,' she added unnecessarily, 'I apologise without reserve.'

Sir Charles inclined his head courteously. 'Please don't refer to it, madam. And in any event the experience for me was an interesting one.'

'I may have been misled by the case I quoted,' said Mrs Fielder-Flemming, rather wistfully. 'It was a strangely close parallel.'

'It was the first parallel that occurred to me, too,' Roger agreed. 'I studied the Molineux case quite closely, hoping to get a pointer from it. But now, if I were asked for a parallel, I should reply with the Carlyle Harris case. You remember, the young medical student who sent a pill containing morphine to the girl Helen Potts, whom it turned out that he had been secretly married for a year. He was by way of being a profligate and a general young rotter too. A great novel, as you know, has been founded on the case, so why not a great crime too?'

'Then why, Mr Sheringham,' Miss Dammers wanted to know, 'do you think that Mr Bendix took the risk of not destroying the forged letter and the wrapper when he had the chance?'

'He very carefully didn't do so,' Roger replied promptly, 'because the forged letter and the wrapper had been calculated not only to divert suspicion from himself but actually to point away from him to somebody else – an employee of Mason's, for instance, or an anonymous lunatic. Which is exactly what they did.'

'But wouldn't it be a great risk, to send poisoned chocolates like that to Sir Eustace?' suggested Mr Chitterwick diffidently. 'I mean, Sir Eustace might have been ill the next morning, or not offered to hand them over at all. Suppose he had given them to somebody else instead of Bendix.'

Roger proceeded to give Mr Chitterwick cause for his diffidence. He was feeling something of a personal pride in Bendix by this time, and it distressed him to hear a great man thus maligned.

'Oh, really! You must give my man credit for being what he is. He's not a bungler, you know. It wouldn't have had any serious results if Sir Eustace had been ill that morning, or eaten the chocolates himself, or if they'd been stolen in transit and consumed by the postman's favourite daughter, or any other unlikely contingency. Come, Mr Chitterwick! You don't imagine he'd send the poisoned ones through the post, do you? Of course not. He'd send harmless ones, and exchange them for the others on the way home. Dash it all, he wouldn't go out of his way to present opportunities to chance.'

'Oh! I see,' murmured Mr Chitterwick, properly subdued.

'We're dealing with a very great criminal,' went on Roger, rather less severely. 'That can be seen at every point. Take the arrival at the club, just for example – that most unusual early arrival (why this early arrival at all, by the way, if he isn't guilty?). Well, he doesn't wait outside and follow his unconscious accomplice in, you see. Not a bit of it. Sir Eustace is chosen because he's known to get there so punctually at half-past ten every morning; takes a pride in it; boasts of it; goes out of his way to keep up the good old custom. So Bendix arrives at ten thirty-five, and there things are. It had puzzled me at the beginning of the case, by the way, to see why the chocolates had been sent to Sir Eustace at his club at all, instead of to his rooms. Now it's obvious.'

'Well, I wasn't so far out with my list of conditions,' Mr Bradley consoled himself. 'But why don't you agree with my rather subtle point about the murderer not being a public school or University man, Sheringham? Just because Bendix happens to have been at Selchester and Oxford?'

'No, because I'd make the still more subtle point that where the code of a public school and University might influence a murderer in the way he murdered another man, it wouldn't have much effect when a woman is to be the victim. I agree that if Bendix had been wanting to dispose of Sir Eustace, he would probably have put him out of the world in a nice, straightforward, manly way. But one doesn't use nice, straightforward, manly ways in one's dealings with women, if it comes to hitting them on the head with a bludgeon or anything in that nature. Poison, I fancy, would be quite in order. And there's very little suffering with a large dose of nitrobenzene. Unconsciousness soon intervenes.'

'Yes,' admitted Mr Bradley, 'that is rather too subtle a point for one of my unpsychological attributes.'

'I think I dealt with most of your other conditions. As regards the methodical habits, which you deduced from the meticulous doses of poison in each chocolate, my point of course is that the doses were exactly equal in order that Bendix could take any two of the chocolates and be sure of having got the right amount of nitrobenzene into his system to produce the symptoms he wanted, and not enough to run any serious risk. That dosing of himself with the poison really was a master-stroke. And it's so natural that a man shouldn't have taken so many chocolates as a woman. He exaggerated his symptoms considerably, no doubt, but the effect on everybody was tremendous.

'We must remember, you see, that we've only got his word for the conversation in the drawing-room, over the eating of the chocolates, just as we've only got his word for it that there was a bet at all. Most of that conversation certainly took place, however. Bendix is far too great an artist not to make all possible use of the truth in his lying. But of course he wouldn't have left her that afternoon till he'd seen her take, or somehow made her take at least six of the chocolates, which he'd know made up more than a lethal dose. That was another advantage in having the stuff in those exact six-minim quantities.'

'In fact,' Mr Bradley summed up, 'our Uncle Bendix is a great man.'

'He really is,' said Roger, quite solemnly.

'You've no doubt at all that he is the criminal?' queried Miss Dammers.

'None at all,' said Roger, astonished.

'Um,' said Miss Dammers.

The conversation then lapsed.

'Well,' said Mr Bradley, 'let's all tell Sheringham how wrong he is, shall we?'

Mrs Fielder-Flemming looked tense. 'I'm afraid,' she said in a hushed voice, 'that he is only too right.'

But Mr Bradley refused to be impressed. 'Oh, I think I can find a hole or two to pick at. You seem to attach a good deal of importance to the motive, Sheringham. Don't you exaggerate? One doesn't poison a wife one's tired of; one leaves her. And really, I find some difficulty in believing *(a)* that Bendix should have been so set on getting hold of more money to pour down the drainpipe of his businesses as to commit murder for it, and *(b)* that Mrs Bendix should have been so close as to refuse to come to her husband's help if he really was so badly pressed.'

'Then I think you fail to estimate the characters of both of them,' Roger told him. 'They were both obstinate as the devil. It was Mrs Bendix, not her husband, who realised that his businesses *were* a drainpipe. I could give you a list a yard long of murders that have been committed with far less motive than Bendix had.'

'Motive allowed again, then. Now you remember that Mrs Bendix had had a lunch appointment for the day of her death, which was cancelled. Didn't Bendix know of that? Because if he did, would he have chosen a day for the delivery of the chocolates when he knew his wife wouldn't be at home for lunch to receive them?'

'Just the point I thought of putting to Mr Sheringham myself,' remarked Miss Dammers.

Roger looked puzzled. 'It seems to me a most unimportant point. If it comes to that, why should he necessarily want to give the chocolates to his wife at lunch-time?'

'For two reasons,' responded Mr Bradley glibly. 'Firstly because he would naturally want to put them to their right purpose as soon as he possibly could, and secondly because his wife being the only person who can contradict this story of the bet, he would obviously want her silenced as soon as practicable.'

'You're quibbling,' Roger smiled, 'and I refuse to be drawn. For that matter, I don't see why Bendix should have known of his wife's lunch appointment at all. They were constantly lunching out, both of them, and I don't suppose they took any particular care to inform each other beforehand.'

'Humph!' said Mr Bradley and stroked his chin.

Mr Chitterwick ventured to raise his recently crushed head. 'You really base your whole case on the bet, Mr Sheringham, don't you?'

'And the psychological deduction I drew from the story of it. Yes, I do. Entirely.'

'So that if the bet could be proved after all to have been made, you would have no case left?'

'Why,' exclaimed Roger, in some alarm, 'have you any independent evidence that the bet was made?'

'Oh, no. Oh, dear me, no. Nothing of the sort. I was merely thinking that if anyone did want to disprove your case, as Bradley suggested, it is the bet on which he would have to concentrate.'

'You mean, quibbling about the motive, and the lunch appointment, and such minor matters, is altogether beside the point?' suggested Mr Bradley amiably. 'Oh, I quite agree. But I was only trying to test his case, you know, not disprove it. And for why? Because I think it's the right one. The Mystery of the Poisoned Chocolates, so far as I'm concerned, is at an end.'

'Thank you, Bradley,' said Mr Sheringham.

'So three cheers for our sleuth-like President,' continued Mr Bradley with great heartiness, 'coupled with the name of Graham Reynard Bendix for the fine run he's given us. Hip, hip – '

'And you say you've definitely proved the purchase of the typewriter, and the contact of Mr Bendix with the sample book at Webster's, Mr Sheringham?' remarked Alicia Dammers, who had apparently been pursuing a train of thought of her own.

'I do, Miss Dammers,' said Roger, not without complacence.

'Would you give me the name of the typewriter shop?'

'Of course,' Roger tore a page from his notebook and copied out the name and address.

'Thank you. And can you give me a description of the girl at Webster's who identified the photograph of Mr Bendix?'

Roger looked at her a little uneasily; she gazed back with her usual calm serenity. Roger's uneasiness grew. He gave her as good a description of Webster's young woman as he could recall. Miss Dammers thanked him unperturbedly.

'Well, what are we going to do about it all?' persisted Mr Bradley, who seemed to have adopted the role of showman for his President. 'Shall we send a delegation to Scotland Yard consisting of Sheringham and myself, to break the news to them that their troubles are over?'

'You are assuming that everybody agrees with Mr Sheringham?'

'Of course.'

'Isn't it customary to put this sort of question to a vote?' suggested Miss Dammers coolly.

'"Carried unanimously,"' quoted Mr Bradley. 'Yes, do let's have the correct procedure. Well, then, Sheringham moves that this meeting do accept his solution of the Poisoned Chocolates Mystery as the right one, and send a delegation of himself and Mr Bradley to Scotland Yard to talk pretty severely to the police. I second the motion. Those in favour...? Mrs Fielder-Flemming?'

Mrs Fielder-Flemming endeavoured to conceal her disapproval of Mr Bradley in her approval of Mr Bradley's suggestion. 'I certainly think that Mr Sheringham has proved his case,' she said stiffly.

'Sir Charles?'

'I agree,' said Sir Charles, in stern tones, equally disproving Mr Bradley's frivolity.

'Chitterwick?'

'I agree too.' Was it Roger's fancy, or did Mr Chitterwick hesitate just a moment before he spoke, as if troubled by some mental reservation which he did not care to put into words? Roger decided that it was his fancy.

'And Miss Dammers?' concluded Mr Bradley.

Miss Dammers looked calmly round the table. 'I don't agree at all. I think Mr Sheringham's exposition was exceedingly ingenious, and altogether worthy of his reputation; at the same time I think it quite wrong. Tomorrow I hope to be able to prove to you who really committed this crime.'

The Circle gaped at her respectfully.

Roger, wondering whether his ears had not really been playing tricks with him, found that his tongue too utterly refused to work. An inarticulate sound oozed from him.

Mr Bradley was the first to recover himself. 'Carried, non-unanimously. Mr President, I think this is a precedent. Does anybody know what happens when a resolution is not carried unanimously?'

In the temporary disability of the President, Miss Dammers took it upon herself to decide. 'The meeting stands adjourned, I think,' she said.

And adjourned the meeting found itself.

chapter fifteen

Roger arrived at the Circle's meeting-room the next evening even more agog than usual. In his heart of hearts he could not believe that Miss Dammers would ever be able to destroy his case against Bendix, or even dangerously shake it, but in any event what she had to say could not fail to be of absorbing interest, even without its animadversions of his own solution. Roger had been looking forward to Miss Dammer's exposition more than to that of any one else.

Alicia Dammers was so very much a reflection of the age.

Had she been born fifty years ago, it is difficult to see how she could have gone on existing. It was impossible that she could have become the woman novelist of that time, a strange creature (in the popular imagination) with white cotton gloves, an intense manner, and passionate, not to say hysterical yearnings towards a romance from which her appearance unfortunately debarred her. Miss Dammers' gloves, like her clothes, were exquisite, and cotton could not have touched her since she was ten (if she ever had been); tensity was for her the depth of bad form; and if she knew how to yearn, she certainly kept it to herself. Passion and purple, one gathered, Miss Dammers found quite unnecessary to herself, if interesting phenomena in lesser mortals.

From the caterpillar in cotton gloves the woman novelist has progressed through the stage of cook-like cocoondom at which Mrs Fielder-Flemming had stuck, to the detached and serious butterfly, not infrequently beautiful as well as pensive, whose decorative pictures the illustrated weeklies are nowadays delighted to publish. Butterflies with calm foreheads, just faintly wrinkled in analytical thought. Ironical, cynical butterflies; surgeon-butterflies thronging the mental dissecting-rooms (and sometimes, if we must be candid, inclined to loiter there a little too long); passionless butterflies, flitting gracefully from one brightly-coloured complex to another. And sometimes completely humourless, and then distressingly boring butterflies, whose gathered pollen seems to have become a trifle mud-coloured.

To meet Miss Dammers and look at her classical, oval face, with its delicately small features and big grey eyes, to glance approvingly over her tall, beautifully dressed figure, nobody whose imagination was still popular would ever have set her down as a novelist at all. And that in Miss Dammers' opinion, coupled with the ability to write good books, was exactly what a properly-minded modern authoress should hope to achieve.

No one had ever been brave enough to ask Miss Dammers how she could hope successfully to analyse in others emotions which she had never experienced in herself. Probably because the plain fact confronted the enquirer that she both could and did. Most successfully.

'We listened last night,' began Miss Dammers, at five minutes past nine on the following evening, 'to an exceedingly able exposition of a no less interesting theory of this crime. Mr Sheringham's methods, if I may so, were a model to all of us. Beginning with the deductive, he followed this as far as it would take him, which was actually to the person of the criminal; he then relied on the inductive to prove his case. In this way he was able to make the best possible use of each method. That this ingenious mixture should have been based on a fallacy and therefore never had any chance of leading Mr Sheringham to the right solution, is rather a piece of bad luck than his fault.'

Roger, who still could not believe that he had not reached the truth, smiled dubiously.

'Mr Sheringham's reading of the crime,' continued Miss Dammers, in her clear, level tones, 'must have seemed to some of us novel in the extreme. To me, however, it was perhaps more interesting than novel, for it began from the same starting-point as the theory on which I myself have been working; namely, that the crime had not failed in its objective.'

Roger pricked up his ears.

'As Mr Chitterwick pointed out, Mr Sheringham's whole case rested on the bet between Mr and Mrs Bendix. From Mr Bendix's story of that bet, he draws the psychological deduction that the bet never existed at all. That is clever, but it is the wrong deduction. Mr Sheringham is too lenient in his interpretation of feminine psychology. I began, I think I may say, with the bet too. But the deduction I drew from it knowing my sister-women perhaps a little more intimately than Mr Sheringham could, was that Mrs Bendix was not quite so honourable as she was painted by herself.'

'I thought of that, of course,' Roger expostulated. 'But I discarded it on purely logical grounds. There's nothing in Mrs Bendix's life to show that she wasn't honest, and everything to show that she was. And when there exists no evidence at all for the making of the bet beyond Bendix's bare word…'

'Oh, but there does,' Miss Dammers took him up. 'I've been spending most of today in establishing that point. I knew I should never really be able to shake you till I could definitely prove that there was a bet. Let me put you out of your agony at once, Mr Sheringham. I've overwhelming evidence that the bet was made.'

'You have?' said Roger, disconcerted.

'Certainly. It was a point you really should have verified yourself, you know,' chided Miss Dammers gently, 'considering its importance to your case. Well, I have two witnesses. Mrs Bendix mentioned the bet to her maid when she went up to her bedroom to lie down, actually saying (like yourself, Mr Sheringham) that the violent indigestion from which she thought herself to be suffering was a judgment on her for having made it. The second witness is a friend of my own, who knows the Bendixes. She saw Mrs Bendix sitting alone in her box during the second interval, and went in to speak to her. In the course of the conversation Mrs Bendix remarked that she and her husband had a bet on the identity of the villain, mentioning the character in the play whom she herself fancied. But (and this completely confirms my own deduction) Mrs Bendix did *not* tell my friend that she had seen the play before.'

'Oh!' said Roger, now quite crestfallen.

Miss Dammers dealt with him as tenderly as possible. 'There were only those two deductions to be made from that bet, and by bad luck you chose the wrong one.'

'But how did you know,' said Roger, coming to the surface for the third time, 'that Mrs Bendix had seen the play before? I only found that out myself a couple of days ago, and by the merest accident.'

'Oh, I've known that from the beginning,' said Miss Dammers carelessly. 'I suppose Mrs Verreker-le-Mesurer told you? I don't know her personally, but I know people who do. I didn't interrupt you last night when you were talking about the amazing chance of this piece of knowledge reaching you. If I had, I should have pointed that the agency by which anything known to Mrs Verreker-le-Mesurer (as I see her) might become known to her friends too, isn't chance at all, but certainty.'

'I see,' said Roger, and sank for the third, and final, time. But as he did so he remembered one piece of information which Mrs Verreker-le-Mesurer had succeeded, not wholly as it seemed but very nearly so, in withholding from her friends; and catching Mr Bradley's ribald eye knew that his thought was shared. So even Miss Dammers was not quite infallible in her psychology.

'We then,' resumed that lady, somewhat didactically, 'have Mr Bendix displaced from his temporary role of villain and back again in his old part of second victim.' She paused for a moment.

'But without Sir Eustace returning to the cast in his original start part of intended victim of the piece,' amplified Mr Bradley.

Miss Dammers rightly ignored him. 'Now here, I think, Mr Sheringham will find my case as interesting as I found his last night, for though we differ so vitally in some essentials we agree remarkably in others. And one of the points on which we agree is that the intended victim certainly was killed.'

'What, Alicia?' exclaimed Mrs Fielder-Flemming. 'You think too that the plot was directed against Mrs Bendix from the beginning?'

'I have no doubt of it. But to prove my contention I must demolish yet another of Mr Sheringham's conclusions.

'You made the point, Mr Sheringham, that half-past ten in the morning was a most unusual time for Mr Bendix to arrive at his club and therefore highly significant. That is perfectly true. Unfortunately you attached the wrong significance to it. His arrival at that hour doesn't necessarily argue a guilty intention, as you assumed. It escaped you (as in fairness I must say it seems to have escaped everyone else) that if Mrs Bendix was the intended victim and Mr Bendix himself not her murderer, his presence at the club at that convenient time might have been secured by the real murderer. In any case I think Mr Sheringham might have given Mr Bendix the benefit of the doubt in so far as to ask him if he had any explanation of his own to offer. As I did.'

'You asked Bendix himself how it happened that he arrived at the club at half-past ten that morning?' Mr Chitterwick said in awed tones. This was certainly the way real detecting should be done. Unfortunately his own diffidence seemed to have prevented Mr Chitterwick from doing any real detecting at all.

'Certainly,' agreed Miss Dammers briskly. 'I rang him up, and put the point to him. From what I gathered, not even the police had thought to put it before. And though he answered it in a way I quite expected, it was clear that he saw no significance in his own answer. Mr Bendix told me that he had gone there to receive a telephone message. But why not have had the message telephoned to his home? you will ask. Exactly. So did I. The reason was that it was not the sort of message one cares about receiving at home. I must admit that I pressed Mr Bendix about this message, and as he had no idea of the importance of my questions he must have considered my taste more than questionable. However, I couldn't help that.

'In the end I got him to admit that on the previous afternoon he had been rung up at his office by a Miss Vera Delorme, who plays a small part in *Heels Up!* at the Regency Theatre. He had only met her once or twice, but was not averse from doing so again. She asked him if he were doing anything important the next morning, to which he replied that he was not. Could he take her out to a quiet little lunch somewhere? He would be delighted. But she was not quite sure yet whether she was free. She would ring him up the next morning between ten-thirty and eleven o'clock at the Rainbow Club.'

Five pairs of brows were knitted.

'I don't see any significance in that either,' finally plunged Mrs Fielder-Flemming.

'No?' said Miss Dammers. 'But if Miss Delorme straightly denies having ever rung Mr Bendix up at all?'

Five pairs of brows unravelled themselves.

'*Oh!*' said Mrs Fielder-Flemming.

'Of course that was the first thing I verified,' said Miss Dammers coolly.

Mr Chitterwick sighed. Yes, undoubtedly this was real detecting.

'Then your murderer had an accomplice, Miss Dammers?' Sir Charles suggested.

'He had two,' retorted Miss Dammers. 'Both unwitting.'

'Ah, yes. You mean Bendix. And the woman who telephoned?'

'Well – !' Miss Dammers looked in her unexcited way round the circle of faces. 'Isn't it obvious?'

Apparently it was not at all obvious.

'At any rate it must be obvious why Miss Delorme was chosen as the telephonist: because Mr Bendix hardly knew her, and would certainly not be able to recognise her voice on the telephone. And as for the real speaker... Well, really!' Miss Dammers looked her opinion of such obtuseness.

'Mrs Bendix!' squeaked Mrs Fielder-Flemming catching sight of a triangle.

'Of course. Mrs Bendix, carefully primed by *somebody* about her husband's minor misdemeanours.'

'The somebody being the murderer of course,' nodded Mrs Fielder-Flemming. 'A friend of Mrs Bendix's then. At least,' amended Mrs Fielder Flemming in some confusion, remembering that real friends seldom murder each other, 'she thought of him as a friend. Dear me, this is getting very interesting, Alicia.'

Miss Dammers gave a small, ironical smile. 'Yes, it's a very intimate little affair after all, this murder. Tightly closed, in fact, Mr Bradley.

'But I'm getting on rather too fast. I had better complete the destruction of Mr Sheringham's case before I build up my own.' Roger groaned faintly and looked up at the hard, white ceiling. It reminded him of Miss Dammers, and he looked down again.

'Really, Mr Sheringham, your faith in human nature is altogether too great, you know,' Miss Dammers mocked him without mercy. 'Whatever anybody chooses to tell you, you believe. A confirmatory witness never seems necessary to you. I'm sure that if some one had come to your rooms and told you he'd seen the Shah of Persia injecting the nitrobenzene into those chocolates you would have believed him unhesitatingly.'

'Are you hinting that somebody hasn't told me the truth?' groaned the unhappy Roger.

'I'll do more than hint it; I'll prove it. When you told us last night that the man in the typewriter-shop had positively identified Mr Bendix as the purchaser of a second-hand No. 4

Hamilton I was astounded. I took a note of the shop's address. This morning, first thing, I went there. I taxed the man roundly with having told a lie. He admitted it, grinning.

'So far as he could make out, all you wanted was a good Hamilton No. 4, and he had a good Hamilton No. 4 to sell. He saw nothing wrong in leading you to supposed that his was the shop where your friend had bought his own good Hamilton No. 4, because he had quite as good a one as any other shop could have. And if it eased your mind that he should recognise your friend from his photograph – well,' said Miss Dammers drily, 'he was quite prepared to ease it as many times as you had photographs to produce.'

'I see,' said Roger, and his thoughts dwelt on the eight pounds he had handed over to that sympathetic, mind-easing shopman in return for a Hamilton No. 4 he didn't want.

'As for the girl in Webster's,' continued Miss Dammers implacably, 'she was just as ready to admit that perhaps she might have made a mistake in recognising that friend of the gentleman who called in yesterday about some notepaper. But really, the gentleman had seemed so anxious she should that it would have seemed quite a pity to disappoint him, like. And if it came to that, she couldn't see the harm in it not even now she couldn't.' Miss Dammers' imitation of Webster's young woman was most amusing. Roger did not laugh heartily.

'I'm sorry if I seem to be rubbing it in, Mr Sheringham,' said Miss Dammers.

'Not at all,' said Roger.

'But it's essential to my own case, you see.'

'Yes, I quite see that,' said Roger.

'Then that evidence is disposed of. I don't think you really had any other, did you?'

'I don't think so,' said Roger.

'You will see,' Miss Dammers resumed, over Roger's corpse, 'that I am following the fashion of withholding the criminal's name. Now that it has come to my turn to speak, I am realising the advantages of this; but really, I can't help fearing that you will all have guessed it by the time I come to my denouement. To me, at any rate, the murderer's identity seems quite absurdly obvious. Before I disclose it officially, however, I should like to deal with a few of the other points, not actual evidence, raised by Mr Sheringham in his argument.

'Mr Sheringham built up a very ingenious case. It was so very ingenious that he had to insist more than once on the perfect planning that had gone to its construction, and the true greatness of the criminal mind that had evolved it. I don't agree,' said Miss Dammers crisply. 'My case is much simpler. It was planned with cunning but not with perfection. It relied almost entirely upon luck: that is to say, upon one vital piece of evidence remaining undiscovered. And finally the mind that evolved it is not great in any way. But it *is* a mind which, dealing with matters outside its usual orbit, would certainly be imitative.

'That brings me to a point of Mr Bradley's. I agree with him to the extent that I think a certain acquaintance with criminological history is postulated, but not when he argues that it is the work of a creative mind. In my opinion the chief features of the crime is its servile imitation of certain of its predecessors. I deduced from it, in fact, the type of mind which is possessed of no originality of its own, is intensely conservative because without the wit to recognise the progress of change, is obstinate, dogmatic, and practical, and lacks entirely any sense of spiritual values. As one who am inclined to suffer myself from something of an aversion from matter, I sensed my exact antithesis behind the whole atmosphere of this case.'

Everybody looked suitably impressed. As for Mr Chitterwick, he could only gasp before these detailed deductions from a mere atmosphere.

'With another point of Mr Sheringham's I have already inferred that I agree: that chocolates were used as the vehicle of the poison because they were meant to reach a woman. And here I might add that I am sure no harm was intended to Mr Bendix himself. We know that Mr Bendix did not care for chocolates, and it is a reasonable assumption that the murderer knew it too; he never expected that Mr Bendix would eat any himself.

'It is curious how often Mr Sheringham hits the mark with small shafts, while missing it with the chief one. He was quite right about the notepaper being extracted from that sample book at Webster's. I'm bound to admit that the possession of the piece of notepaper had worried me considerably. I was at a complete loss there. Then Mr Sheringham very handily presented us with his explanation, and I have been able today to destroy his application of it to his own theory and incorporate it in my own. The attendant who pretended out of innocent politeness to recognise the photograph Mr Sheringham showed her, was able to recognise in earnest the one I produced. And not only recognise it,' said Miss Dammers with the first sign of complacence she had yet shown, 'but identify the original of it actually by name.'

'Ah!' nodded Mrs Fielder-Flemming, much excited.

'Mr Sheringham made a few other small points, which I thought it advisable today to blunt,' Miss Dammers went on, with a return to her impersonal manner. 'Because most of the small firms in which Mr Bendix figures on the board of directors are not in a flourishing state, Mr Sheringham deduced not only that Mr Bendix was a bad businessman, with which I am inclined to agree, but that he was desperately in need of money. Once again Mr Sheringham failed to verify his deduction, and once again he must pay the penalty in finding himself utterly wrong.

'The most elementary channels of enquiry would have brought Mr Sheringham the information that only a very small proportion of Mr Bendix's money is invested in these concerns which are really a wealthy man's toys. By far the greater part is still where his father left it when he died, in government stock and safe industrial concerns so large that even Mr Bendix could never aspire to a seat on the board. And from what I know of him, Mr Bendix is quite a big enough man to recognise that he is not the business genius his father was, and has no intention of spending on his toys more than he can comfortably afford. The real motive Mr Sheringham gave him for his wife's death therefore completely disappears.'

Roger bowed his head. For ever afterwards, he felt, would genuine criminologists point the finger of contempt at him as the man who failed to verify his own deductions. Oh, shameful future!

'As for the subsidiary motive, I attach less importance to that but on the whole I am inclined to agree with Mr Sheringham. I think Mrs Bendix must have become a dreadful bore to her husband, who after all was a normal man, with a normal man's reactions and scale of values. I should be inclined to think that she morally drove him into the arms of his actresses, in search of a little light companionship. I'm not saying he wasn't deeply in love with her when he married her; no doubt he was. And he'd have had a naturally deep respect for her then.

'But it's an unfortunate marriage,' observed the cynical Miss Dammers, 'in which the respect outstays its usefulness. A man wants a piece of humanity in his marriage-bed; not an object of deep respect. But I'm bound to say that if Mrs Bendix did bore her husband before the end, he was gentleman enough not to show it. The marriage was generally considered an ideal one.'

Miss Dammers paused for a moment to sip at the glass of water in front of her.

'Lastly, Mr Sheringham made the point that the letter and wrapper were not destroyed, because the murderer thought they would not only not harm him but definitely help him. With that too I agree. But I do not draw the same deduction from it that Mr Sheringham did. I should have said that this entirely confirms my theory that the murder is the work of a second-rate mind, because a first-rate mind would never consent to the survival of any clue which could be easily destroyed, however helpful it might be expected to prove, because he would know how often such clues, deliberately left to mislead, have actually led to the criminal's undoing. And I would draw the subsidiary deduction that the wrapper and letter were not expected to be just generally helpful, but there was some definite piece of misleading information contained in them. I think I know what that piece of information was.

'That is all the reference I have to make to Mr Sheringham's case.'

Roger lifted his bowed head, and Miss Dammers sipped again at her water.

'With regard to this matter of the respect Mr Bendix had for his wife,' Mr Chitterwick hazarded, 'isn't there something of an anomaly there, Miss Dammers? Because I understood you to say at the very beginning that the deduction you had drawn from that bet was that Mrs Bendix was not quite so worthy of respect as we had all imagined. Didn't that deduction stand the test, then?'

'It did, Mr Chitterwick, and there is no anomaly.'

'Where a man doesn't suspect, he will respect,' said Mrs Fielder-Flemming swiftly, before Alicia could think of it.

'Ah, the horrid sepulchre under the nice white paint,' remarked Mr Bradley, who didn't approve of that sort of thing, even from distinguished dramatists. 'Now we're getting down to it. Is there a sepulchre, Miss Dammers?'

'There is,' Miss Dammers agreed, without emotion. 'And now, as you say, Mr Bradley, we're getting down to it.'

'Oh!' Mr Chitterwick positively bounced on his chair. 'If the letter and wrapper *could* have been destroyed by the murderer...and Bendix wasn't the murderer...and I suppose the porter needn't be considered... Oh, *I* see!'

'I wondered when somebody would,' said Miss Dammers.

chapter sixteen

'From the very beginning of this case,' Miss Dammers proceeded, imperturbable as ever, 'I was of the opinion that the greatest clue the criminal had left us was one of which he would have been totally unconscious: the unmistakable indications of his own characters. Taking the facts as I found them, and not assuming others as Mr Sheringham did to justify his own reading of the murderer's exceptional mentality – ' She looked challengingly towards Roger.

'Did I assume any facts that I couldn't substantiate?' Roger felt himself compelled to answer her look.

'Certainly you did. You assumed for instance that the typewriter on which the letter was written is now at the bottom of the Thames. The plain fact that it is not, once more bears out my own interpretation. Taking the established facts as I found them, then, I was able without difficulty to form the mental picture of the murderer that I have already sketched out for you. But I was careful not to look for somebody who would resemble my picture and then build up a case against him. I simply hung the picture up in my mind, so to speak, in order to compare it with any individual toward whom suspicion might seem to point.

'Now, after I had cleared up Mr Bendix's reason for arriving at his club that morning at such an unusual hour, there remained so far as I could see only one obscure point, apparently of no importance, to which nobody's attention seemed to have been directed. I mean, the engagement Sir Eustace had had that day for lunch, which must have subsequently been cancelled. I don't know how Mr Bradley discovered this, but I am quite ready to say how I did. It was from that same useful valet who gave Mrs Fielder-Flemming so much interesting information.

'I must admit in this connection that I have advantages over the other members of this Circle so far as investigations regarding Sir Eustace were concerned, for not only did I know Sir Eustace himself so well but I knew his valet too; and you may imagine that if Mrs Fielder-Flemming was able to extract so much from him with the aid of money alone, I myself, backed not only by money but by the advantage of a previous acquaintance, was in a position to obtain still more. In any case, it was not long before the man casually mentioned that four days before the crime Sir Eustace had told him to ring up Fellows' Hotel in Jermyn Street and reserve a private room for lunch-time on the day on which the murder subsequently took place.

'That was the obscure point, which I thought it worth while to clear up if I could. With whom was Sir Eustace going to lunch that day? Obviously a woman, but which of his many women? The valet could give me no information. So far as he knew, Sir Eustace actually had not got any women at the moment, so intent was he upon the pursuit of Miss Wildman (you must excuse me, Sir Charles), her hand and her fortune. Was it Miss Wildman herself then? I was very soon able to establish that it wasn't.

'Does it strike you that there is a reminiscent ring about this cancelled lunch appointment on the day of the crime? It didn't occur to me for a long time, but of course there is. Mrs

Bendix had a lunch engagement for that day too, which was cancelled for some reason unknown on the previous afternoon.'

'*Mrs Bendix!*' breathed Mrs Fielder-Flemming. Here was a juicy triangle.

Miss Dammers smiled faintly. 'Yes, I won't keep you on the tenterhooks, Mabel. From what Sir Charles told us I knew that Mrs Bendix and Sir Eustace at any rate were not total strangers, and in the end I managed to connect them. Mrs Bendix was to have lunched with Sir Eustace, in a private room, at the somewhat notorious Fellows' Hotel.'

'To discuss her husband's shortcomings, of course?' suggested Mrs Fielder-Flemming, more charitably than her hopes.

'Possibly, among other things,' said Miss Dammers nonchalantly. 'But the chief reason, no doubt was because she was his mistress.' Miss Dammers dropped this bombshell among the company with as little emotion as if she had remarked that Mrs Bendix was wearing a jade-green taffeta frock for the occasion.

'Can you – can you substantiate that statement?' asked Sir Charles, the first to recover himself.

Miss Dammers just raised her fine eyebrows. 'But of course. I shall make no statements that I can't substantiate. Mrs Bendix had been in the habit of lunching at least twice a week with Sir Eustace, and occasionally dining too, at Fellows' Hotel, always in the same room. They took considerable precautions and used to arrive not only at the hotel but in the room itself quite independently of each other; outside the room they were never seen together. But the waiter who attended them (always the same waiter) has signed a declaration for me that he recognised Mrs Bendix, from the photographs published after her death, as the woman who used to come there with Sir Eustace Pennefather.'

'He signed a declaration for you, eh?' mused Mr Bradley. 'You must find detecting an expensive hobby too, Miss Dammers.'

'One can afford one expensive hobby, Mr Bradley.'

'But just because she lunched with him...' Mrs Fielder-Flemming was once more speaking with the voice of charity. 'I mean, it doesn't necessarily mean that she was his mistress, does it? Not, of course, that I think any less of her if she was,' she added hastily, remembering the official attitude.

'Communicating with the room in which they had their meals is a bedroom,' replied Miss Dammers, in a desiccated tone of voice. 'Invariably after they had gone, the waiter informed me, he found the bedclothes disarranged and the bed showing signs of recent use. I imagine that would be accepted as clear enough evidence of adultery, Sir Charles?'

'Oh, undoubtedly, undoubtedly,' rumbled Sir Charles, in high embarrassment. Sir Charles was always exceedingly embarrassed when women used words like 'adultery' and 'sexual perversions' and even 'mistress' to him, out of business hours. Sir Charles was regrettably old-fashioned.

'Sir Eustace, of course,' added Miss Dammers in her detached way, 'had nothing to fear from the King's Proctor.'

She took another sip of water, while the others tried to accustom themselves to this new light on the case and the surprising avenues it illuminated.

Miss Dammers proceeded to illuminate them still further, with powerful beams from her psychological searchlight. 'They must have made a curious couple those two. Their widely differing scales of values, the contrast of their respective reactions to the business that brought them together, the possibility that not even in a common passion could their minds establish any point of real contact. I want you to examine the psychology of the situation as closely as you can, because the murder was derived directly from it.

'What can have induced Mrs Bendix in the first place to become that man's mistress I don't know. I won't be so trite as to say I can't imagine, because I can imagine all sorts of ways in which it may have happened. There is a curious mental stimulus to a good but stupid woman in a bad man's business. If she has a touch of the reformer in her, as most good women have, she soon becomes obsessed with the futile desire to save him from himself. And in seven cases out of ten her first step in doing so is to descend to his level.

'Not that she considers herself at first to be descending at all; a good woman invariably suffers for quite a long time from the delusion that whatever she does, her own particular brand of goodness cannot become smirched. She may share a reprobate's bed with him, because she knows that only through her body at first can she hope to influence him, until contact is established through the body with the soul and he may be led into better ways than a habit of going to bed in the daytime; but the initial sharing doesn't reflect on her own purity in the least. It is a hackneyed observation but I must insist on it once more: good women have the most astonishing powers of self-deception.

'I do consider Mrs Bendix as a good woman, before she met Sir Eustace. Her trouble was that she thought herself so much better than she was. Her constant references to honour and playing the game, which Mr Sheringham quoted, show that. She was infatuated with her own goodness. And so, of course, was Sir Eustace. He had probably never enjoyed the complaisance of a really good woman before. The seduction of her (which was probably very difficult) would have amused him enormously. He must have had to listen to hour after hour's talk about honour, and reform, and spirituality, but he would have borne it patiently enough for the exquisite revenge on which he had set his heart. The first two or three visits to Fellows' Hotel must have delighted him.

'But after that it became less and less amusing. Mrs Bendix would discover that perhaps her own goodness wasn't standing quite so firm under the strain as she had imagined. She would have begun to bore him with her self-reproaches; bore him dreadfully. He continued to meet her there first because a woman, to his type, is always a woman, and afterwards because she gave him no choice. I can see exactly what must inevitably have happened. Mrs Bendix begins to get thoroughly morbid about her own wickedness, and quite loses sight of her initial zeal for reform.

'They use the bed now because there happens to be a bed there and it would be a pity to waste it, but she has destroyed the pleasure of both. Her one cry now is that she must put herself right with her own conscience either by running away with Sir Eustace on the spot, or, more probably, by telling her husband, arranging for divorce (for, of course, he will never forgive her, *never*), and marrying Sir Eustace as soon as both divorces are through. In any case, although she almost loathes him by now nothing else can be contemplated but that the rest of her life must be spent with Sir Eustace and his with her. How well I know that type of mind.

'Naturally, to Sir Eustace, who is working hard to retrieve his fortunes by a rich marriage, this scheme has small appeal. He begins by cursing himself for having seduced the damned woman at all, and goes on to curse still more the damned woman for having been seduced. And the more pressing she becomes, the more he hates her. Then Mrs Bendix must have brought matters to a head. She has heard about the Wildman girl affair. That must be stopped at once. She tells Sir Eustace that if he doesn't break it off himself, she will take steps to break it off for him. Sir Eustace sees the whole thing coming out, his own appearance in a second divorce court, and all hopes of Miss Wildman and her fortune have gone for ever. Something has got to be done about it. But what can be done? Nothing short of murder will stop the damned woman's tongue.

'Well – it's high time somebody murdered her anyhow.

'Now I'm on rather less sure ground, but the assumptions seems to me sound enough and I can produce a reasonable amount of proof to support them. Sir Eustace decided to get rid of the woman once and for all. He thinks it over carefully, remembers to have read about a case, several cases, in some criminological book, each of which just failed through some small mistake. Combine them, eradicate the small mistake from each, and so long as his relations with Mrs Bendix are not known (and he is quite certain they aren't) there is no possibility of being found out. That may seem a long guess, but here's my proof.

'When I was studying him, I gave Sir Eustace every chance of plying his blandishments on me. One of his methods is to profess a deep interest in everything that interests the woman. Naturally therefore he discovered a profound, if hitherto latent, interest in criminology. He borrowed several of my books, and certainly read them. Among the ones he borrowed is a book of American poisoning cases. In it is an account of every single case that has been mentioned as a parallel by members of this Circle (except of course Marie Lafarge and Christina Edmunds).

'About six weeks ago, when I got in one evening my maid told me that Sir Eustace, who hadn't been near my flat for months, had called; he waited for a time in the sitting-room and then went. Shortly after the murder, having also been struck by the similarity between this and one or two of those American cases, I went to the bookstall in my sitting-room to look them up. The book was not there. Nor, Mr Bradley, was my copy of Taylor. But I saw them both in Sir Eustace's rooms the day I had that long conversation with his valet.'

Miss Dammers paused for comment.

Mr Bradley supplied it. 'Then the man deserves what's coming to him,' he drawled.

''I told you this murder wasn't the work of a highly intelligent mind,' said Miss Dammers.

'Well, now, to complete my reconstruction. Sir Eustace decides to rid himself of his encumbrance, and arranged what he thinks a perfectly safe way of doing so. The nitrobenzene, which appears to worry Mr Bradley so much, seems to me a very simple matter. Sir Eustace has decided upon chocolates as the vehicle, and chocolate liqueurs at that. (Mason's chocolate liqueurs, I should say, are a favourite purchase of Sir Eustace's. It is significant that he had bought several one-pound boxes recently.) He is searching, then, for some poison with a flavour which will mingle well enough with that of the liqueurs. He is bound to come across oil of bitter almonds very soon in that connection, actually used as it is in confectionery, and from that to nitrobenzene, which is more common, easier to get hold of, and practically untraceable, is an obvious step.

'He arranges to meet Mrs Bendix for lunch, intending to make a present to her then of the chocolates which are to come to him that morning by post, a perfectly natural thing to do. He will already have the porter's evidence of the innocent way in which he acquired them. At the last minute he sees the obvious flaw in this plan. If he gives Mrs Bendix the chocolates in person, and especially at lunch at Fellows' Hotel, his intimacy with her must be disclosed. He hastily racks his brains and finds a very much better plan. Getting hold of Mrs Bendix, he tells her some story of her husband and Vera Delorme.

'In characteristic fashion Mrs Bendix loses sight of the beam in her own eye on learning of this mote in her husband's and at once falls in with Sir Eustace's suggestion that she shall ring Mr Bendix up, disguising her voice and pretending to be Vera Delorme, and just find out for herself whether or not he will jump at the chance of an intimate little lunch for the following day.

'And tell him you'll ring him up at the Rainbow tomorrow morning between ten-thirty and eleven,' Sir Eustace adds carelessly. 'If he goes to the Rainbow, you'll be able to know for certain that he's dancing attendance on her at any hour of the day.' And so she does. The presence of Bendix is therefore assured for the next morning at half-past ten. Who in the world is to say that he was not there by purest chance when Sir Eustace was exclaiming over that parcel?

'As for the bet, which clinched the handing over of the chocolates, I cannot believe that this was just a stroke of luck for Sir Eustace. That seems too good to be true. Somehow, I'm sure, though I won't attempt to show here (that would be mere guesswork), Sir Eustace arranged for that bet in advance. And if he did, the fact in no way destroys my initial deduction from it, that Mrs Bendix was not so honest as she pretended; for whether it was arranged or whether it wasn't, the plain fact is left that it is dishonest to make a bet to which you know the answer.

'Lastly, if I am to follow the fashion and cite a parallel case, I decide unhesitatingly for John Tawell, who administered prussic acid in a bottle of beer to his mistress, Sarah Hart, when he was tired of her.'

The Circle looked at her admiringly. At last, it seemed, they really had got to the bottom of the business.

Sir Charles voiced the general feeling. 'If you've got any solid evidence to support this theory, Miss Dammers...' He implied that in that case the rope was as good as round Sir Eustace's thick red neck.

'Meaning that the evidence I've given already isn't solid enough for the legal mind?' enquired Miss Dammers equably.

'Psy – psychological reconstructions wouldn't carry *very* much weight with a jury,' Sir Charles took refuge behind the jury in question.

'I've connected Sir Eustace with the piece of Mason's notepaper,' Miss Dammers pointed out.

'I'm afraid on that alone Sir Eustace would get the benefit of the doubt.' Sir Charles was evidently deprecating the psychological obtuseness of that jury of his.

'I've shown a tremendous motive, and I've connected him with a book of similar cases and a book of poisons.'

'Yes. Oh, quite so. But what I mean is, have you any real evidence to connect Sir Eustace quite definitely with the letter, the chocolates, or the wrapper?'

'He has an Onyx pen, and the inkpot in his library used to be filled with Harfield's Ink,' Miss Dammers smiled. 'I've no doubt it is still. He was supposed to have been at the Rainbow the whole evening before the murder, but I've ascertained that there is a gap of half an hour between nine o'clock and nine-thirty during which nobody saw him. He left the dining-room at nine, and a waiter brought him a whisky and soda in the lounge at half-past. In the interim nobody knows where he was. He wasn't in the lounge. Where was he? The porter swears he did not see him go out, or come in again; but there is a back way which he could have used if he wanted to be unnoticed, as of course he did. I asked him myself, as if by the way of a joke, and he said that he had gone up to the library after dinner to look up a reference in a book of big-game hunting. Could he mention the names of any other members in the library? He said there weren't any; there never were; he'd never seen a member in the library all the time he belonged to the club. I thanked him and rang off.

'In other words, he says he was in the library, because he knows there would be no other member there to prove he wasn't. What he really did during that half hour, of course, was to slip out the back way, hurry down to the Strand to post the parcel (just as Mr Sheringham saw Mr Bendix hurrying down), slip in again, run up to the library to make sure nobody was there, and then go down to the lounge and order his whisky and soda to prove his presence there later. Isn't that more feasible than your version of Mr Bendix, Mr Sheringham?'

'I must admit that it's no less so,' Roger had to agree.

'Then you haven't any solid evidence at all?' lamented Sir Charles. 'Nothing that would really impress a jury?'

'Yes, I have,' said Miss Dammers quietly. 'I've been saving it up till the end because I wanted to prove my case (as I consider I have done) without it. But this is absolutely and finally conclusive. Will everybody examine these please.'

Miss Dammers produced from her bag a brown-paper-covered parcel. Unwrapping it, she brought to light a photograph and a quarto sheet of paper which looked like a typed letter.

'The photograph,' she explained, 'I obtained from Chief Inspector Moresby the other day, but without telling him the specific purpose for which I wanted it. It is of the forged letter, actual size. I should like everybody to compare it with this typed copy of the letter. Will you look at them first, Mr Sheringham, and then pass them round? Notice particularly the slightly crooked s's and the chipped capital H.'

In dead silence Roger pored over the two. He examined them for a full two minutes, which seemed to the others more like two hours, and then passed them on to Sir Charles on his right.

'There isn't the slightest doubt that those two were done on the same machine,' he said soberly.

Miss Dammers showed neither less nor more emotion than she had displayed throughout. Her voice carried exactly the same impersonal inflection. She might have been announcing her discovery of a match between two pieces of dress material. From her level tone it could never have been guessed that a man's neck depended on her words no less than on the rope that was to hang him.

'You will find the machine in Sir Eustace's rooms,' she said.

Even Mr Bradley was moved. 'Then as I said, he deserves all that's coming to him,' he drawled, with a quite impossible nonchalance, and even attempted a yawn. 'Dear me, what a distressing bungler.'

Sir Charles passed on the evidence. 'Miss Dammers,' he said impressively, 'you have rendered a very great service to society. I congratulate you.'

'Thank you, Sir Charles,' replied Miss Dammers, matter-of-factly. 'But it was Mr Sheringham's idea, you know.'

'Mr Sheringham,' intoned Sir Charles, 'sowed better than he knew.'

Roger, who had hoped to add another feather to his cap by solving the mystery himself, smiled in a somewhat sickly way.

Mrs Fielder-Flemming improved the occasion. 'We have made history,' she said with fitting solemnity. 'When the whole police force of a nation had failed, a woman had uncovered the dark mystery. Alicia, this is a red-letter day, not only for you, not only for this Circle, but for Woman.'

'Thank you, Mabel,' responded Miss Dammers. 'How very nice of you to say so.'

The evidence passed slowly round the table and returned to Miss Dammers. She handed it on to Roger.

'Mr Sheringham, I think you had better take charge of these. As President, I leave the matter in your hands. You know as much as I do. As you may imagine, to inform the police officially myself would be extremely distasteful. I should like my name kept out of any communication you make to them, entirely.'

Roger was rubbing his chin. 'I think that can be done. I could just hand these things over to him, with the information where the machine is, and let Scotland Yard work the case up themselves. These, and the motive, with the evidence of the porter at Fellows' Hotel of which I shall have to tell Moresby, are the only things that will really interest the police, I think. Humph! I suppose I'd better see Moresby tonight. Will you come with me, Sir Charles? It would add weight.'

'Certainly, certainly,' Sir Charles agreed with alacritty.

Everybody looked, and felt, very serious.

'I suppose,' Mr Chitterwick dropped shyly into all this solemnity, 'I suppose you couldn't put it off for twenty-four hours, could you?'

Roger looked his surprise. 'But why?'

'Well, you know…' Mr Chittterwick wriggled with diffidence. 'Well – I haven't spoken yet, you know.'

Five pairs of eyes fastened on him in astonishment. Mr Chitterwick blushed warmly.

'Of course. No, of course.' Roger was trying to be as tactful as he could. 'And – well, that is to say, you want to speak, of course?'

'I have a theory,' said Mr Chitterwick modestly. 'I – I don't *want* to speak, no. But I have a theory.'

'Yes, yes,' said Roger, and looked helplessly at Sir Charles.

Sir Charles marched to the rescue. 'I'm sure we shall all be most interested to hear Mr Chitterwick's theory,' he pronounced. 'Most interested. But why not let us have it now, Mr Chitterwick?'

'It isn't quite complete,' said Mr Chitterwick, unhappy but persistent. 'I should like another twenty-four hours to clear up one or two points.'

Sir Charles had an inspiration. 'Of course, of course. We must meet tomorrow and listen to Mr Chitterwick's theory, of course. In the meantime Sheringham and I will just call in at Scotland Yard and – '

'I'd much rather you didn't,' said Mr Chitterwick, now in the deeps of misery. 'Really I would.'

Again Roger looked helplessly at Sir Charles. This time Sir Charles looked helplessly back.

'Well – I suppose another twenty-four hours wouldn't make *much* difference,' said Roger with reluctance. 'After all this time.'

'Not *very* much difference,' pleaded Mr Chitterwick.

'Well, not very much difference certainly,' agreed Sir Charles, frankly puzzled.

'Then have I your word, Mr President?' persisted Mr Chitterwick, very mournfully.

'If you put it like that,' said Roger, rather coldly.

The meeting then broke up, somewhat bewildered.

chapter seventeen

It was quite evident that, as he had said, Mr Chitterwick did not want to speak. He looked appealingly round the circle of faces the next evening when Roger asked him to do so, but the faces remained decidedly unsympathetic. Mr Chitterwick, expressed the faces plainly, was being a silly old woman.

Mr Chitterwick cleared his throat nervously two or three times and took the plunge.

'Mr President, ladies and gentlemen, I quite realise what you must be thinking, and I must plead for leniency. I can only say in excuse of what you must consider my perversity, that convincing though Miss Dammers' clever exposition was and definite as her proofs appeared, we have listened to so many apparently convincing solutions of this mystery and been confronted with so many seemingly definite proofs, that I could not help feeling that perhaps even Miss Dammers' theory might not prove on reflection to be not quite so strong as one would at first think.' Mr Chitterwick, having surmounted this tall obstacle, blinked rapidly but was unable to recall the next sentence he had prepared so carefully.

He jumped it, and went on a little. 'As the one to whom has fallen the task, both a privilege and a responsibility, of speaking last, you may not consider it out of place if I take the liberty of summing up the various conclusions that have been reached here, so different in both their methods and results. Not to waste time however in going over old ground, I have prepared a little chart which may show more clearly the various contrasting theories, parallels, and suggested criminals. Perhaps members would care to pass it round.'

With much hesitation Mr Chitterwick produced the chart on which he had spent so much careful thought, and offered it to Mr Bradley on his right. Mr Bradley received it graciously, and even condescended to lay it on the table between himself and Miss Dammers and examine it. Mr Chitterwick looked artlessly gratified.

'You will see,' said Mr Chitterwick, with a shade more confidence, 'that practically speaking no two members have agreed on any one single matter of importance. The divergence of opinion and method is really remarkable. And in spite of such variations each member has felt confident that his or her solution was the right one. This chart, more than any words of mine could, emphasises not only the extreme openness, as Mr Bradley would say, of the case before us, but illustrates another of Mr Bradley's observations too, that is how surprisingly easy it is to prove anything one may desire, by a process either of conscious or of unwitting selection.

'Miss Dammers, I think,' suggested Mr Chitterwick, 'may perhaps find that chart especially interesting. I am not myself a student of psychology, but even to me it was striking to notice how the solution of each member reflected, if I may say so, that particular member's own trend of thought and character. Sir Charles, for instance, whose training has naturally led him to realise the importance of the material, will not mind if I point out that the angle from which he viewed the problem was the very material one of *cui bono*, while the equally material evidence of the notepaper formed for him its salient feature. At the other end of the scale, Miss Dammers herself regards the case almost entirely from a psychological viewpoint and takes as its salient feature the character, as unconsciously revealed, of the criminal.

'Between these two, other members have paid attention to psychological and material evidence in varying proportions. Then again the methods building up the case against a suspected person have been widely different. Some of us have relied almost entirely on inductive methods, some almost wholly on deductive; while some, like Mr Sheringham, have blended the two. In short, the task our President set us has proved a most instructive lesson in comparative detection.'

Mr Chitterwick cleared his throat, smiled nervously, and continued. 'There is another chart which I might have made, and which I think would have been no less illuminating than this one. It is a chart of the singularly different deductions drawn by different members from the undisputed facts in the case. Mr Bradley might have found particular interest in this possible chart, as a writer of detective stories.

'For I have often noticed,' apologised Mr Chitterwick to the writers of detective stories *en masse*, 'that in books of that kind it is frequently assumed that any given fact can admit of only one single deduction, and that invariably the right one. Nobody else is capable of drawing any deductions at all but the author's favourite detective, and the ones he draws (in the books where the detective is capable of drawing deductions at all which, alas, are only too few) are invariably right. Miss Dammers mentioned something of the

Solver	*Motive*	*Angle of view*	*Salient feature*	*Method of proof*	*Parallel case*	*Criminal*
Sir Charles Wildman	Gain	*Cui bono*	Notepaper	Inductive	Marie Lafarge	Lady Pennefather
Mrs Fielder-Flemming	Elimination	*Cherchez la femme*	Hidden triangle	Intuitive and Inductive	Molineux	Sir Charles Wildman
Bradley (1)	Experiment	Detective novelist's	Nitrobenzene	Scientific deduction	Dr Wilson	Bradley
Bradley (2)	Jealousy	Character of Sir Eustace	Criminological knowledge of murderer	Deductive	Christina Edmunds	Woman unnamed
Sheringham	Gain	Character of Mr Bendix	Bet	Deductive and Inductive	Carlyle Harris	Bendix
Miss Dammers	Elimination	Psychology of all participants	Criminal's character	Psychological deduction	Tawell	Sir Eustace Pennefather
Police	Conviction, or lust of killing	General	Material clues	Routine	Horwood	Unknown fanatic or lunatic

MR CHITTERWICK'S CHART

kind one evening herself, with her illustration of the two bottles of ink.

'As an example of what really happens therefore, I should like to cite the sheet of Mason's notepaper in this case. From that single piece of paper the following deductions have at one time or another been drawn:

1. That the criminal was an employee or ex-employee of Mason & Sons.
2. That the criminal was a customer of Mason & Sons.
3. That the criminal was a printer, or had access to a printing-press.
4. That the criminal was a lawyer, acting on behalf of Mason & Sons.
5. That the criminal was a relative of an ex-employee of Mason & Sons.
6. That the criminal was a would-be customer of Webster's, the printers.

'There have been plenty of other deductions of course from that sheet of paper, such as that the chance possession of it suggested the whole method of the crime, but I am only calling attention to the ones which were to point directly to the criminal's identity. There are no less than six of them, you see, and all mutually contradictory.'

'I'll write a book for you, Mr Chitterwick,' promised Mr Bradley, 'in which the detective shall draw six contradictory deductions from each fact. He'll probably end up by arresting seventy-two different people for the murder and committing suicide because he finds afterwards that he must have done it himself. I'll dedicate the book to you.'

'Yes, do,' beamed Mr Chitterwick. 'For really, it wouldn't be far from what we've had in this case. For example, I only called attention to the notepaper. Besides that there were the poison, the typewriter, the postmark, the exactness of the dose – oh, many more facts. And from each one of them not much less than half-a-dozen different deductions have been drawn.

'In fact,' Mr Chitterwick summed up, 'it was as much as anything the different deductions drawn by different members that proved their different cases.'

'On second thoughts,' decided Mr Bradley, 'my detectives in future will be the kind that don't draw any deductions at all. Besides, that will be so much easier for me.'

'So with these few remarks on the solutions we have already heard,' continued Mr Chitterwick, 'which I hope members will pardon me, I will hurry on to my explanations of why I asked Mr Sheringham so urgently last evening not to go to Scotland Yard at once.'

Five faces expressed silent agreement that it was about time Mr Chitterwick was heard on that point.

Mr Chitterwick appeared to be conscious of the thoughts behind the faces, for his manner became a little flurried.

'I must first deal very briefly with the case against Sir Eustace Pennefather, as Miss Dammers gave it us last night. Without belittling her presentation of it in any way at all, I must point out that her two chief reasons for fixing the guilt upon him seemed to me to be firstly that he was the type of person whom she had already decided the criminal must be, and secondly that he had been conducting an intrigue with Mrs Bendix and certainly would have seemed to have some cause for wishing her out of the way – *if* (but only if) Miss Dammers' own view of the progress of that intrigue was the correct one.

'But the typewriter, Mr Chitterwick!' cried Mrs Fielder-Flemming, loyal to her sex.

Mr Chitterwick started. 'Oh, yes; the typewriter. I'm coming to that. But before I reach it, I should like to mention two other points which Miss Dammers would have us believe are important material evidence against Sir Eustace, as opposed to the psychological. That he should be in the habit of buying Mason's liqueur chocolates for his – his female friends hardly seems to me even significant. If everyone who is in the habit of buying Mason's liqueur chocolates is to be suspect, then London must be full of suspects. And surely even so unoriginal a murderer as Sir Eustace would seem to be, would have taken the elementary precaution of choosing some vehicle for the poison which is not generally associated with his name, instead of one that is. And if I may venture the opinion, Sir Eustace is not quite such a dunderhead as Miss Dammers would seem to think.

'The second point is that the girl in Webster's should have recognised, and even identified, Sir Eustace from his photograph. That also doesn't appear to me, if Miss Dammers doesn't mind my saying so, nearly as significant as she would have us believe. I have ascertained,' said Mr Chitterwick, not without pride (here too was a piece of real detecting) 'that Sir Eustace Pennefather buys his notepaper at Webster's, and has done so for years. He was in there about a month ago to order a fresh supply. It would be surprising, considering that he has a title, if the girl who served him had not remembered him; it cannot be considered significant,' said Mr Chitterwick quite firmly, 'that she does.

'Apart from the typewriter, then, and perhaps the copies of the criminological books, Miss Dammers' case has no real evidence to support it at all, for the matter of the broken alibi, I am afraid, must be held to be neither here nor there. I don't wish to be unfair,' said Mr Chitterwick carefully, 'but

I think I am justified in saying that Miss Dammers' case against Sir Eustace rests entirely and solely upon the evidence of the typewriter.' He gazed round anxiously for possible objections.

One came, promptly. 'But you can't possibly get round that,' exclaimed Mrs Fielder-Flemming impatiently.

Mr Chitterwick looked a trifle distressed. 'Is "get round" quite the right expression? I'm not trying wilfully or maliciously to pick holes in Miss Dammers' case just for amusement. You must really believe that. Please think that I am actuated only by a desire to bring this crime home to its real perpetrator. And with that end alone in view, I can certainly suggest an explanation of the typewriter evidence which excludes the guilt of Sir Eustace.'

Mr Chitterwick looked so unhappy at what he conceived to be Mrs Fielder-Flemming's insinuation that he was merely wasting the Circle's time, that Roger spoke to him kindly.

'You can?' he said gently, as one encourages one's daughter on drawing a cow, which if not much like a cow is certainly unlike any other animal on earth. 'That's very interesting, Mr Chitterwick. How do you explain it then?'

Mr Chitterwick, responding to treatment, shone with pride. 'Dear me! You can't see it really? Nobody sees it?'

It seemed that nobody saw it.

'And yet the possibility of such a thing has been before me right from the beginning of the case,' crowed the now triumphant Mr Chitterwick. 'Well, well!' He arranged his glasses on his nose and beamed round the Circle, his round red face positively aglow.

'Well, what is the explanation, Mr Chitterwick?' queried Miss Dammers, when it seemed that Mr Chitterwick was going to continue beaming in silence for ever.

'Oh! Oh, yes; of course. Why, to put it one way, Miss Dammers, that you were wrong and Mr Sheringham was right, in your respective estimates of the criminal's ability. That there was, in fact, an extremely able and ingenious mind behind this murder (Miss Dammers' attempts to prove the contrary were, I'm afraid, another case of special pleading). And that one of the ways in which this ingenuity was shown, was to arrange the evidence in such a way that if any one were to be suspected it would be Sir Eustace. That the evidence of the typewriter, in a word, and of the criminological books was, as I believe the technical word is, *"rigged."'* Mr Chitterwick resumed his beam.

Everybody sat up with what might have been a concerted jerk. In a flash the tide of feeling towards Mr Chitterwick had turned. The man *had* got something to say after all. There actually was an idea behind that untimely request of the previous evening.

Mr Bradley rose to the occasion, and he quite forgot to speak quite so patronisingly as usual. 'I say – dam' good, Chitterwick! But can you substantiate that?'

'Oh, yes. I think so,' said Mr Chitterwick, basking in the rays of appreciation that were being shone on him.

'You'll be telling us next you know who did it,' Roger smiled.

Mr Chitterwick smiled back. 'Oh, I know *that.*'

'What!' exclaimed five voices in chorus.

'I know that, of course,' said Mr Chitterwick modestly. 'You've practically told me that yourselves. Coming last of all, you see, my task was comparatively simple. All I had to do was to sort out the true from the false in everybody else's statements, and – well, there *was* the truth.'

The rest of the Circle looked their surprise at having told Mr Chitterwick the truth without knowing it themselves.

Mr Chitterwick's face took on a meditative aspect. 'Perhaps I may confess now that when our President first propounded his idea to us, I was filled with dismay. I had had no practical experience of detecting, I was quite at a loss as to how to set about it, and I had no theory of the case at all. I could not even see a starting-point. The week flew by, so far as I was concerned, and it left me exactly where I had been at the beginning. On the evening Sir Charles spoke he convinced me completely. The next evening, for a short time, Mrs Fielder-Flemming convinced me too.

'Mr Bradley did not altogether convince me that he had committed the murder himself, but if he had named any one else then I should have been convinced; as it was, he convinced me that his – his discarded mistress theory,' said Mr Chitterwick bravely, 'must be the correct one. That indeed was the only idea I had had at all, that the crime might be the work of one of Sir Eustace's – h'm! – discarded mistresses.

'But the next evening Mr Sheringham convinced me just as definitely that Mr Bendix was the murderer. It was only last night, during Miss Dammers' exposition, that I at last began to realise the truth.'

'Then I was the only one who didn't convince you, Mr Chitterwick?' Miss Dammers smiled.

'I'm afraid,' apologised Mr Chitterwick, 'that is so.'

He mused for a moment.

'It is really remarkable, quite remarkable, how near in some way or other everybody got to the truth of this affair. Not a single person failed to bring out at least one important fact, or make at least one important deduction correctly. Fortunately, when I realised that the solutions were going to differ so widely, I made copious notes of the preceding ones and kept them up to date each evening as soon as I got home. I thus had a complete record of the productions of all these brains, so much superior to my own.'

'No, no,' murmured Mr Bradley.

'Last night I sat up very late, poring over these notes, separating the true from the false. It might perhaps interest members to hear my conclusions in this respect?' Mr Chitterwick put forward the suggestion with the utmost diffidence.

Everybody assured Mr Chitterwick that they would be only too gratified to hear where they had stumbled inadvertently on the truth.

chapter eighteen

Mr Chitterwick consulted a page of his notes. For a moment he looked a little distressed. 'Sir Charles,' he began. 'Er – Sir Charles...' It was plain that Mr Chitterwick was finding difficulty in discovering any point at all on which Sir Charles had been right, and he was a kindly man. He brightened. 'Oh, yes, of course. Sir Charles was the first to point out the important fact that there had been an erasure on the piece of notepaper used for the forged letter. That was – er – very helpful.

'Then he was right too when he put forward the suggestion that Sir Eustace's impending divorce was really the mainspring of the whole tragedy. Though I am afraid,' Mr Chitterwick felt compelled to add, 'that the inference he drew was not the correct one. He was quite right in feeling that the criminal, in such a clever plot, would take steps to arrange an alibi, and that there was, in fact, an alibi in the case that would have to be circumvented. But then again it was not Lady Pennefather's.

'Mrs Fielder-Flemming,' continued Mr Chitterwick, 'was quite right to insist that the murder was the work of somebody with a knowledge of criminology. That was a very clever inference, and I am glad,' beamed Mr Chitterwick, 'to be able to assure her that it was perfectly correct. She contributed another important piece of information too, just as vital to the real story underlying this tragedy as to her own case, namely that Sir Eustace was not in love with Miss Wildman at all but was hoping to marry her simply for money. Had that not been the case,' said Mr Chitterwick, shaking his head, 'I fear, I very much fear, that it would have been Miss Wildman who met her death instead of Mrs Bendix.'

'Good God!' muttered Sir Charles; and it is perhaps as great a tribute as Mr Chitterwick was ever to receive that the KC accepted this startling news without question.

'That clinches it,' muttered Mr Bradley to Mrs Fielder-Flemming. 'Discarded mistress.'

Mr Chitterwick turned to him. 'As for you, Bradley, it's astonishing how near you came to the truth. Amazing!' Mr Chitterwick registered amazement. 'Even in your first case, against yourself, so many of your conclusions were perfectly right. The final result of your deductions from the nitrobenzene, for instance; the fact that the criminal must be neat-fingered and of a methodical and creative mind; even, what appeared to me at the time just a trifle far-fetched, that a copy of Taylor would be found on the criminal's shelves.

'Then beyond the fact that No. 4 must be qualified to "must have had an opportunity of secretly obtaining a sheet of Mason's notepaper," all twelve of your conditions were quite right, with the exception of 6, which does not admit of an alibi, and 7 and 8, about the Onyx pen and Harfield's ink. Mr Sheringham was right in that matter with his rather more subtle point of the criminal's probable unobtrusive borrowing of the pen and ink. Which is exactly what happened, of course, with regard to the typewriter.

'As for your second case – well!' Mr Chitterwick seemed to be without words to express his admiration of Mr

Bradley's second case. 'You reached to the truth in almost every particular. You saw that it was a woman's crime, you deduced the outraged feminine feelings underlying the whole affair, you staked your whole case on the criminal's knowledge of criminology. It was really most penetrating.'

'In fact,' said Mr Bradley, carefully concealing his gratification, 'I did everything possible except find the murderess.'

'Well, that is so, of course,' deprecated Mr Chitterwick, somehow conveying the impression that after all finding the murderess was a very minor matter compared with Mr Bradley's powers of penetration.

'And then we come to Mr Sheringham.'

'Don't!' implored Roger. 'Leave him out.'

'Oh, but your reconstruction was very clever,' Mr Chitterwick assured him with great earnestness. 'You put a new aspect on the whole affair, you know, by your suggestion that it was the right victim who was killed after all.'

'Well, it seems that I erred in good company,' Roger said tritely, with a glance at Miss Dammers.

'But you didn't err,' corrected Mr Chitterwick.

'Oh?' Roger showed his surprise. 'Then it was all aimed against Mrs Bendix?'

Mr Chitterwick looked confused. 'Haven't I told you about that? I'm afraid I'm doing this in a very muddle-headed way. Yes, it is partially true to say that the plot was aimed against Mrs Bendix. But the real position, I think, is that it was aimed against Mrs Bendix and Sir Eustace jointly. You came very near the truth, Mr Sheringham, except that you substituted a jealous husband for a jealous rival. Very near indeed. And of course you were entirely right in your point that the method was not suggested by the chance possession of the notepaper or anything like that, but by previous cases.'

'I'm glad I was entirely right over something,' murmured Roger.

'And Miss Dammers,' bowed Mr Chitterwick, 'was most helpful. *Most* helpful.'

'Although not convincing,' supplemented that lady drily.

'Although I'm afraid I did not find her altogether convincing,' agreed Mr Chitterwick, with an apologetic air. 'But it was really the theory she gave us that at last showed me the truth. For she also put yet another aspect on the crime, with her information regarding the – h'm! – the affair between Mrs Bendix and Sir Eustace. And that really,' said Mr Chitterwick, with another little bow to the informant, 'was the foundation-stone of the whole business.'

'I didn't see how it could fail to be,' said Miss Dammers. 'But I still maintain that my deductions from it are the correct ones.'

'Perhaps if I may just put my own forward?' hesitated Mr Chitterwick, apparently somewhat dashed.

Miss Dammers accorded a somewhat tart permission.

Mr Chitterwick collected himself. 'Oh, yes; I should have said that Miss Dammers was quite right in one important particular, her assumption that it was not so much the affair between Mrs Bendix and Sir Eustace that was at the bottom of the crime, as Mrs Bendix's character. That really brought about her own death. Miss Dammers, I should imagine, was perfectly right in her tracing out of the intrigue, and her imaginative insight into Mrs Bendix's reactions – I think that is the word?' Mr Chitterwick inquired diffidently of authority. 'Mrs Bendix's reactions to it, but not, I consider, in her deductions regarding Sir Eustace's growing boredom.

'Sir Eustace, I am led to believe, was less inclined to be bored than to share the lady's distress. For the real point, which happened to escape Miss Dammers, is that Sir Eustace was quite infatuated with Mrs Bendix. Far more so than she with him.

'That,' pronounced Mr Chitterwick, 'is one of the determining factors in this tragedy.'

Everybody pinned the factor down. The Circle's attitude towards Mr Chitterwick by this time was one of intelligent expectation. Probably no one really thought that he had found the right solution, and Miss Dammers' stock had not been appreciably lowered. But certainly it seemed that the man had at any rate got something to offer.

'Miss Dammers,' proceeded the object of their attention, 'was right in another point she made too, namely that the inspiration of this murder, or perhaps I should say the method of it, certainly came from that book of poisoning cases she mentioned, of which her own copy (she tells us) is at present in Sir Eustace's rooms – planted there,' added Mr Chitterwick, much shocked, 'by the murderess.

'And another useful fact she established. That Mr Bendix had been lured (really,' apologised Mr Chitterwick, 'I can use no other word) to the Rainbow Club that morning. But it was not Mrs Bendix who telephoned to him on the previous afternoon. Nor was he sent there for the particular purpose of receiving the chocolates from Sir Eustace. The fact that the lunch appointment had been cancelled was altogether outside the criminal's knowledge. Mr Bendix was sent there to be a witness to Sir Eustace receiving the parcel; that was all.

'The intention was, of course, that Mr Bendix should have Sir Eustace so connected in his mind with the chocolates that if suspicion should ever arise against any definite person, that of Mr Bendix would be directed before long to Sir Eustace himself. For the fact of his wife's intrigue would be bound to come to his knowledge, as indeed I understand privately that it has, causing him naturally the most intense distress.'

'So that's why he's been looking haggard,' exclaimed Roger.

'Without doubt,' Mr Chitterwick agreed gravely. 'It was a wicked plot. Sir Eustace, you see, was expected to be dead by then and incapable of denying his guilt, and such evidence as there was had been carefully arranged to point to murder and suicide on his part. That the police never suspected him (that is, so far as we know), simply shows that investigations do not always take the turn that the criminal expects. And in this case,' observed Mr Chitterwick with some severity, 'I think the criminal was altogether too subtle.'

'If that was her very involved reason for ensuring the presence of Mr Bendix at the Rainbow Club,' agreed Miss Dammers with some irony, 'her subtlety certainly overreached itself.' It was evident that not only on the point of psychology did Miss Dammers not find herself ready to accept Mr Chitterwick's conclusions.

'That, indeed, is exactly what happened,' Mr Chitterwick pointed out mildly. 'Oh, and while we are on the subject of the chocolates, I ought to add that the reason why they were sent to Sir Eustace's club was not only so that Mr Bendix might be a witness of their arrival, but also, I should imagine, so that Sir Eustace would be sure to take them with him to his lunch appointment. The murderess of course would be sufficiently conversant with his ways to know that he would almost certainly spend the morning at his club and go straight on to lunch from there; the odds were enormous that he would take the box of Mrs Bendix's favourite chocolates with him.

'I think we may regard it as an instance of the criminal's habitual overlooking of some vital point that is to lead eventually to detection, that this murderess completely lost sight of the possibility that the appointment for lunch might be cancelled. She is a particularly ingenious criminal,' said Mr Chitterwick with gentle admiration, 'and yet even she is not immune from this failing.'

'Who is she, Mr Chitterwick?' ingenuously asked Mrs Fielder-Flemming.

Mr Chitterwick answered her with a positively roguish smile. 'Everybody else has withheld the name of the suspect till the right moment. Surely I may be allowed to do so too.

'Well, I think I have cleared up most of the doubtful points now. Mason's notepaper was used, I should say, because chocolates had been decided on as the vehicle and Mason's were the only chocolate manufacturing firm who were customers of Webster's. As it happened, this fitted very well, because it was always Mason's chocolates that Sir Eustace bought for his – er – his friends.'

Mrs Fielder-Flemming looked puzzled. 'Because Mason's were the only firm who were customers of Webster's? I'm afraid I don't understand.'

'Oh, I *am* explaining all this badly,' cried Mr Chitterwick in much distress, assuming all blame for this obtuseness. 'It had to be some firm on Webster's books, you see, because Sir Eustace has his notepaper printed at Webster's, and he was to be identified as having been in there recently if the purloined piece was ever connected with the sample book. Exactly, in fact, as Miss Dammers did.'

Roger whistled. 'Oh, I see. You mean, we've all been putting the cart before the horse over this piece of notepaper?'

'I'm afraid so,' regretted Mr Chitterwick with earnestness. 'Really, I'm very much afraid so.'

Insensibly opinion was beginning to turn in Mr Chitterwick's favour. To say the least, he was being just as convincing as Miss Dammers had been, and that without subtle psychological reconstructions and references to 'values'. Only Miss Dammers herself remained outwardly sceptical; but that, after all, was only to be expected.

'Humph!' said Miss Dammers, sceptically.

'What about the motive, Mr Chitterwick?' nodded Sir Charles with solemnity. 'Jealousy, did you say? I don't think you've quite cleared up that yet, have you?'

'Oh, yes, of course.' Mr Chitterwick actually blushed. 'Dear me, I meant to make that clear right at the beginning. I *am* doing this badly. No, not jealousy, I'm inclined to fancy. Revenge. Or revenge at any rate so far as Sir Eustace was concerned, and jealousy as regards Mrs Bendix. From what I can understand, you see, this lady is – dear me,' said Mr Chitterwick, in distress and embarrassment, 'this is very delicate ground. But I must trespass on it. Well – though she had concealed it successfully from her friends, this lady had been very much in love with Sir Eustace, and become – er – had become,' concluded Mr Chitterwick bravely, 'his mistress. That was a long time ago.

'Sir Eustace was very much in love with her too, and though he used to amuse himself with other women it was understood by both that this was quite permissible so long as there was nothing serious. The lady, I should say, is very modern and broad-minded. It was understood, I believe, that he was to marry her as soon as he could induce his wife (who was quite ignorant of this affair) to divorce him. But when this was at last arranged, Sir Eustace found that owing to his extreme financial stringency, it was imperative that he should marry money instead.

'The lady was naturally very disappointed, but knowing that Sir Eustace did not care at all for – er – was not really in love with Miss Wildman and the marriage would only be, so far as he was concerned, one of convenience, she reconciled herself to the future and, quite seeing Sir Eustace's necessity, did not resent the introduction of Miss Wildman – whom indeed,' Mr Chitterwick felt himself compelled to add, 'she considered as quite negligible. It never occurred to her to doubt, you see, that the old arrangement would hold good, and she would still have Sir Eustace's real love with which to content herself.

'But then something quite unforeseen happened. Sir Eustace not only fell out of love with her. He fell unmistakably in love with Mrs Bendix. Moreover, he succeeded in making her his mistress. That was quite recently, since he began to pay his addresses to Miss Wildman. And I think Miss Dammers has given us a true picture of the results in Mrs Bendix's case if not in that of Sir Eustace.

'Well, you can see the position then, so far as this other lady was concerned. Sir Eustace was getting his divorce, marriage with the negligible Miss Wildman was now out of the question, but marriage with Mrs Bendix, tortured in her conscience and seeing in divorce from her husband and marriage with Sir Eustace the only means of solving it – marriage with Mrs Bendix, the real beloved, and even more eligible than Miss Wildman so far as the financial side was concerned, was to all appearances inevitable. I deprecate the use of hackneyed quotations as much as anybody, but really I feel that if I permit myself to add that hell has no fury like – '

'Can you prove all this, Mr Chitterwick?' interposed Miss Dammers coolly on the hackneyed quotation.

Mr Chitterwick started. 'I – I think so,' he said, though a little dubiously.

'I'm inclined to doubt it,' observed Miss Dammers briefly.

Somewhat uncomfortable, under Miss Dammers' sceptical eye, Mr Chitterwick explained. 'Well, Sir Eustace, whose acquaintance I have been at some pains to cultivate recently...' Mr Chitterwick shivered a little, as if the acquaintance had not been his ideal one. 'Well, from a few indications that Sir Eustace has unconsciously given me... That is to say, I was questioning him at lunch today as adroitly as I could, my conviction as to the murderer's identity having been formed at last, and he did unwittingly let fall a few trifles which...'

'I doubt it,' repeated Miss Dammers bluntly.

Mr Chitterwick looked quite nonplussed.

Roger hurried to the rescue. 'Well, shelving the matter of proof for the moment, Mr Chitterwick, and assuming that your reconstruction of the events is just an imaginative one. You'd reached the point where marriage between Sir Eustace and Mrs Bendix had become inevitable.'

'Yes; oh, yes,' said Mr Chitterwick, with a grateful look towards his saviour. 'And then of course, this lady formed her terrible decision and made her very clever plan. I think I've explained all that. Her old right of access to Sir Eustace's rooms enabled her to type the letter on his typewriter one day when she knew he was out. She is quite a good mimic, and it was easy for her when ringing up Mr Bendix to imitate the sort of voice Miss Delorme might be expected to have.'

'Mr Chitterwick, do any of us know this woman?' demanded Mrs Fielder-Flemming abruptly.

Mr Chitterwick looked more embarrassed than ever. 'Er – yes,' he hesitated. 'That is, you must remember it was she who smuggled Miss Dammers' two books into Sir Eustace's rooms too, you know.'

'I shall have to be more careful about my friends in the future, I see,' observed Miss Dammers, gently sarcastic.

'An ex-mistress of Sir Eustace's, eh?' Roger murmured, conning over in his mind such names as he could remember from that lengthy list.

'Well, yes,' Mr Chitterwick agreed. 'But nobody has any idea of it. That is – Dear me, this is very difficult.' Mr Chitterwick wiped his forehead with his handkerchief, and looked extremely unhappy.

'She'd managed to conceal it?' Roger pressed him.

'Er – yes. She'd certainly managed to conceal the true state of matters between them, very cleverly indeed. I don't think anybody suspected it at all.'

'They apparently didn't know each other?' Mrs Fielder-Flemming persisted. 'They were never seen about together?'

'Oh, at one time they were,' said Mr Chitterwick, looking in quite a hunted way from face to face. 'Quite frequently. Then, I understand, they thought it better to pretend to have quarrelled and – and met only in secret.'

'Isn't it time you told us this woman's name, Chitterwick?' boomed Sir Charles down the table, looking judicial.

Mr Chitterwick scrambled desperately out of this fire of questions. 'It's very strange, you know, how murderers never will let well alone, isn't it?' he said breathlessly. 'It happens so often. I'm quite sure I should never have stumbled on the truth in this case if the murderess had only left things as they were, in accordance with her own admirable plot. But this trying to fix the guilt on another person... Really, from the intelligence displayed in this case, she ought to have been above that. Of course her plot *had* miscarried. Been only half-successful, I should say. But why not accept the partial failure? Why tempt Providence? Trouble was inevitable – inevitable – '

Mr Chitterwick seemed by this time utterly distressed. He was shuffling his notes with extreme nervousness, and wriggling in his chair. The glances he kept darting from face to face were almost pleading. But what he was pleading for remained obscure.

'Dear me,' said Mr Chitterwick, as if at his wits' end. 'This is very difficult. I'd better clear up the remaining point. It's about the alibi.

'In my opinion the alibi was an afterthought, owing to a piece of luck. Southampton Street is near both the Cecil and the Savoy, isn't it? I happen to know that this lady has a friend, another woman, of a somewhat unconventional nature. She is continually away on exploring expeditions and so on, usually quite alone. She never stays in London more than a night or two, and I should imagine she is the sort of woman who rarely reads the newspapers. And if she did, I think she would certainly not divulge any suspicion they might convey to her, especially concerning a friend of her own.

'I have ascertained that immediately preceding the crime this woman, whose name by the way is Jane Harding, stayed for two nights at the Savoy Hotel, and left London, on the morning the chocolates were delivered, for Africa. From there she was going on to South America. Where she may be now I have not the least idea. Nor, I should say, has any one else. But she came to London from Paris, where she had been staying for a week.

'The – er – criminal would know about this forthcoming trip to London, and so hurried to Paris. (I am afraid,' apologised Mr Chitterwick uneasily, 'there is a good deal of guesswork here.) It would be simple to ask this other lady to post the parcel in London, as the parcel postage is so heavy from France, and just as simple to ensure it being delivered on the morning of the lunch appointment with Mrs Bendix, by saying it was a birthday present, or some other pretext, and – and – must be posted to arrive on that particular day.' Mr Chitterwick wiped his forehead again and glanced pathetically at Roger. Roger could only stare back in bewilderment.

'Dear me,' muttered Mr Chitterwick distractedly, 'this is *very* difficult. – Well, I have satisfied myself that – '

Alicia Dammers had risen to her feet and was unhurriedly picking up her belongings. 'I'm afraid,' she said, 'I have an appointment. Will you excuse me, Mr President?'

'Of course,' said Roger, in some surprise.

At the door Miss Dammers turned back. 'I'm so sorry not to be able to stay to hear the rest of your case, Mr Chitterwick. But really, you know, as I said, I very much doubt whether you'll be able to prove it.'

She went out of the room.

'She's perfectly right,' whispered Mr Chitterwick, gazing after her in a petrified way. 'I'm quite sure I can't. But there isn't the faintest doubt. I'm afraid, not the faintest.'

Stupefaction reigned.

'You – you *can't* mean…?' twittered Mrs Fielder-Flemming in a strangely shrill voice.

Mr Bradley was the first to get a grip on himself. 'So we did have a practising criminologist amongst us after all,' he drawled in a manner that was never Oxford. 'How quite interesting.'

Again silence held the Circle.

'So now,' asked the President helplessly, 'what the devil do we do?'

Nobody enlightened him.

ANTHONY BERKELEY

DEATH IN THE HOUSE

When Lord Wellacombe, the Secretary of State for India, collapses in the House of Commons and dies, everyone suspects a stroke. His death causes political waves as a successor is sought and there is the question of a bill to be put through. But then tests show Wellacombe to have been poisoned and not by any conventional method – a thorn covered in South American poison is discovered under the dead man's coat collar. Is this the work of an international terrorist or someone closer to home?

'Anthony Berkeley is the supreme master not of the "twist" but of the "double-twist"!' – *The Sunday Times*

JUMPING JENNY

A Roger Sheringham case.

Gentleman sleuth Roger Sheringham is at a fancy-dress party where the theme is murderers and victims. The fun takes a sinister turn however when a real victim is discovered hanging on the roof. Is it suicide – or a perfect murder?

Anthony Berkeley

The Layton Court Mystery

A Roger Sheringham case.

Mr Victor Stanworth, an apparently carefree sixty-year-old, is entertaining a party of friends at his summer residence, Layton Court. When one morning he is found shot dead in the library it is hard to believe it is either suicide or murder. As one of the country-house guests, gentleman sleuth Roger Sheringham resolves to solve the murder. As he pursues the truth he does not conceal any of the evidence, and the reader is able to follow his detection work to the conclusion of this original mystery story.

Murder in the Basement

A Roger Sheringham case.

'Don't come down, Molly. There – there's something pretty beastly here. I must get a policeman.'

When Reginald and Molly Dane return from their honeymoon to a new house, they are curious to explore the cellar. Reginald notices a corner where the bricks have been inexpertly put back to cover a hole dug in the floor. Convinced he will find treasure he takes a pickaxe to it – but discovers a body of a woman in a shallow grave, not treasure in a chest. Chief Inspector Moresby and gentleman sleuth Roger Sheringham are soon on the case. What was the vicitm's identity? Why was she shot through the back of the head and why was she buried naked except for a pair of gloves?

ANTHONY BERKELEY

THE SILK STOCKING MURDERS

A Roger Sheringham case.

Gentleman sleuth and novelist Roger Sheringham would not have ordinarily been curious about the suicide of chorus girl Miss Unity Ransome. However when he receives a cry for help from a country parson attempting to trace his missing daughter Janet in London he finds himself involved. And when three other young women are found hanged dead by silk stockings, Sheringham realises that what he is investigating is actually murder.

TRIAL AND ERROR

Lawrence Todhunter is in search of a victim. After an academic conversation with friends he decides that he is going to commit a murder – and so he does. Todhunter's carefully chosen prey is a glamorous actress and he pulls off the killing with aplomb. When another man is arrested for the crime Todhunter resolves to confess but is staggered when no one believes him. He will have to prove himself guilty...

'First class reading...the detection is enthralling!'
– *Times Literary Supplement*

PAYMENT

Please tick currency you wish to use:

☐ £ (Sterling) ☐ $ (US) ☐ $ (CAN) ☐ € (Euros)

Allow for shipping costs charged per order plus an amount per book as set out in the tables below:

CURRENCY/DESTINATION

	£(Sterling)	$(US)	$(CAN)	€(Euros)
Cost per order				
UK	1.50	2.25	3.50	2.50
Europe	3.00	4.50	6.75	5.00
North America	3.00	3.50	5.25	5.00
Rest of World	3.00	4.50	6.75	5.00
Additional cost per book				
UK	0.50	0.75	1.15	0.85
Europe	1.00	1.50	2.25	1.70
North America	1.00	1.00	1.50	1.70
Rest of World	1.50	2.25	3.50	3.00

PLEASE SEND CHEQUE OR INTERNATIONAL MONEY ORDER
payable to: HOUSE OF STRATUS LTD or HOUSE OF STRATUS INC. or card payment as indicated

STERLING EXAMPLE

Cost of book(s): .... Example: 3 x books at £6.99 each: £20.97

Cost of order: .... Example: £1.50 (Delivery to UK address)

Additional cost per book: .... Example: 3 x £0.50: £1.50

Order total including shipping: .... Example: £23.97

VISA, MASTERCARD, SWITCH, AMEX:

☐☐☐☐☐☐☐☐☐☐☐☐☐☐☐☐☐☐☐☐

Issue number (Switch only):

☐☐☐

Start Date: ☐☐/☐☐

Expiry Date: ☐☐/☐☐

Signature: ______________________

NAME: ______________________

ADDRESS: ______________________

COUNTRY: ______________________

ZIP/POSTCODE: ______________________

Please allow 28 days for delivery. Despatch normally within 48 hours.

Prices subject to change without notice.
Please tick box if you do not wish to receive any additional information. ☐